GABRIELLE

Marianne walked in front of her daughter to meet her eyes. "I want you to have a good time tonight," she commanded in the Acadian accent that set her apart from other French residents of Louisiana. "I want you to meet some nice men. Dance. Be happy."

Gabrielle stared at her hands in her lap. Happiness was not something she was used to, except when Jean was around.

"He may never return," Marianne said. "If he does, he may not wish for marriage. Don't waste your young life waiting for someone who might not appear."

Gabrielle couldn't imagine a life without Jean. She dreamed of him at night, ached for the touch of his arms about her, his lips hot upon hers.

"Promise me you will enjoy the attention of men tonight," her mother demanded. "Promise me that if they call on you tomorrow, you will not discourage them as you have in the past."

Gabrielle nodded. It was the sixth of January, Twelfth Night, the Epiphany, the begining of the Carnival season. It was also her twenty-first birthday. It was time to enjoy life, to find happiness.

If only she could escape the pain gripping her heart.

Dear Romance Reader,

In July, we launched the Ballad line with four new series, and each month we'll present both new and continuing stories set everywhere from medieval England to the American West—the kind of passionate, romantic stories you love best, written by the most gifted authors. At the back of each book, we'll tell you when you can find subsequent books in the series that have captured your heart.

This month talented Cindy Harris introduces the charming new *Dublin Dreams* series. When an anonymous benefactor brings together four penniless women in one stately Dublin square, none of them expect to find love. Yet in the first book, the widow of a dissolute gambler meets her romantic match when she has **A Bright Idea.** Next, rising star Linda Lea Castle presents the second of a trio of spirited *Bogus Brides.* In **Mattie and the Blacksmith,** a schoolteacher who longs to be properly courted discovers that the most unlikely suitor may be the one who steals her heart.

Fabulous new author Lynne Hayworth is also back with the second installment of the *Clan Maclean* series, **Autumn Flame.** Will a spirited pickpocket make a proper wife for the overseer of a Virginia plantation? Finally, Cherie Claire concludes the atmospheric *Acadians* trilogy with the story of **Gabrielle,** a woman who will risk anything to save the bold privateer who has claimed her, body and soul. Enjoy!

Kate Duffy
Editorial Director

The Acadians

GABRIELLE

Cherie Claire

ZEBRA BOOKS

KENSINGTON PUBLISHING CORP.

http://www.zebrabooks.com

To my father, Paul Fernard Dastugue, Jr.

Merci beaucoup *to my Tobeez friends, and especially my Canadian cousin Susanne McDonald-Boyce, for invaluable support this past year and for reminding me to* "Lâche pas la patate!"

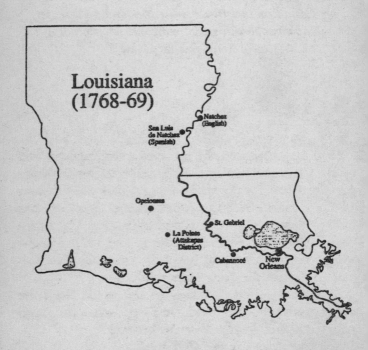

Louisiana
(1768-69)

Natchez
(English)

San Luis
de Natchez
(Spanish)

Opelousas

St. Gabriel

La Pointe
(Attakapas
District)

Cabannocé

New
Orleans

Chapter One

Nothing surpassed the sight of a ship primed and ready for sail, Delphine Delaronde thought as she gazed at her father's schooner. *La Belle Amie*'s decks had been scrubbed, her ropes hauled tight, and the anchor cleansed of its rust and barnacles. The ship's copper glistened in the afternoon sun while a slight winter breeze teased at her sails, newly washed and laid to dry on the New Orleans docks.

Delphine sighed, thinking of the possibilities the two-masted schooner held. One step across the gangplank and her troubles would be over.

"No, you can't come with me."

Delphine turned at the sound of her father's voice. His tall, dark figure cast a shadow over her petite frame, still childlike despite her thirteen years. Delphine instinctively placed her hands at her hips, preparing for an argument. Her father, one of the finest sea captains in the Louisiana Territory, was a constant challenge.

"My studies will be finished by Christmas. You said you would take me one day when I was old enough."

A smile began in the creases of Jean Bouclaire's lips, accented by the deep dimple in his right cheek, just left of a thick, dark mustache. Delphine doubted he would relent and agree to take her on board, but she knew he admired her tenacity and spunk. It was, after all, a family trait.

Then a carriage passed and his smile disappeared.

"You shouldn't be here," Jean said, grabbing her elbow and moving her out of sight. "Your mother and I agreed we would not meet in public."

The familiar anger and frustration rose in Delphine's chest until she felt her cheeks flush. Her mother had agreed to many things, but lately kept none of her promises.

Jean gently pushed her across the gangplank onto the ship. "Tell your mother you were aboard and I will give your presents I brought back from the West Indies to Carmeline."

"Nonsense," Delphine replied. "You brought presents for Carmeline, too."

"That doesn't mean she can't have more," Jean said, grinning as he helped her onto the ship.

The minute Delphine's feet hit the deck, her spirits lifted. She could feel the currents of the mighty Mississippi churn beneath the ship, feel the promise of exotic shores whispered on the wind.

"I am thirteen now," she insisted. "It's time you took me with you."

Jean shook his head in frustration, weary of the

endless argument Delphine presented. Yet the tiny lines breaking at the sides of his dark eyes told her he was glad to see her.

"Should I worry for my job, Captain? Perhaps Delphine wishes to be made first mate?"

Delphine sensed Philibert Bertrand's presence before he came into view. An enormous man who rivaled her father in height, Phil joined Jean in casting a heavy shadow over her. The two men crossed their arms and scrutinized her, trying their best to keep their laughter at bay.

"We could put her to scrubbing the decks," Jean offered.

"Better yet, the top of the mast needs painting," Phil injected.

Delphine lifted her chin as high as she could manage to match the tall men's gazes. "I will do anything that's commanded of me."

"Great," Jean said, leaning close. "Then go home and go back to your studies."

Delphine felt tears burn at the back of her eyes. Jean glanced at the docks and, finding no one present, pulled her into his arms and held her tight.

"Soon, *mon petite,*" he whispered to the top of her head. "Soon."

Her head barely met his shoulder so she lay her cheek upon his chest and breathed in the briny scent that lingered on his clothes. His warm embrace felt so incredibly good, like a long drink at the well after weeks of traveling. How long had it been since someone held her close? How long had it been since someone cared?

"Let us go below before someone sees us," Jean said, releasing her.

Delphine followed her father down the steps to the main cabin. As she passed Phil, Jean's business partner and best friend, he quickly offered his own hug and planted a kiss on her forehead.

"Good to see you, Phiney," he said, calling her by the nickname he had given her since a babe.

"And you too, Noncle Phil."

They entered the small cabin with its wide expanse of glass at the stern. The portholes on each side of the room had been opened and a chilling breeze ruffled the maps lying across a four-poster bed. A bowl of fruit planted in its center was the only thing keeping the papers from blowing out the window into the river.

"You bought a bed?" Delphine exclaimed, staring at the mahogany woodwork.

"Never mind the bed," Jean said. "What are you doing here? I thought we had an agreement."

"I wanted to see you," she said, her mind studying the intricate pattern of the silk coverlet. "Carmeline spotted your ship this morning on the way to market."

"I was planning on visiting tonight. Have I ever come to New Orleans and not come to see you?"

Delphine slid the soft fabric between her fingers. Silk? On her father's bed? The fact that he had a bed was startling enough, but the delicate material was a puzzle. Her father usually preferred a hammock, both on ship and off, with cotton blankets to keep him warm.

"No," she said, focusing on his question. "But the

whole thing is preposterous. You're my father. The whole world knows it. Why must we keep it a secret?"

Jean wrapped his arms about her shoulders and pulled her into his chest and she felt her troubles disappear. He was such a commanding man. Tall, yes, but large in every other way. His hands alone were the size of melons, his arms like tight coils of rope. The world with all its social demands disappeared the moment he enveloped her in his broad, strong embrace.

"I love you," Delphine whispered, feeling the tears return. "And I want to be with you. I don't give a hoot about society or anything else. Please take me with you."

Jean released her and cupped her chin with one hand while caressing her wild black curls with the other.

"I have no right to you, Phiney," he said.

"You have as much right as any father."

Clouds passed over his sea-black eyes and his voice grew solemn. "In the eyes of the world I am not your father."

Pushing away, Delphine walked the length of the bed, tracing the intricate lines of the wood with her forefinger. "In the eyes of my mother, you mean."

She heard her father sigh. "Your mother made a choice," he said gravely. "And we all must live with the consequences."

My mother made a bad choice! Delphine wanted to scream. One that was destroying her life.

"Why didn't she marry you when she found herself with your child?" Delphine asked. "You asked her. Why didn't she choose you?"

It was fruitless, she knew, questions always followed by the same answers. Yet Delphine couldn't help wondering how her mother, an educated woman of Creole society, could have made such a grave error in judgment.

"You know why." Jean brushed back the curls from her cheeks. "Why marry a smuggler with no social standing and no wealth when there are richer, more prominent men about the streets of New Orleans? Your mother got what she wanted: money and a title. And Count Delaronde thought he was getting an heir. Your mother saw to that."

The sound of her "father's" name caused a bad taste in her mouth. She had never met the Compte Delaronde, nor ever wished to do so. After Delphine's birth, the man had collected all of their funds, including her mother's dowry, and returned to France. Her mother was still married to him, but he would never acknowledge her.

"If he thought I was his child, why did he abandon us?"

Again, she knew the answer, wondered why she continued to broach the subject. Yet how could she not? It all seemed so unfair. The man who should have been her father, the man who loved her and provided for the household, had to visit at night, unseen for fear of scandal, while her titled father played at court in France, never offering a *piastre* of support.

Jean turned her around gently so she faced the mirror, another feminine addition to the stark, masculine cabin. When Delphine glanced into the glass, she saw what Count Delaronde must have seen the day of her birth.

She sported thick, black curls the color of midnight, the kind of crimped hair found only on a few. It cascaded down her back, tied with a ribbon at her nape, and framed her face in natural rivulets. Although Jean's hair reached only his collar and fell partly in waves, the resemblance was unmistakable.

Delphine's eyes, too, mirrored her father's in their color and intensity. And gracing her right cheek was a dimple to match his.

As Carmeline always said, only fools and the blind would doubt her parentage.

"But Count Delaronde's gone," Delphine whispered. "And you're here."

"And I always will be," Jean said to her reflection. "But people will talk and there is no sense in feeding a fire. You must be schooled and reared like a proper young lady, without the scandal my liaison would bring."

Delphine rolled her eyes. She knew her father hated when she did so, but her schooling and etiquette instruction were laughable. Most of the money Jean had given her mother for such services was used to supplement her mother's wardrobe and decadent lifestyle. A tutor had been hired, a half-educated man fresh off the docks from French Haiti who preferred sampling the Delaronde wine to teaching languages and reading. Her etiquette instruction consisted of Delphine offering charity work to the Ursuline nuns, who continually insisted that pious behavior and supreme sacrifices, to their benefit of course, would save her soul, a soul created by a night of sin between a fortune-hunting woman and a drunken pirate.

As if he read her mind, Jean turned her so she faced him.

"No matter what has come of this," he said firmly, "I never regret what happened. Never."

Delphine wished she hadn't brought up the painful subject for the hundredth time. It was a delicate matter, after all, one a young girl shouldn't discuss with her father who couldn't be seen in public with her. Still, it warmed her heart to hear him speak such rare words of affection. Captain Jean Bouclaire was not a man of passionate declarations. Actions, maybe, but rarely words of love.

It didn't matter. One look into his eyes and Delphine realized the depths of his adoration. And that was all she needed.

The flag flying across the stern whipped in the breeze, tapping on the windows with its tip. The movement brought Delphine's attention back to the marvelous bed and its elegant coverlet. Glancing up and over her father's shoulder, realization hit.

"It's a woman," Delphine announced. "There's a woman in your life."

How was it that Jean feared no man, yet his daughter could render him helpless in an instant? One minute his heart ached for her pain, worried for her happiness. The next minute she had seen right through him.

"What are you talking about?" he asked her, although he knew she had guessed his secret.

"The bed," Delphine said with a satisfied grin.

"Silk bedding and a mirror. Why else would you have purchased such things?"

"How about comfort?" Jean continued. "Don't you think your father deserves some of the finer things in life?"

Delphine took his large hand in hers and squeezed, a simple gesture that nearly undid him. Nothing in his life matched the love of his precious daughter. He would conquer oceans if it meant keeping her safe.

"I think you deserve to be happy," Delphine answered softly. "I hope this means you will marry that woman."

Jean's heart constricted. The bed and other furnishings were purchased in the West Indies with the idea of proposing marriage to Gabrielle Gallant, but he refused to admit to such a plan, even to himself. Jean still wasn't convinced that what he had to offer Gabrielle was worthy of her.

"What woman?" he asked, fearing Delphine would give her a name.

"The Acadian woman you talked about so much on your last trip. The one who lives on the frontier with her family. The one with the angelic name."

Now Jean knew he was sunk. If he spoke her name, his actions would have meaning, Delphine would expect results. But who was he fooling? Inside his breast pocket was an emerald ring the perfect color to accent Gabrielle's long, ivory fingers.

"Gabrielle Gallant," Jean said, his heart quickening at the sound of her name. He had met her at the Spanish fort at Natchez, immediately entranced by her haunting eyes, silky raven hair, and unpretentious airs. When her family had moved on in search of her father, Jean had followed, often managing to steal a kiss or two. Now, she was in the Attakapas region to the west of New Orleans, waiting on her father's frontier land grant in the hopes of his return. Jean hoped she waited for his return as well.

"She's the one," Delphine said, casually sitting on the bed as if it were her own.

The Gallants were Acadians, expelled from their Canadian homes by the English thirteen years before. During their *grand dérangement,* when thousands of Acadians were shipped throughout the English colonies, the three daughters and their mother had been separated from their father and sent to the colony of Maryland. When the Gallant family heard that Joseph Gallant was in the Louisiana Territory, they traveled to New Orleans in the hopes of reunion. Only Joseph had also heard of their existence and boarded a ship bound for Maryland. The family passed each other in the Gulf of Mexico—two ships passing in the night, as the saying goes. Now, Gabrielle and her family waited for Joseph Gallant's return to Louisiana, living on his land grant, hoping he would safely cross the southeastern region to their eager arms.

Gabrielle Gallant. Her image haunted Jean's dreams, filled his every waking moment and left him with a scalding desire. He literally ached for his Acadian woman. As soon as he visited with Delphine and saw to her needs, he would depart for the Attakapas Poste and ask Gabrielle Gallant for her hand.

"That is her, right?" Delphine asked.

"That is *she,* " Jean corrected her. "What kind of schooling are you receiving?"

Delphine picked up a pear from the bowl and smirked. "Pierre Lamont is a drunk. I've learned a lot about the different types of wine by following his empty bottles around the house. He's useless. He made me clean his boots yesterday. And I don't like the way he looks at me, just like the way he stares at a fine piece of meat."

The blood rose in Jean's neck until he thought a vein might burst.

"Why is your mother spending my money on a half-wit and a miscreant?" he shouted.

Delphine's eyes widened as she took a tentative bite of her pear. Jean knew she feared divulging too much about her mother and he hated putting her in the middle of such unpleasantries. But he had to know.

"She spends it on clothes instead," Delphine whispered. "We had nothing to eat last week because she spent the remainder of our market money on a new hat, some new man she's trying to impress. Said he was the answer to our prayers. Carmeline sold some of the silver, but Maman doesn't know about it. She wouldn't anyway. We never entertain anymore."

Jean had heard enough. He buttoned his waistcoat and pulled on his coat. Grabbing the papers on the bed and Delphine's hand, they headed for the deck.

"I'm taking Phiney home," he barked to Phil.

"Shouldn't you let me do that?" Phil asked. "At least, wait until dark. You might be seen."

But Jean would not be satisfied until Louise Delaronde explained herself, and he didn't give a damn who saw him escort his daughter home. He handed Phil the transport papers and helped Delphine cross the gangplank to the docks.

"Finish unloading the goods for me," he said over his shoulder. "And give the men shore leave until tomorrow."

When they had hailed a carriage and were seated inside, Delphine burst into tears. "Don't yell at Maman," she pleaded. "She blames me enough as it is."

Jean framed her face with his hands and slid his thumbs underneath her eyes to catch her tears. "You are not to blame for anything," he insisted, hoping to keep control of his anger for fear of upsetting her further. "You are not to blame because two people had too much wine one night at a garden party. You are not to blame because your fool mother can never be thankful for what she has, cannot see the riches before her."

"But it will only make it worse," Delphine said between sobs.

"How can it be worse?" Jean almost shouted. "I give your mother a handsome income. She has no right to rob you of an education."

"I don't want an education," Delphine said, wiping her nose with her sleeve. "I want to go with you. I hate it here."

Jean tilted her chin up so their eyes met. "You won't after I get finished talking to your mother. You will be happier getting a formal education, meeting young men, and going to dances and balls."

Delphine jerked her head from his hand and stared out the carriage window. Her tears had stopped, replaced by poorly hidden anger.

"What kind of life could I possibly offer you?" Jean

insisted. "A ship of smelly, rugged men is no place for a young lady."

"It's a place for Gabrielle."

Hardly, Jean thought. God knew he was plagued with doubts over inviting Gabrielle into his life.

"I haven't asked her yet," he said. "And I may never."

The carriage stopped at the same moment Delphine's eyes turned back toward his, and the pain reflected there pierced him to his core.

"Papa," she said softly. "Gabrielle and I love you. Why won't you let us into your life?"

Jean leaned forward so he could touch her delicate cheek. He longed to tell her he wanted nothing better than to carry her away with him, to spend his days surrounded by the women he loved. But it was because of this love that he kept them onshore. He knew what dangers existed at sea. How could he risk his precious daughter and Gabrielle for his selfish desires?

As she had so many times before, Delphine saw right through him.

"We love you," she whispered. "Don't sacrifice our happiness because we're women."

The carriage doors opened before a house in dire need of repairs. The footman offered his hand to Delphine, but Jean bounded from the carriage and helped his daughter onto the *banquette*. He slipped the footman the fare and entered the house without knocking, his leather boots pounding on the cypress planks beneath his feet.

"Captain Bouclaire," Carmeline uttered, nearly

dropping the vase of flowers in her hands. "The Countess isn't expecting you."

Still holding tightly to Delphine's hand, Jean paused in the hallway and examined the light-skinned slave who was ten years Delphine's senior.

"Where is she?" He tried to keep his voice from exhibiting his anger, but years of Louise's games and mistreatment of Delphine burned in his temple.

"She's, uh . . ." Carmeline glanced quickly at the parlor doors, then hung her head. "I don't know."

Jean had a good idea what was happening behind the parlor doors, so he released Delphine, entered the parlor, and quickly closed the doors behind him. Louise, dressed in her finest with plenty of bosom exposed, was seated on the chaise while a young man in uniform kneeled before her, planting kisses on her forearm. They both jumped to their feet upon his entry.

"What on earth are you doing?" Jean shouted.

Louise's mouth fell open in shock while the man straightened his jacket. But it didn't take the countess long to recover.

"Jean, how dare you march in here—"

"How dare I?" Jean returned. "How dare you spend my hard-earned money on frivolities while subjecting Delphine to a life of hardship? And who the hell is this drunkard Pierre Lamont staring at my daughter like she's his property?"

"You have no right to accuse me or make demands," Louise insisted. "No right at all."

Jean leaned so close to her he nearly gagged on her perfume. Startled by his large presence, Louise retreated a few steps.

"I have every right," Jean said, finally stating the words aloud. "I am her father."

"How dare you, monsieur!"

Turning to acknowledge the voice of the uniformed man, Jean found almost a boy before him.

"Who's this?" he asked. "Your new footman?"

The man's eyes grew bright with fury and Jean heard Louise gasp behind him. So this was the answer to her prayers, a boy too ignorant to understand the plotting of a woman starved for constant adoration and funds to feed her insatiable appetite for parties and fancy dresses.

"Stay out of this," Jean warned the man.

"I will not," the man said, stepping forward. "The lady wishes you to leave."

"The lady?" Jean laughed. "If you had any sense, young man, you would bolt this instant. Before you have a chance to mature, this 'lady' will bleed you dry."

To his credit, the man stood his ground. "I will say it once more, monsieur, the lady wishes you to leave."

Jean crossed his arms across his chest, truly captivated at the nerve of such a young adversary. But courage was one thing, sense quite another.

"My name is Captain Bouclaire," he said, hoping the man would get the hint and leave.

"I know who you are."

The hairs on Jean's neck began to tingle. He was tiring of the fool. "Then you know better than to tell me what to do in this house."

"Marcel," Louise said with a catch in her voice. "I will summon you later. Jean and I will discuss this in private."

"You will not discuss it at all," Marcel continued. "You have asked him to leave and I will see that he does."

The anger that had consumed Jean earlier returned in a startling force. Another word from the idiot's mouth and Jean feared he would punch the boy senseless.

"Marcel," Louise whispered. "Please."

"Yes, Marcel," Jean added firmly. "You must leave."

Marcel stepped forward. "You have insulted this household with your presence," he said. "Your acknowledgment of Delphine places scandal on this fine lady's head. I will not allow it."

"Louise," Jean said as calmly as he could manage. "Tell this child to leave my sight before I rip every limb from his body."

"Marcel," Louise began, but the man would hear nothing of it.

"I demand at your hands immediate personal satisfaction," he said, removing his gloves from his epaulette.

"And you shall have it," Jean agreed, stepping so close to the boy all thought of his striking Jean disappeared. Marcel moved backward a step, his confidence failing.

"Tomorrow then," he said in a less cocky tone. "Behind the Faed house on the outskirts of town. At dawn."

Before Jean could answer, the boy turned and quickly bowed to Louise, then exited the parlor.

"What have you done?" Louise exclaimed as the front door opened and closed.

"What have *I* done?"

Jean glanced at the beautiful woman who turned heads wherever she ventured. He knew why he had sought her out that night at the party, but all he felt for her now was contempt.

"What have *you* done?" he shouted. "You have robbed my daughter of an education and a decent upbringing, you're wasting food money on useless trinkets. And now you've reduced yourself to robbing the cradle for affection."

"Don't you dare hurt Marcel," Louise said, thrusting her chin forward. "He wants to take care of us, which is more than you have been able to do with your putrid income."

Jean wished it was Louise facing him the next morning in a duel. He was tired of her endless demands, her resentments and accusations. More than anything, he was tired of being blamed for her husband's abandonment. He wanted to shake sense into the woman, but knew it to be fruitless. She would always despise him. Resent his freedom. Resent the fact that Delphine loved him so.

"Your boy will not die tomorrow," Jean said. "But when I come back from the Attakapas Poste, I'm taking Delphine with me. I can stomach this situation no longer."

Louise surprised him by not refusing his request. Maybe he had fooled himself into believing she had cared for her daughter all these years. Now that a young, handsome provider had entered the picture, Delphine was no longer needed.

"I pity you, Louise," Jean said. "You're throwing away your only chance at happiness."

A wild look of apprehension crossed her features before she resumed her usual, haughty demeanor. "You're mistaken, Jean," she said softly. "I gave away my chance at happiness the night I lay with you."

Jean heard the words the same moment he saw them register on his daughter's face in the hall. At that moment his courageous Delphine appeared as breakable as the vase still held tightly in Carmeline's hands.

"Funny," Jean said, staring into Delphine's eyes. "That's the only part of our relationship I don't regret."

Delphine attempted a smile, but Jean knew her heart had shattered. No kind words could ever replace the fact that her mother did not care.

As he passed her in the hall, he tilted her chin upward with his finger. "Three weeks, Phiney," he said, then planted a kiss on her forehead. "Be ready to leave in three weeks."

Chapter Two

Gabrielle stared at herself in the mirror, wondering how she had managed to constrict her bosom into such a small amount of fabric. She attempted a sigh, only to be reminded of the stays pressing against her ribs.

"How do women wear such clothes every day?" she asked her mother. "I feel as if I will either faint or my seams will rip."

"Madame Vincent said this was the latest style for young women," Marianne Gallant said. "She knows about such things."

"Yes, she does," Gabrielle said wistfully. Juliette Vincent, a wealthy Creole in her own right, had married the richest man in the southwestern Louisiana district. Although the Attakapas Poste was considered frontier, one would hardly realize it standing in the elegant Vincent household.

"It was kind of her to honor your twenty-first birthday at her Twelfth Night celebration," Marianne reminded her. "And lend you one of her finest gowns for the occasion."

Gabrielle examined her reflection in the glass and had to admit the emerald silk gown was exquisite. The offending stays beneath her bodice flattened her abdomen and emphasized her bosom nicely.

"You look magnificent," Marianne said. "Such a picture for your twenty-first birthday."

Gabrielle winced. "That's the second time you said that."

"Said what, my dear?"

Gabrielle turned toward her mother, a graceful beauty even though years of living in exile, separated from her husband, had lined her ebony hair with gray. Marianne had suffered several horrors since being forced from their Nova Scotian home thirteen years before—separation from family, intense poverty, fevers. But the last four months had been the hardest by far.

When they had reached Louisiana almost a year before, and learned that Joseph had left for Maryland in search of them, they decided to wait for his return. They had traveled west to the Opelousas Poste first, then south to La Poste in the Attakapas. But in the meantime, Gabrielle's younger sister Rose had married an American named Coleman Thorpe and was now with child. She and their older sister, Emilie, and her husband Lorenz, remained in Opelousas.

Staring into that face that had been her strength for years, Gabrielle knew what her mother was trying to do: the same thing she had done for her two sisters, who were now living in matrimonial bliss. She wanted Gabrielle wed and happy. Anything to relieve the pain of their splintered family.

"You said twenty-first twice," Gabrielle explained. "Are you trying to tell me something?"

Marianne shrugged and shook the lint off Gabrielle's skirt. "I want you to enjoy yourself tonight, being your birthday and all."

"There it is again." Gabrielle laughed, turning back toward the mirror to fix her hair. "If I didn't know better, Maman, I'd think you were trying to tell me I've become an old maid."

As she pulled her long black hair off her face, Gabrielle caught her mother's eyes in the mirror and her heart stilled. "Is that what you're saying?"

Marianne rested her hands on her daughter's shoulders and squeezed while placing her cheek against hers. It was the standard Gallant maternal gesture that preceded a lecture.

"You're not an old maid," Marianne said. "You're a young, vibrant, beautiful woman."

"But . . . ?" Gabrielle offered.

"But you will not be young forever."

Suddenly, Gabrielle understood her meaning. If anyone comprehended the agony of waiting for a man, it was her mother. Since they had begun living on her husband's land grant, Marianne religiously waited by the banks of Bayou Teche hoping to see Joseph Gallant appear around the bend. Every day, she ventured out, waiting for his arrival. Every day she returned home alone.

They had received word he was in Georgia heading toward the Louisiana Territory, but months had passed and still he had not arrived. For the first time since Gabrielle and her family had been shipped from their home thirteen years before, she had doubts she would see her father again. Too much time had passed and so much wilderness lay between Georgia and New Orleans.

But Joseph wasn't the only man Gabrielle waited for in the Attakapas Poste.

"Jean said he would be back," Gabrielle whispered to their reflection.

Marianne led Gabrielle to a chair and began fixing her hair for the ball.

"What if he does come back?" Marianne said. "Gabrielle, you know I care for Jean very much and I approve of you marrying him, but the truth is, he's not the marrying type. Not to mention that it's been months since you last saw him."

Her mother spoke the truth, but Gabrielle refused to listen. There had to be a way for them to be together. She loved Jean and knew he loved her as well.

"He's a sailor," Marianne continued. "I know how much you love the sea, but you can't raise a family aboard a ship. What kind of life can he offer you?"

An exciting one, Gabrielle thought, her heart leaping at the prospect of returning to the sea. God, how she missed the ocean.

Then she remembered the reason for her family's separation, and guilt consumed her. She couldn't let her selfish desires rule her head this time. And she couldn't leave her mother alone, even if Jean returned.

"What do you want me to do?" Gabrielle asked, her heart breaking.

Marianne walked in front of her daughter to meet her eyes. "I want you to have a good time tonight," she commanded in the Acadian accent that set her apart from other French residents of Louisiana. "I want you to meet some nice men. Dance. Be happy."

Gabrielle stared at her hands in her lap. Happiness was not something she was used to, except when Jean was around.

"Gabrielle."

Her mother's stern tone demanded her attention. Gabrielle looked up to find her mother's arms crossed against her chest, the same gesture she used when Gabrielle got into trouble as a child. And she had gotten into trouble endlessly.

"He may never return," Marianne said. "If he does, he may not wish for marriage. Don't waste your young life waiting for something that might not happen. For someone who might not appear."

Gabrielle swallowed hard at the words. She prayed her mother wasn't speaking her own thoughts. "You haven't wasted yours," Gabrielle said softly.

It was more of a question than a statement, and Gabrielle wished with all her soul that her mother was not speaking doubts after thirteen long, tormenting years. If her mother doubted Joseph's return, all was lost.

Marianne slipped her fingers through Gabrielle's hair, still unpinned and hanging loose. She cupped her daughter's face and smiled. "No, *'ti-monde*. I haven't wasted one minute of my life. And I will wait until my dying day for your father's return."

Gabrielle released a breath; she hadn't realized she had stopped breathing while waiting for her mother's answer. She rose and slipped into her mother's arms, placing her cheek on Marianne's shoulders while tears streamed forth.

"Oh, my dear, I didn't mean to make you cry," Marianne said.

Still holding each other, they began to sway, the way they had done since Gabrielle was a baby. Emilie used to laugh at the way they embraced, but Gabrielle always found it comforting.

"If you don't regret waiting for Papa," Gabrielle whispered over her mother's shoulder, "why do you wish for me . . . ?"

Releasing her, Marianne wiped the tears from her face. "Because I have known passion. I have known the joys of waking up next to your father. I have children to comfort me in my old age. What will you have, Gabrielle, if you give up your chance at happiness for a man who may never materialize?"

Gabrielle couldn't imagine a life without Jean. She dreamed of him at night, ached for the touch of his arms about her, his lips hot upon hers. But her mother had a valid point. If only she could convince her heart to forget.

"Promise me you will enjoy the attention of men tonight," her mother demanded. "Promise me that if they call on you tomorrow, you will not discourage them as you have in the past."

As she contemplated her mother's words, images of Jean appeared before her eyes.

"Promise me," her mother urged.

Gabrielle nodded. It was the sixth of January,

Twelfth Night, the Epiphany, the beginning of the Carnival season. It was also her twenty-first birthday. It was time to enjoy life, to find happiness.

If only she could escape the pain gripping her heart.

Jean followed the house servant into the foyer of the Vincent home, realizing his surprise visit to his friend was an inopportune one. The Vincent house was abuzz with activity, and music could be heard from the dining room mixed with the soft hum of conversation.

"If this is a bad time, I can call on Monsieur Vincent tomorrow," Jean offered the servant.

"Don't be ridiculous, you old fool."

Jean turned and found Antoine Vincent, dressed in his finest suit, strolling down the hallway. "I will take care of my good friend," he said to the servant, then opened an adjoining door to his study and motioned for them to enter.

The Vincent house hardly matched the sophistication of New Orleans society, yet the rugged raised cottage held an aspect of elegance rarely seen among the city's elite. There were only three rooms to the house: one for dining, one for Antoine's study, and the other a bedroom. Yet all three were spacious and opened onto galleries, providing a nice breeze even on the hottest of afternoons. Surrounding the house were a courtyard and a series of gardens leading down to the bayou. If Jean had to live on land, the Vincent house at La Pointe in the Attakapas Poste would be his first choice.

"What brings you here, my friend?" Antoine asked,

pouring Jean a glass of brandy. "What precious cargo have you acquired this time that you wish for me to buy? I'm surprised you made it up the bayou with the drought we've been experiencing. Water levels have been dangerously low."

Jean accepted the glass and downed the contents in one swallow. The liquor left a satisfying burn down the back of his throat, a dulling sensation he had gotten used to in the past two weeks. Jean had managed to drink all of his stashes in the sail from New Orleans. Anything to deaden the pain.

"What is it?"

Jean felt Antoine's hand on his shoulder. Although he despised speaking of his pain, he had to confide in someone. He had to know of Gabrielle.

"I'm in a bit of trouble," Jean said.

To his credit, Antoine said nothing and refilled both their glasses. Jean tossed back the contents, then walked toward the fireplace and placed an elbow on the mantel.

"I killed a man," Jean explained. "There's a price on my head."

Shock registered on Antoine's face, more from the latter piece of information than the first. "How?"

Jean leaned his head back and shut his eyes, letting the brandy work its magic. After two weeks, he still couldn't believe what had transpired that ill-fated morning.

"It was a duel," Jean began. "Louise had taken a lover, practically a boy. I barged in one day, barking orders, and he challenged me to protect her honor." Jean smirked. "As if that woman had any honor."

"Duels don't make men criminals." Antoine

refilled his glass. "You said you have a price on your head."

"The boy's father is a top-ranked Spanish official with connections to the new governor." Jean's blood boiled remembering how Edouard Prevost had called him a murderer while his fool son died in his arms. If anyone was the cause of the boy's death, it was his idiot father.

"I gave him several chances to back out of the duel," Jean explained. "I never meant to go through with it. The boy must have heard of my prowess with the foils for he was ready to retract the challenge. Only his bastard of a father wouldn't hear of it, kept insisting he had to finish the duel."

"What happened?"

Jean sat down in the chair opposite his friend. "We crossed swords. I injured him, giving him an excuse to stop the fight. But his father wouldn't let him back down, kept telling him he would be humiliated if he didn't finish the fight." Jean tossed back the brandy. "What father would rather see his son dead than reasonably end a duel?"

"The world is full of fools," Antoine offered.

"I gave up then," Jean continued. "I wasn't going to kill the boy. He didn't have a chance against me. I turned to leave, his father yelled something to the boy, and he lunged at me."

"From behind?"

Jean nodded, still amazed that a soldier would do such a dishonest thing in a duel between gentlemen, but fathers had that power over sons.

"I raised my sword to meet his, the grass was wet

from the early morning fog, he slipped and fell against my blade. He died almost instantly."

Antoine slapped his hands against his knees. "It was an accident. Surely you had witnesses."

"Philibert was my second," Jean said softly.

Antoine said nothing, but ran his fingers through his curly sandy hair. Jean knew what he was thinking. Philibert was the finest swordsman and sailor Jean knew. He was also the finest of men. But there had been a scandal back in France, and scandals of that nature were hard to overcome. In a court of law, Philibert's character would always come into question, especially against a man close to the governor.

"And the boy's father claims this to be murder?"

"The bastard would rather blame a pirate than admit he sent his son to his death. I'm an easy target, Antoine. It only took hours before New Orleans was covered with posters asking for my capture."

Antoine rose and scratched his head while he paced. "I will write letters. I will see what influence I have in this matter."

"I appreciate your help," Jean said. "In the meantime I must leave the territory. Before I do, I want to ask a favor."

His friend stopped and met his eyes. "Anything."

"Write to Delphine, send her money, and have her write back to you. I must know she is well. Please pass this information on to her."

"Of course."

Jean stood, wondering if the weight pressing on his heart was the effect of the brandy or the knowledge that he would never see Gabrielle again. And Gabrielle was so close, only a small walk up the bayou.

"There is one other thing."

A knock sounded at the door and Juliette Vincent, adorned with jewels around her neck and feathers in her hair, popped her head inside the study. "Antoine, dear, your guests are waiting."

Antoine turned and offered Jean an apologetic smile. "It's our annual Twelfth Night gala," he said gravely. "I'm afraid I must make an appearance."

The two men turned back toward Juliette in an effort to make introductions, but Juliette had rushed back to the party.

"Perhaps you would like to join me," Antoine said. "We could find a quiet corner and continue our conversation."

Jean hated asking his friend to inquire about Gabrielle and her mother, but he had to know they were safe and settled. By now, her father had arrived, her sisters and their husbands had joined them, and they had returned to a normal family life. It was doubtful they needed his assistance, but he had to know.

"I'm not properly dressed," Jean said, gazing down at his usual attire of a loose-fitting shirt, breeches, black coat, and leather boots.

"Nonsense," Antoine replied, pulling a mask from his pocket. "It's Carnival. Anything goes. We shall pretend you are costumed as a pirate."

Twelve dances. Gabrielle had counted them. With twelve different men. Now that she had performed her duty, smiled politely, and offered plenty of compliments to the long array of boasting men who had filled her dance card, she wanted to go home. None of the men had caught her fancy. None of them could compare to Jean.

"Having fun?" Felicité Hébert whispered.

"Of course," Gabrielle answered. "Aren't you?"

The two women grinned at their inside joke. Both had been asked to join the Vincent's prelude to the Carnival season, an honor among young, available girls not privileged enough to join Poste society on their own. They were this year's Juliette Vincent marriage project. Juliette had discovered her "orphaned Acadians" and vowed to have them wed by Easter to prosperous cattle owners in the area.

"I still haven't mastered that horrid dance," Felicité whispered as they watched the guests glide through the steps of a rigid dance.

"Give me a fiddle and a *dance rounde* any day," Gabrielle concurred.

"Have you met anyone you like?" Felicité asked. "I saw you speaking at great length with Charles Maase."

"You saw me listening at great length." Gabrielle let her guard down for an instant and smiled. "He is such a bore, yet he never stops talking. Someone needs to inform him that what he is saying is of no interest to anyone."

The girls began to giggle, which drew the attention of Juliette standing guard over the room like a queen. They quickly resumed a dignified countenance, bringing their masks up over their eyes.

"And what about you?" Gabrielle asked. "I saw you speaking with Pierre Doucet's son."

Again, the two broke out in giggles, turning away from the crowd to keep from being seen.

"I can't help it," Felicité said. "I know I'm supposed to catch a rich husband at these parties, but I prefer the stable boy. He is rather cute, don't you think?''

Silvestre Doucet was not only handsome, but modest as well, a trait Gabrielle found more appealing than money. He was also an Acadian, someone who would understand Felicité's moods. Like Gabrielle, Felicité had been separated from her father during their exile from Grand Pré. After being sent to the colony of Georgia, her mother was sold into indentured servitude and she and her sister sent to work at another plantation. Her sister died of smallpox within months and Felicité ran away only to find her mother buried in an unmarked grave. The Doucets, a neighboring Acadian family, took her in and brought her to Louisiana, where she lived as a member of their family.

But Felicité was prone to depression, falling into melancholy without warning. Gabrielle had hoped the parties would cheer her up.

''You could always bow to the moon three times tonight and see if his face appears,'' Gabrielle said with a smile. ''Or place your garter beneath your pillow and say a prayer to St. Francis.''

Felicité returned the smile. They both thought the seasonal superstitions preposterous, but likely would perform the rituals that night anyway. Gabrielle knew whose face would appear to her within the moon. Of that she had no doubt.

''Do you think Madame Vincent would mind if I married Silvestre?'' Felcité asked, her smile gone. ''His family has been so good to me. I feel like a daughter anyway.''

Gabrielle leaned forward so no one else would hear. "Marry whomever you please."

Brightened by the prospect of love, Felicité beamed, dropping her mask and beginning a long conversation about Silvestre and his plans for an indigo farm. But despite her friend's excitement, Gabrielle failed to hear a word of it. Behind her, only steps away, was the voice of her dreams, the man she had been waiting for for several agonizing months.

She knew it was Jean. She would recognize that baritone voice anywhere. And the sound came from above her shoulder. Few men matched Jean's height and girth.

Gabrielle's heart quickened. Still clutching the mask to her face, she thought to turn and greet him, but Felicité was in the middle of an animated explanation and she hadn't the heart to interrupt her good spirits. If Gabrielle appeared too eager to gain Jean's attention, not only would Felicité guess her feelings, nearly everyone present would too. A lady didn't make casual introductions, Madame Vincent had instructed her. She had to be properly introduced by a third party, even if they had met before. "A true lady is judged by discretion," Juliette had said, which seemed a waste of time to Gabrielle, but she obeyed nonetheless.

"So what is the other favor you wish to ask of me?" Gabrielle heard Antoine Vincent ask Jean.

Nodding her head to Felicité, Gabrielle concentrated hard on the conversation at her back. The two men were so close, she could make out almost every word.

"There's a family at the Poste that I wish to inquire about," Jean said.

"And you want me to inquire for you?" Antoine asked.

"Yes."

"Why not do it yourself?"

Gabrielle could feel her heart thumping in her chest as she waited for Jean's answer.

"Considering everything," Jean said, "I think it's best I not approach her. It's a delicate situation."

"A woman, you mean?" Antoine asked with a chuckle.

Jean answered with a nervous laugh. "Something like that."

Pain replaced apprehension, a stabbing pain that tore at Gabrielle's soul. Did he mean what she thought he meant? Was their friendship merely a pirate's flirtation onshore?

"Gabi, are you not feeling well?" Felicité asked.

Gabrielle looked into her friend's eyes, suddenly aware of their previous conversation. She wondered if her face exhibited the myriad feelings raging inside her, and clutched the mask tightly.

"So, what does Silvestre think of you attending these balls?" Gabrielle asked, trying to keep the panic from her voice.

Felicité began another long explanation and Gabrielle again strained to hear the conversation at her back.

"I never knew you to be one to run away from a clutching female," Antoine said. "You were always good at casting off your fish once you got them hooked."

The stays locked around Gabrielle's middle threatened to suffocate her. Her friend's voice, the music, and the dancers seemed to swirl around her like a whirlpool.

"If it's all the same to you," she heard Jean say, "I'd rather not see this woman."

Spots appeared before Gabrielle's eyes. She dropped her mask, grabbed her friend's forearm, and squeezed to get her attention.

"Excuse me, Felicité, but I have to get some air."

"Gabi, you look pale."

Felicité gazed around the room, looking for assistance. The nearest men were Antoine and Jean. If Jean was to see her, know that she had overheard . . .

Before Felicité could summon help, Gabrielle slipped through the open door onto the gallery and sought refuge in the neighboring gardens. Trying hard to resume a steady breath, she made her way down the stone path to the bayou and rested on a bench near an oak tree.

It couldn't be true, Gabrielle thought wildly, staring at the placid bayou before her. He did love her, she knew it. She couldn't be just another flirtation to him, another fish to be caught and cast away.

But he had said those words. She had heard him.

Gabrielle rose and began to pace. Her head screamed from the pounding, and the punch she had consumed soured in her belly. How could she have been so stupid? How did she not see Jean for who he was?

"He's a pirate, you idiot," she whispered to the night. "What did you expect?"

Gabrielle thought of the first night she had spoken

with Jean, when she and her family had first arrived
in Louisiana and been sent to a fort at Natchez near
the English territory. They had sat aboard his boat
on the Mississippi River, a full spring moon sending
down a cascade of silver upon the water.

He had laughed when she called him a pirate, said
he was a smuggler at best, another Frenchmen making a living off the wilds of Louisiana. He talked of
his daughter, his love for her evident in his voice,
confessed his scandalous liaison with her mother.
They shared so many things that night, vowed to be
friends. He'd even kissed her, gently.

Of course, what gentleman would have kissed a lady
at night, unchaperoned? She should have seen the
nature of his character then, realized his improper
advances for what they were.

But Gabrielle had wanted him to kiss her. She'd
wanted him to kiss her in Opelousas when he visited
there. If he stood before her now, she'd want him to
kiss her again. She loved him. He was everything she
wanted in a man and she'd thought he felt the same
for her.

Gabrielle closed her eyes to fight off the pain crush-
ing her heart and ripping through her head. Her
mother had been right, after all. Jean wasn't the marrying type. Now she knew he wasn't the honorable
type either.

"How could I have been so naive?" she said to the
misty night air.

Suddenly, voices sounded from the galleries and
Gabrielle knew she had to return to the party or risk
being found outside alone. What would Juliette think
of that indiscretion? With one hand rubbing her

pounding head and the other against the tight bodice that pressed at her ribs, Gabrielle didn't care what anyone thought at that moment. She only wanted to be done with the party, to return home, be rid of the suffocating gown, and head straight to bed.

And she never wanted to see Captain Jean Bouclaire again.

The voices drifted from the right of the house, the opposite direction from where she had fled. Gabrielle lifted her skirts and headed up the path toward the left side of the house. She would return to the gallery and slip inside, hide behind her mask, and beg Juliette to let her return home and nurse her headache.

She wasn't three feet on her way when she collided with an enormous male chest.

Chapter Three

What was he thinking, Jean wondered, when he asked Antoine to check on Gabrielle? He should have known his friend would suspect him of improper conduct with a woman. Now he was caught in a lie. He couldn't reveal her name to Antoine because he'd risk ruining Gabrielle's reputation, but he couldn't inquire as to her health either. He'd have to make excuses and inquire about her another way.

Thankfully, before Antoine had time to ask her name, he was called away by his wife, which allowed Jean the opportunity to steal away to the peaceful gardens. The last thing he needed that night was Juliette pairing him up with a giggling woman for a dance.

Jean wasn't ten feet from the house when a dark-haired socialite bounded into his chest.

"Whoa," he said, grabbing her forearms to steady her. "Where's the fire?"

When the woman looked up, Jean could only stare in amazement. Gabrielle appeared before him like a dream, dressed in a cloud of verdant silk, her black hair woven in braids atop her head. Her expressive, deep-set eyes widened at the sight of him. God, but she was more beautiful than he had imagined during those lonely nights at sea.

How foolish of him to think he could visit the Atta-kapas Poste and not see her. Her image was as necessary to him as breathing; he realized that as she stood before him. Yet Jean also knew leaving would be ten times harder now. For both of them.

"Gabrielle," he whispered.

For several moments, they stared at one another, Gabrielle not uttering a sound. Then her eyes turned cold. If he wasn't mistaken, she was angry.

"What are you doing here?" he asked.

She remained speechless, seemingly condemning him with her massive bronze-colored eyes. He heard voices coming from the other side of the house. Gabrielle jerked her arms from his grasp, sent him one last reproachful look, and hurried up the path.

As she brushed past him, Jean felt as if the wind had been ripped from his sails. What had just happened between them? Despite his logical mind telling him not to continue their relationship, to leave the area and let Gabrielle live a normal life married to a man who could offer her a better existence, Jean had to know.

He had to see her one last time.

"Where were you?" Felicité asked her as soon as Gabrielle had crossed the threshold into the house. "We have been worried sick."

"Where is Madame Vincent?" Gabrielle inquired. "I must go home."

Gabrielle heard the rustle of Juliette's petticoats before she saw her arrive. When Juliette met her eyes, her brow creased in worry. "What is wrong, child?"

"I must go home immediately," Gabrielle told her, swallowing hard to tame her beating heart. "Please, I have a dreadful headache."

Juliette placed a maternal hand on her forehead and nodded. "Of course, dear. I will send the Doucet boy for a carriage."

As soon as Juliette had left, Gabrielle felt Felicité's hand in hers, placing a glass of water and a handkerchief in her palm. "You really scared me, Gabi. I have never seen you turn so pale."

Gabrielle sipped the water, realizing her throat was parched. "I will be fine, Felicité. I just need to go home."

Juliette returned and took Gabrielle's elbow and discreetly led her through the crowded room toward the front door. "The carriage is being summoned," Juliette said. "I will have Antoine escort you home."

"That won't be necessary," came a man's voice to their rear.

Whatever calming effect the water had on Gabrielle's heart, the sound of Jean's voice sent it back to a rapid beating. Why was he torturing her when it was clear he never wanted to see her again? What possible reason would he have to share a carriage ride with her when he wished to break off their friendship?

"That's very kind of you, Captain Bouclaire," Juliette said. "But you haven't been properly introduced."

Gabrielle turned, waiting for Jean to acknowledge

that they were old friends, a fact that would make it harder for her to refuse him as an escort.

"Then introduce us," Jean said to their hostess.

Gabrielle didn't think Jean could offer more hurtful words than he had in the ballroom, but claiming they didn't know each other stabbed her to her core. Now, she was to endure his company on the ride home. It was unbearable.

"Silvestre Doucet can escort me home, Madame Vincent," she said, shocking all present. It was the epitome of rudeness, but Jean's feelings were the least of her concern.

The look Jean sent her was scalding. "Silvestre Doucet is a boy," he said. "This is still a frontier, despite the fact that most of the Indians are gone. You need protection."

"I agree," Juliette said, gazing at her with equally condemning eyes. "This is Captain Jean Bouclaire, Gabrielle, an old friend of the family."

Jean bowed, still staring at her sternly. "Mademoiselle."

"This is Mademoiselle Gallant," Juliette added, "who is much more polite when she's in better spirits."

"Captain," Gabrielle uttered, offering a curtsy. Thinking back to her hostess's unending kindness, she added, "My apologies."

The house servant appeared, announcing to Juliette that the carriage had arrived. Gabrielle gritted her teeth and allowed Jean to lead her down the hallway to the front gallery and help her into the carriage seat. She bid Juliette farewell and waved to Felicité at the door. Then Jean joined her on the seat and whipped the horses into action.

They had traveled well out of reach of the house before Jean spoke. He sat so close their arms touched, sending wild sensations through her despite her anger. When he turned to speak, his breath was warm against her cheek. Gabrielle felt her vow never to see him again evaporating.

"Are you ill?" he asked, truly concerned. "Is that why you were so cold to me?"

Gabrielle didn't know how to answer. She still fumed from the knowledge that she meant little more to him than an escapade at port. But something deep inside her refused to believe he didn't care.

"What else should I be?" she said. "We haven't been introduced until tonight."

Jean hesitated, staring at the road before them. "I didn't know how else to respond."

"You didn't want her to know that we knew each other."

Jean turned back and stared at her hard. "What is that supposed to mean?"

"It could mean a lot of things, Jean." Gabrielle gripped the handkerchief tightly between her fingers. "Perhaps, you don't want your upper-class friends to know you cavort with a woman of my station."

Jean jerked the reins so tightly, the horses nearly reared up. They pawed the ground in agitation. "That's the most absurd thing I've ever heard you say. Since when have I ever cared about class distinctions?"

"Then how about you not wanting them to know we had a friendship. Perhaps if Antoine and Juliette knew of our secret kisses, they might expect you to do something honorable and we couldn't have that.''

She knew her voice had risen considerably, that the bitterness lying at the pit of her stomach had emerged in her tongue, but she didn't realize she had mentioned the prospect of them marrying until the last words had been uttered. Gabrielle turned away from him, furious with herself for speaking her feelings. The last thing she needed was further humiliation.

''What I was doing *was* honorable,'' Jean said softly. His voice, too, betrayed his anger, but there was something else, a hint of regret perhaps?

''I know why you were there tonight,'' he continued. ''Juliette always has her favorites at Carnival and this year it's you. So who were you looking to catch, Gabrielle, one of the Masse brothers or Dauterive's oldest son, who's set to inherit that nice piece of land on the bayou?''

She couldn't believe this. He was angry at her for considering other men's advances when she had not heard a word from him in months? Was he disappointed that he hadn't had the chance to break off their relationship?

''She asked me to join her celebration, and yes, Felicité and I are her current apprentices,'' Gabrielle said as calmly as she could manage, despite the fury brewing inside her. ''Since I didn't have other *commitments,* I hardly see why you should object.''

Jean whipped the horses back into action, his jaw tense. ''I don't object,'' he said, although the tension in his face said otherwise. ''But I do object to you being angry with me for interfering in your marital plans."

Gabrielle couldn't believe her ears. He wanted to break their relationship, to steal away without so much as a goodbye, yet he blamed her for being angry on some ridiculous desire to marry another? The night could not get any worse.

"Why are you here?" Gabrielle asked, her heart ready to break into two. "Why did you come to the Poste?"

Jean said nothing, continued staring at the road ahead. They were passing Raymond Sonnier's house, her neighbor. It would be only a few more minutes before they reached home.

"How are you and your mother?" Jean finally asked.

So we're down to polite pleasantries, Gabrielle thought. So be it. More than likely Jean would deposit her at her door and never be heard from again.

"We are fine," she told him.

"And your father?"

The pain that gripped Gabrielle's heart was so intense, she feared it would stop beating. For the first time since she'd overheard Jean speaking, tears formed in her eyes.

"He hasn't come yet," she whispered.

Jean turned and wrapped an arm about her shoulders before she had time to object. He pulled her so close she could feel his mustache brush her forehead. "Oh Gabi," he said so heatedly, she thought she would melt for sure. "I'm sorry."

Gabrielle rested her head against his cheek and breathed in his heavenly scent, a mixture of hard work and the promise of the open sea. For a moment, before logic reared its head, she savored the feel of him, inhaled the comfort of his warm embrace.

Reminded again of his words to Antoine, Gabrielle pulled away. Through the cypress trees lining the bayou she could make out her home, a light shining in the main room. Marianne was probably waiting for her arrival, waiting for news that Gabrielle had met the man of her dreams and was on the road to happy matrimony. What would she tell her mother now?

"And what of your sisters?" Jean asked, returning his hands to the reins.

"Rose is not well enough to travel so they plan to stay in Opelousas for a few more months. The baby is expected in the late spring so she and Emilie will join us after the birth."

"Coleman, Lorenz, are they well?"

More tears gathered at the thought of her brothers-in-law, men she missed almost as much as Jean.

"They write often," she said quietly. "They harvested a good crop. They ask about you all the time. Wonder when you're coming to visit."

"We were going to be partners in a fur business," Jean said.

Gabrielle had heard of this great idea the three men had. Lorenz and Coleman would gather furs and skins from the frontier and Jean would bring them to market in New Orleans.

"And now you're not?"

Jean stopped the carriage in front of the house, turned, and placed an elbow on the back of the seat. While his hand caressed the side of her cheek and neck, his dark eyes studied her hard. When their eyes finally met, Gabrielle swore that he still cared. She could read the love in his eyes.

Something was wrong. He couldn't have meant what he said to Antoine. He couldn't wish to dismiss her as an unimportant fling onshore, not with the affection staring at her now.

But did words lie?

"Just say goodbye, Jean," Gabrielle said softly. "You're good at casting off your fish once you get them hooked. Or how about I save you the trouble and cast off on my own?"

Jean's eyes widened at her words, but she didn't give him time to answer. She hopped from the carriage seat, hurried up the path, and slipped through the door.

For the second time that night, Jean felt like a boat drifting without a helm. All his well-laid plans to check on Gabrielle and leave the territory had disintegrated, ruined by a prideful conversation between two men. He shouldn't have asked Antoine to inquire about Gabrielle. Hell, he shouldn't have let his friend lead him into a ridiculous conversation about women in general. He had acted like a schoolboy, denying a perfectly harmless association with Gabrielle as if acknowledging their friendship would place scandal on her head.

Lying on the carriage floorboard was Gabrielle's handkerchief, cast aside in her hurry to enter the house. Jean picked it up and raised it to his lips, savoring the smell of lavender. Who was he fooling? Their association was anything but friendly. She owned his heart, one hundred percent.

Maybe it was best this way. She would hate him,

but she would stop waiting for his return and marry another. There'd been plenty of prosperous young men at the ball tonight. Gabrielle with her exquisite dark looks and luminous eyes would have no trouble snaring a good husband. She would live in a safe house with a good income, surrounded by her family. It was far more than Jean could offer.

But how would he ever live without her?

Jean closed his eyes in an effort to relieve the pain tearing at his heart. He had to return the horses, but somehow he couldn't bear leaving Gabrielle's house.

"Bonsoir, Captain,'' came a voice from his right.

Jean looked up to find Charles Maase on horseback at his side. He hadn't heard the man approach.

"Are you feeling all right, Jean?" Charles asked. "You don't look well, old man."

Jean straightened in his seat and tried not to appear agitated by the interruption or the remark as to his age. "I'm fine, Charles. What are you doing here?"

Charles dismounted and tied his reins to the fence lining the road in front of the Gallant house. "I was worried about Gabrielle. I heard she left early, and I wanted to make sure she was home safe."

For a moment, Jean wanted to crack his perfect young face with his fist. But this was what Gabrielle needed, a handsome, successful man as her husband. He just didn't feel like facing the bastard tonight of all nights.

"She's fine," Jean said stiffly. "I'm sure she's gone straight to bed."

What was he doing? He needed to encourage Gabrielle's suitors, not send them away. But something about Charles made his blood boil. Or would every man cause him to react this way? More than likely.

"Well, I will check on her anyway, since I'm here."

Charles tipped his tricornered hat to Jean and strode confidently toward the door. Before he had taken three steps, Jean leaped from the carriage seat and joined him on the path.

"She forgot her handkerchief," Jean said when Charles stared at him in surprise.

They reached the door together, Jean stepping aside for Charles to knock. To Charles's even greater surprise, Marianne answered and greeted Jean warmly with an embrace.

"Jean," she exclaimed, kissing both his cheeks. "It is so good to see you again. Where have you been all these months?"

"In the West Indies, Marianne. Trying to keep my daughter in petticoats."

Marianne turned toward Charles and offered her hand in greeting. Apparently, they knew each other. Jean's jealousy heated his blood once again.

"Charles, how nice to see you at this hour." Marianne opened the door wider. "Do come in, both of you."

Gabrielle stood by the wall, nervously twisting the knot of a shawl wrapped around her shoulders, fury and pain still gleaming in her eyes. Jean wanted nothing more than to draw her into his arms and kiss away her misunderstanding. "We must talk," he whispered as he passed her on the way to a chair on the far side of the room.

"Sit," Marianne said more to her daughter than

to the men, who easily made themselves comfortable. "We were just about to have coffee."

Gabrielle slowly made her way to a chair and began pouring the men coffee while Marianne asked Jean about his travels and his daughter. He, in turn, asked about the family and news of Joseph.

"I'm afraid we're short a cup," Gabrielle said, her voice breaking slightly.

"We should leave," Jean said, sending Charles a knowing look. "It is late."

Charles, however, refused his gaze. "Gabrielle, I was wondering if you would join me tomorrow for a picnic," he said, oblivious to her discomfort. "I have some news I'd like to share. The Vincents will be there. Please say you'll come."

It took everything in Jean's power not to grab the upstart and throw him from the room, preferably face first in the mud. He almost did, when Marianne interrupted his thoughts.

"Jean," she said. "I need to make a fresh pot of coffee and the pump is difficult to manage. Would you help me in the kitchen?"

"Of course." Jean rose and helped Marianne with the tray, following her out of the house along a passageway to the kitchen. They entered the small building, which was separate from the house in case of fires, and Marianne lit a candle.

When Jean turned and looked into her face, he noticed two startling things. First, the last few months had aged Marianne considerably, her hair more noticeably gray and lines of worry and heartache etched about her eyes. Second, Marianne was not pleased with his behavior, nor the condition of her daughter. She crossed her arms and gazed at him like a judge about to administer a sentence.

"It was a misunderstanding," Jean said, feeling her eyes burn into his soul and feeling every bit as guilty.

"You have been gone a long time, Jean," Marianne said softly. "And Gabrielle has waited every day for your return. If you don't wish for more of this friendship, then please let her be. Don't keep her hoping for something that will never happen."

Listening to Marianne talk, Jean knew she spoke from experience. The last thing he wanted was to hurt his precious Gabrielle or cause the Gallant family further pain.

"I'm leaving tomorrow," he assured Marianne. "I doubt I will return."

He expected her to approve. Instead, Marianne frowned and shook her head. "Why?"

There were many reasons, but mainly one, and he didn't have the heart to tell her he was wanted for murdering a man the same age as Gabrielle.

"It's best this way," Jean said, escaping her piercing eyes. "Let Gabrielle marry some prosperous man like Charles, someone with a fat land grant and a hundred head of cattle. When the children come, you'll be close by to help, instead of wondering what port your grandchild is being born in."

Marianne placed a loving hand on his cheek, forcing his gaze back to hers. "That is what I have always wanted for Gabrielle," she said gently. "Her home and farm close to me, grandchildren at my beck and call, a steady income. But that is not what is best for her. Surely, you of all people know that."

Jean nodded, kissing the work-worn fingers at his

cheek. He did know that Gabrielle loved the sea, and that if any woman would be his perfect mate, it was Gabrielle. Still, he said nothing, turning and filling the water pitcher. They worked in silence while the coffee dripped, then returned to the main house and the animated conversation of Charles Maase.

"So, if I find the chief's midden, I can prove that they were cannibals," he said to Gabrielle. "Then there will be no more doubts as to the fact that the Attakapas consumed their enemies."

"And how do you propose to prove that?" Jean asked, placing the coffee tray in front of him.

"If the Attakapas Indians were cannibals, they would have placed their enemy's bones in their burial mounds." Charles poured himself a cup of coffee. "I've been told they ate the men they killed and prized their bones as evidence of their prowess. I believe they would have buried their warriors with such enemy bones and I plan to dig through the midden and find them."

"You plan to desecrate a sacred grave to prove a point?" Jean asked.

Charles shrugged while he stirred sugar into his cup. "What does it matter, now? The Attakapas have all but disappeared."

"There are some working on area plantations and I've seen a small group of them at the Poste store," Gabrielle inserted. "I don't think they would like it if someone disturbed their ancestors' resting place."

Charles gave Gabrielle an astonished look. "They're Indians, Gabrielle. They're not like us."

Now, Jean really wanted to lay the young pup flat, grab the ruffles at his collar, and squeeze. It was that Old World, upper-class thinking that was making Louisiana as suffocating as France these days, and Charles Maase fit the class model perfectly. Jean leaned forward to give the man a piece of his mind, but Marianne beat him to it.

"The English ran us out of our homes, Charles," Marianne explained. "I would hate to think they are desecrating our ancestors' graves in Nova Scotia merely because we are not like them."

Charles smiled nervously. It was not his intent to insult the mother of the woman he wished to court. Jean enjoyed watching him squirm.

"I certainly didn't mean it that way, Madame Gallant," Charles said. "Examining the Indian midden is scientific research, I assure you."

"Do you know where this midden is?" Jean asked. Again, Charles shifted nervously in his seat. "No, but I have been told it's on the north shore of Spanish Lake, near the entrance to the bayou. I plan to go there and examine the area."

"I know where the midden is," Jean said. "But it's not at Spanish Lake. There are several middens there, but they are not of the chief."

Charles brightened. "Then you must come with us. Show us where it is."

For the first time since he'd entered the Gallant household, Gabrielle looked his way. Her brown eyes seemed to beseech him to join them, to beg him not to let her face the picnic alone with this arrogant man. Or was he merely fooling himself? Still, there was so much to explain. How could he possibly leave the territory with her thinking so ill of him?

"I'll join you if you promise to leave the midden unharmed."

Charles almost backed down, then his eyes twinkled and he agreed. Jean knew he would only return to the midden another day, but if he played his cards right, the joke would be on Charles.

When Charles began to explain his theory of the Attakapas to Marianne, Gabrielle stood and picked up the tray. "I'm going to get some of the cake I baked this morning," she said to her mother and headed for the back door.

"Jean," her mother said. "We need more water and you know how tricky the pump can be."

Thankful for the interruption and the chance to be alone with Gabrielle, Jean stood and grabbed the water pitcher. Careful not to disturb the water inside, he followed Gabrielle into the night air.

"We have plenty of water," Gabrielle said without looking at him.

Jean tossed the pitcher's contents into the nearby brush. "Not anymore."

When they'd reached the kitchen and the illumination of the candlelight, Gabrielle turned her eyes toward him, enormous chestnut eyes brimming with pain. "Why are you doing this? If you wish to rid yourself of my company, why are you here tonight?"

He slipped his fingers between her silky hair and the bottom of her ear and brushed his thumb across her cheek. "I don't wish to rid myself of you, Gabi," he whispered, taking in the delicious sight of her. "You misunderstood. I have to leave the territory. I didn't want to see you because I knew how hard it would be to say goodbye again."

She huffed and turned toward the coffeepot, obviously not believing a word. Even angry, with her back to him, Gabrielle incited all his senses. He couldn't help himself; he had to touch her. Jean placed his hands at her waist, pulled her slightly toward him, and breathed in her scent. He kissed the top of her head and savored the feel of her body resting against his.

When Jean's large hands gripped her waist, Gabrielle sighed in defeat, realizing she could no longer fight her desire to touch him. As if of its own accord her body betrayed her, forcing her to lean backward into Jean's embrace, her head resting in the curve of his neck. The sudden movement caused her to lose her balance, and she reached for something to steady herself. What her hand found was a rock-hard thigh.

Mon dieu, she thought as she realized the virility of the man behind her, the man she adored, the man now laying a trail of kisses beneath her earlobe. She commanded herself to remove her hand from his leg, to demand that he stop, to force herself not to humiliate herself further, but her curiosity won over her mind. She couldn't help herself. The feel of his firm thigh beneath her hand made her breathing ragged, her heart race.

She wanted him, of that she was certain. One word from his lips and she would follow him anywhere. But the pain in her heart remained. She had to gather her strength, had to push him away.

Gabrielle turned in an effort to say something, to try to regain her composure. When she looked into his face, meeting dark eyes sparkling with flecks of red, what she saw renewed her instinct that something else was at work here.

"What has happened?" she asked.

Jean appeared as if he would reveal his troubles, but then the worry in his eyes disappeared, replaced by a painful look that mirrored Gabrielle's inner turmoil. He pulled her close, his lips only a breath away.

"You have," he whispered, before he claimed her lips with his.

Chapter Four

In the past when Jean had sneaked a kiss, it had been gentle, almost chaste, with just a hint of passion lurking behind the indiscretion. Now, there was no doubt as to his intentions and desires. His lips devoured hers with a forceful hunger, his hands eagerly caressing everything in their path.

Gabrielle met that hunger head on. She instantly wrapped her arms around his neck, allowing him better access to her lips and body. Jean immediately took the opportunity to press her tightly against his expansive chest and parted her lips to deepen the kiss. When his tongue danced lightly with hers, Gabrielle felt her knees weaken and her core ignite into flames.

His lips seemed to set fires every place they rested. Sometimes he dropped teasing nips on her lips, grabbing the plump skin with his teeth and sucking. Sometimes he offered deep kisses that explored the reaches of her mouth with his tongue. The longer he dwelled at her lips, the closer she pressed against him until she could feel every inch of his desire.

Jean left her lips but the separation was brief. He began kissing her cheeks and neck, then nibbling on her earlobe and biting the tender skin at her throat. His enormous hands savored the length of her silky back, pressing her hips hard against him while she dug her fingers into the midnight curls at his nape.

"Oh Gabi," he whispered in between kisses. "I have missed you so much."

When his kisses continued, Gabi knew she was lost. She would follow him anywhere; he only had to ask. He consumed every ounce of her being, devouring her with his relentless passion. And Gabrielle surrendered gladly.

"Oh God," Jean said, when he paused to take a breath. "How will I ever live without you?"

Reminded that she was only a resting place for this pirate, a passionate respite for Jean until he rejoined the sea, Gabrielle forced her mind to clear. She planted both hands on his chest and pushed him away.

She intended to send him from her house and life, but before she had a chance to speak, Jean grabbed her arms and pulled her forward again. "Don't," he said so sternly shivers ran up her arm. "You don't understand."

That was an understatement, Gabrielle thought. One minute she was certain Jean thought nothing more of her than a playful diversion onshore. The next minute she was sure he loved her, that something unspoken was tearing them apart.

Jean released her as if he suddenly realized the

impropriety that had transpired between them. He stepped back slightly, but the darkness lingered in his eyes.

"Don't hate me," he said softly. "I couldn't stand it if I knew you thought ill of me."

"What do you want me to think?" Gabrielle pleaded, still holding on to his coat's lapel for fear of him leaving. She wanted answers. Anything that would make sense.

"I didn't mean what I said to Antoine tonight."

Gabrielle wanted to believe it, but her heart still ached from the words he had spoken. "What did you mean then?"

Jean said nothing, placed a hand at her face, and caressed her cheek. His eyes spoke the words she had wanted to hear, but her heart still refused to accept the love reflected there. He looked as if he wanted to explain, then thought better of it. Instead, he kissed her one last time, a slow, seductive journey into heaven, then rested his forehead against hers as if branding her image to memory.

"Bonsoir, mon amour," he whispered.

Before Gabrielle could react and grasp his lapel once again, she felt his warmth leave her arms and the sound of his boots echoing on the path leading back to the house. Like the sea birds that flew inland with the winter storms, Jean had glided into her life and disappeared just as fast.

Gabrielle lingered in the kitchen, unable to return to the house and the small talk demanded of Charles Maase. She knew she was behaving rudely to her guest, but she didn't have the strength to face another person that night. She brushed a strand of hair behind an ear only to find half of her braid hanging in disarray. No doubt her dress was in a similar state. Another good reason not to return to company.

"What has happened?" Marianne asked when she entered the kitchen. "Jean bolted out of the house, insisting Charles go with him. Are you not feeling well?"

Gabrielle laughed nervously. She knew her mother wasn't blind. "I don't know what happened, Maman," Gabrielle said. "Nothing makes sense."

Marianne placed an arm about her daughter's shoulders and held her tight. "Why don't we sample some of this coffee we have just brewed and you can tell me everything."

Gabrielle nodded, glad to have a willing ear. But she doubted her mother would comprehend Jean's actions any more than she did.

Jean's *radeau* sat high in the water, free from the merchandise he usually brought over from Plaquemine. An empty boat ordinarily gave him reason to celebrate, reminding him that silver jingled in his pocket. Today, the makeshift bayou boat served as a symbol of his failures. There would be no more trips to the Interior, no more smuggling among the residents of Louisiana, no more visits to those he cared for.

"Will you and that pitiful excuse for a boat be leaving today?" Antoine asked him, pouring Jean another cup of coffee. The two were enjoying breakfast at the gallery table overlooking the bayou.

"Yes," Jean answered his friend, leaning back in

his chair. "My men are aboard my ship in Côte Blanche Bay, waiting to set sail for the Caribbean."

"Pity," Antoine said. "I was hoping we would enlist your help. Charles and Juliette have a picnic planned and it requires navigating a few bayous."

Jean had agreed to accompany Charles on his ridiculous outing, but after his lack of control with Gabrielle in the kitchen, he'd thought it best to leave that morning. If only her kisses and the feel of her body in his embrace would stop haunting his thoughts.

"What was the name of that family you wished for me to check on?" Antoine asked.

"Doesn't matter," Jean said tersely to the inside of his cup. "I have seen to it already."

"Already?" Antoine dropped some sugar into his coffee and stirred while grinning slyly. "When did you do this, while driving Gabrielle home last night?"

Jean didn't have to look at his friend to know he was on to his lie. There was little Antoine Vincent could not decipher, the precise reason why the Creole had amassed enormous wealth at such a young age. But Jean was not willing to discuss his personal life— with anyone.

"I should have known," Antoine continued. "Gabrielle isn't just another beauty. She's very unusual, witty, subtly cunning. And so intelligent. There's something wonderful about her I can't explain."

"Then don't."

Jean hoped Antoine would get the message and change the subject, but his friend insisted on continuing. "She's Juliette's pet this season, you know. Juliette has her eye on Charles as a suitor. He's not a bad choice, owns a healthy piece of land, although I do wish the boy would quit talking so much.''

Jean rose and walked to the edge of the gallery, leaning on one of the four columns. ''At present, I wish *you* would quit talking.''

''There are rumors, Jean.'' Antoine's voice changed tone and Jean turned to meet his friend's eyes. ''Marianne Gallant spends every day waiting by the bayou's edge for her husband.''

''And?''

Antoine rose and leaned against a neighboring column so they stood eye to eye. ''She sits by an oak tree on her land grant. Waits there every day, all day, morning until night.''

''She was separated from her husband during the exile,'' Jean said in her defense, wondering why a waiting wife would be cause for alarm. ''Surely you know the details. He is on his way back to her from Maryland. Why wouldn't she wait for his return?''

''It's been too long,'' Antoine insisted. ''He should have returned months ago. She's refusing to face facts. Besides, even if Joseph Gallant is alive and on his way west, which I doubt, it's not healthy for a woman to spend so much time waiting by the side of a tree for her husband's return. There are people who have seen her arrive at daybreak only to return home long after dark.''

Marianne had seemed perfectly sane to Jean the night before, but her actions did sound mysterious.

''Gabrielle's life is not much better than her mother's,'' Antoine said softly. ''She rarely leaves her house, sometimes waits by her mother's side for hours. This is why Juliette has taken her under her wing.''

Guilt consumed Jean. He had promised Gabrielle he would return by fall, only to be delayed in Hispaniola. Now that he was here, he could only lose control and passionately assault her, then desert her the next day. Thrusting his hands into his pockets, he stared at the placid bayou before him, disliking his friend for passing on such worrisome news.

''Why are you telling me this?'' he asked.

Antoine shrugged. ''Call it a hunch. I thought perhaps it might be a way to get you to stay. You could, you know. Have Philibert operate that island of yours, run goods through the Interior with his help. No one would be the wiser as to who you are.''

''Except the dozens of customers I visit in this region.''

''We'll work it out. Pay off the officials who might become wise.''

Jean leaned his head back against the column and sighed. ''And then what? I've been little better than a pirate all these years, running contraband through the territory. Now, I'm a fugitive. Regardless of where I live or what I do, I cannot offer anything to a woman, most of all Gabrielle Gallant.''

He turned toward his friend hoping he would get the point and drop the painful subject. Instead, he found Antoine grinning. ''What?'' Jean demanded.

''You used to laugh at me,'' Antoine said. ''Remember how silly you thought me when I fell for Juliette? You said any man who loved a woman was a fool. Of course, at the time, you had Louise as an example.''

Jean had a feeling he knew where the conversation

was heading and he wanted no part of it. He moved for the door, but not before Antoine's words hit their mark.

"You're in love with Gabrielle, aren't you?"

Pausing on the threshold, Jean was reminded of Delphine's similar entreaties that day on his ship. Everyone seemed so damned intent on him losing his heart.

"I'm not the type women marry," Jean said sternly. "I have nothing to offer them. Tell Juliette to find Gabrielle a proper husband, someone without a price on his head."

"Someone like Charles Maase?"

Again, the arrow hit its target. Jean closed his eyes to try to tame the rage beating in his chest. For a moment, he didn't care that Antoine witnessed his true feelings. Jean didn't care if the whole world knew. He turned and left Antoine with one final thought before leaving the gallery. "If you let her marry that insipid, arrogant fool, I will visit you one night and slit your throat in your sleep."

Jean didn't wait for Antoine's retort, but he heard his friend's chuckle all the way through the house. Gritting his teeth and staring furiously at the floor, Jean didn't see the person in front of him before it was too late. He bounded into Gabrielle, who had just entered the house.

Just as he had the night before, Jean grabbed Gabrielle's arms to steady himself. When he realized the object of his collision, Jean's hopes of leaving the district disappeared. She stood before him in her usual Acadian dress, a hand-woven striped skirt and a vest of indigo blue that emphasized her generous hips and abundant bosom. A shawl graced her shoulders, and she carried a *garde de soleil* to keep the sun off her resplendent face. As usual with Gabrielle, a haunting sadness lingered in her eyes, but it failed to diminish her amazing beauty.

Whatever self-control he still possessed from the night before waned when he thought of Antoine's cautionary remarks. He still knew so little of the Gallants' situation. How could he leave them waiting hopelessly for Joseph's return while the rest of the family were delayed in Opelousas?

"We seem to have an unusual way of meeting each other," Gabrielle said, pulling her arms from his embrace. "Perhaps we should be introduced properly again."

Jean heard her words, but he was too busy absorbing every detail of her exquisite face. God, but Gabrielle was the most tempting woman he had ever known. His body craved to touch her, to pull their bodies together as one as they had the night before. He wanted to make endless love to her aboard his ship in the bed he had purchased just for her.

"Captain," Charles bellowed as he crossed the front threshold. "I'm so glad to see you're still here. For a moment, I thought you might not come after what you said last night."

Now was the time to regain control of his senses, to insist on meeting his ship, but he couldn't bear leaving Gabrielle's company. He felt as hopeless as an opium addict.

"Of course he's coming with us," Gabrielle said, crossing her arms about her chest, her eyes pinning his with a harsh stare. "He promised."

No matter what tragedy had befallen his angel, Gabrielle burned with an inner strength. Any man who didn't see her iron backbone, despite the darkness that routinely haunted her expressive eyes, was a fool. She was so like his daughter.

"When do we start for this grave desecration?" Jean asked.

Charles's smile disappeared, even though Jean had acquiesced. He knew the boy thought of this outing as a way to impress Gabrielle, which only reiterated his desire to go on the silly picnic. And if all worked out as he planned, he would be able to sneak some time alone with Gabrielle.

For the second time in her life, Gabrielle boarded Jean's *radeau,* a wide, flat-bottomed boat used for transporting goods up the Mississippi and through the southwestern swamps and marshes. There was a makeshift sail and a raised deck in the center for sleeping. One thing was missing from the crude craft, Gabrielle noticed. The bottle of rum Jean used to hang from the mast to announce that he was in town to conduct business was absent, making her doubly curious as to why Jean was visiting the Poste.

Charles offered his hand and helped her aboard. "Be careful, Gabrielle," he warned her like a brother, which made her want to laugh. The only place Gabrielle felt truly comfortable was on the water. In fact, it was Felicité's father who had taught her to sail as a child back in Nova Scotia, taking her with him on his fishing trips throughout Minas Basin.

Gabrielle easily walked to the bow of the boat and

sat down, amazed at how being aboard a crude vessel on a slow-moving bayou could cheer her spirits. Then she remembered the first time she'd boarded Jean's *radeau,* and her heart ached. They had laughed and shared wine and stories, just before he carried her to shore and left her with a kiss. She had given him a necklace that night for luck, a cross she had carved of mahogany. She wondered if he still had it.

The boat lurched as Juliette and Antoine climbed aboard, followed by a talkative Charles. Felicité had chosen to remain at home, no doubt spending time with Silvestre. The only one left to board was Jean, who seemed intent on supervising the contents of the picnic.

"All done, old man?" Charles asked Jean as he approached the boat.

The look Jean sent Charles made Gabrielle want to laugh, so she turned and studied the opposite bank. Jean never told her his age, but it was clear he was past thirty. Slivers of gray were beginning to appear in the hair above his ears—not that it mattered to Gabrielle. She loved everything about him.

While Antoine and Jean released the boat's ties at the dock and began poling the boat from shore, Gabrielle leaned back and enjoyed the feel of the breeze on her face, the water rushing beneath the boat's surface. She heard steps moving up the side of the *radeau* to the bow and she quickly breathed in the moment, knowing that Charles would soon arrive at her side, interrupt her solitude, and begin a lengthy conversation.

"Enjoying yourself?"

Gabrielle turned and found two leather boots at

her side. With a quick glance to the boat's stern, she saw Antoine and Charles polling the rear while Jean took the bow.

"Yes," she replied, wondering what to say next. So much lay between them.

"I'm sorry about last night," Jean said.

"Which part?"

Jean laughed. "Certainly not the last part."

She didn't regret it either, despite the fact that she might be the biggest fool in the Poste, but that didn't stop the pain from stabbing her heart.

"I'm sorry about the ball," Jean said quickly, as if he sensed her thoughts. "Antoine loves to tease me about women, so I . . . I mean, he knows I've never wanted a relationship and I didn't want him thinking . . . Oh hell, it was just two men talking."

Gabrielle wished he would shut up. Her heart had taken enough abuse without his ramblings adding to it. "I understand," she said tersely.

"No, you don't," Jean answered in an equally stern voice.

"You want to leave and not worry that I will pine after you," she said. "So, go then. I assure you I will not wither away and die."

Nothing could be farther from the truth, but Gabrielle was tired of his pretensions. Still, if she could only ignore the nagging image in the back of her mind that swore something else was at work here.

"Why is your mother spending so much time at the bayou's edge?" Jean asked.

Now, she was to endure his take on the rumors circulating through town, comments that her mother was slowly going insane, that something was amiss with Gabrielle too, a lovely young woman who refused to be courted by the area's men.

"You really are insufferable, you know that?" she said softly so the others wouldn't hear. "You breeze into town in the hopes of not seeing me, then get angry because another man wishes for my company. Now, you're feeling guilty because my father hasn't arrived and you've heard rumors that my mother is touched in the head." She leaned close and whispered the words aching to be released. "You can go to hell, Captain Jean Bouclaire."

Gabrielle stood, lifted her skirts, and made her way back toward the raised platform in the center of the craft. Charles immediately headed for her and grabbed for her elbow to assist her, but she pulled away.

"I'm perfectly capable of walking on a boat, Charles," she said a bit too harshly. "I was raised on the sea."

A silence befell the group and Gabrielle mentally kicked herself for being so rude. Again. Thankfully, Juliette came to her rescue. "So, tell us where we are heading, Jean."

"A magical place," Jean said softly. "Near Bayou Portage there is a cypress tree that the Chitimacha Indians consider holy."

Charles stopped polling. "I thought we were heading toward the midden of the Attakapas Chief."

"All in good time," Jean answered.

"What is holy about a tree?" Juliette asked.

"There is a legend that a fair-skinned, intelligent man appeared out of nowhere to the Chitimachas, well versed in their language and traditions," Jean explained. "He taught them many useful things. One day, he said he had to leave and do his father's work. Before he left, he told the tribe that if they ever needed rain to ask the tree for assistance. Then he climbed to the top and disappeared."

"Sounds like a made-up story to teach religion," Juliette said. "Are you sure you didn't hear this from missionaries?"

"When I was a little boy," Antoine added, "my father used to travel out to Bayou Portage and ask the tree whenever we needed rain."

"And did he get it?" Juliette asked.

Antoine and Jean exchanged knowing glances and smiles. "See for yourself," Antoine said.

"Rain would come in handy," Juliette said. "My rose bushes are suffering in this drought. Never have I seen such a dry winter."

They traveled almost an hour before coming upon the "holy tree," an old red cypress, its branches draping over the bayou. Near it lay a midden, a mound of dirt covered in small shells that the local Indians used as burial grounds. Charles examined it, but lost interest when it turned out to be Chitimacha, a peaceful tribe who had warred with their more aggressive neighbors, the Attakapas. The Chitimacha weren't suspected of being cannibals.

"Legend also has it that when an Indian died, they cut the person's hair," Antoine said. "When a young, beautiful girl—the loveliest girl in the village—died at this very spot, her lover cut her hair and hung it from the tree by the midden. And that's where all the moss comes from."

Juliette laughed at the reference to the gray moss

hanging from the trees. "I thought it was supposed to be the beards of the Spanish," she said.

"That too," he said with a wink and a smile.

Antoine led the group toward the famed cypress tree, but Jean caught Gabrielle's arm before she had a chance to step off the boat.

"Don't," he said, then motioned for her to join him in the makeshift cabin. "We'll be along shortly," Jean announced to the group.

Charles frowned when he realized Gabrielle was staying behind, but his curiosity got the better of him and he followed Antoine and Juliette up the bayou's bank to the enormous tree. Gabrielle, however, was not too pleased to be alone in Jean's company.

"I thought I made it clear," she began.

They stood so close she could smell a hint of tonic about him. God, but he looked and smelled wonderful in his traditional black coat and the billowing shirt that emphasized his broad, strong chest. It was everything Gabrielle could do to keep her hands at her side.

"Gabrielle," Jean whispered emotionally, sending shivers up her spine. "I am already in hell."

There it was again, that painful expression, that reminder that something was amiss. She knew him too well to miss such a sign. But why wouldn't he tell her?

"What has happened?" she pleaded.

From the shore Antoine opened an umbrella and began to say a prayer at the base of the tree. Gabrielle knew the two men were enjoying a joke at Charles's expense, but a holy tree that caused rain? Then Jean grabbed her arm and pulled her inside the cabin.

"What are you doing?" Gabrielle asked.

''Wait,'' he said, listening.

Within seconds, the sky turned dark and thunder blasted overhead. Gabrielle watched in amazement as torrents of rain pounded the small boat.

Chapter Five

Gabrielle forgot her troubles for a moment as the magic of the rain enveloped them. "How did you do that?"

The dimple Gabrielle had grown to love resurfaced. "I told you, it's a magical place."

She didn't believe him, although how else could they explain the rain? He couldn't have orchestrated such an event. Instead, she focused on the specks of red sparkling in his dark eyes.

"I thought you were playing a trick on Charles," she said.

"I am," Jean said with a grin. "We are warm and dry and he's the only one without an umbrella."

A thundercloud passed and rain beat hard against the roof of the cabin. "Poor Charles," Gabrielle said halfheartedly. "I wonder if he's out there talking Antoine and Juliette's ears off."

"No doubt he's busy digging through the midden for signs of cannibals, despite the rain," Jean said with a laugh.

She so enjoyed their light banter, but curiosity got the better of her. "Really, Jean, how did you do that?"

Jean opened a miniature door leading to a hollow area inside the boat and brought out a bottle of wine, two cups and some cheese, the same things he had offered her that night in Natchez. They sat so close their knees touched.

"I didn't do a thing," he said as he poured her a glass of wine. "Antoine's father did hear of the legend. Antoine showed me the tree the first time I came to the Attakapas Poste. Amazing, isn't it?"

Gabrielle sipped her wine, enchanted by the sound of the rain on the bayou. It had been so long since it had last rained. But how long had it been since she and Jean laughed together?

"I've missed this," she whispered.

"The rain?"

Gabrielle reached out and ran a finger into the crease in his cheek. "I've missed the happier times."

Jean captured her hand and pressed it against his lips, and his smile disappeared. "Why is your mother spending so much time at this oak tree everyone's talking about?"

Gabrielle didn't want to retreat back to the problems at hand, she wanted to remain laughing and savoring the smell of the first rain in weeks. But like the clouds that appeared suddenly, so did a darkness fall across her heart.

"Don't do that, *chérie,*" Jean said. "I love to see you smile. Your face lights up when you're happy. Don't retreat back to your gloom."

When was the last time she was happy, she wondered? The last time Jean came to visit. "You're the only one who can make me happy."

Jean rubbed her fingers across his lips. "I have to leave," he whispered. "I need to know you and your mother are well, are taken care of. I must know that you're happy or have prospects of being so."

Gabrielle pulled her fingers free. "Why do you have to leave?"

"Why is your mother acting this way?"

She shook her head, weary of the secrets. "Jean Bouclaire, you are the most irritating man I have ever met."

Jean tossed back his wine. "My daughter would agree. Now, why is your mother causing rumors?"

"She's waiting for my father," Gabrielle said, her voice rising. "She had a vision that he would return by the bayou and she would be waiting for him by an oak tree."

"A vision?" Jean asked.

Her mother seeing future events wasn't something she confessed every day. But if Jean could make it rain, surely he was open to other unexplained phenomena.

"My mother has visions," she said. "She foresaw danger the day the English asked every man in Grand Pré to come to the church for a meeting. The day they trapped them all inside and burned our homes." Gabrielle paused to swallow the lump in her throat. Thirteen years and that afternoon remained as clear as yesterday. "She knew they were going to exile us. I don't know how, but she knew. And she knew we would be separated from my father."

"And now she thinks Joseph will return."

"She had a vision that he would arrive by boat and

that Emilie and Rose would be by her side." Gabrielle paused again, wondering how that was possible when her sisters were in Opelousas. "She saw Rose big with child, and this was before Rose was married."

Jean nodded, absorbing the unusual story. "But Rose won't be arriving until after the baby comes."

"I know," Gabrielle said, taking a sip of wine. "Perhaps Maman saw two visions at once."

"And where are you in this vision?"

Gabrielle searched his eyes wondering if he wished her happily wed to another. Again, what shone back was puzzling. She was so confused. "I wasn't in the vision," she said.

Jean pondered her words and silently refilled their cups while thunder cracked overhead. Gabrielle wondered why the others hadn't returned. Then she realized her mother was out in the rain. Waiting.

"She really loves him," Gabrielle said. "My parents fell in love the first time they saw each other. My grandmother told me they met at a dance, but I know they met a week earlier out in the fields. They kept it a secret for days because they didn't want to be chaperoned. After the dance, they asked to get married right away. I'd bet my life that Emilie was conceived that week in the fields of Grand Pré. My parents could never stop touching one another. They were so in love."

Gabrielle thought of the first time she'd laid eyes on Jean Bouclaire. Never once did she doubt the power of first attraction.

"How does a woman stop waiting for the man she loves?" Gabrielle asked him, feeling her heart constrict with every word.

Jean placed his wine at his feet and leaned close, enveloping her cheeks with his hands. "You mustn't wait for me," he said heatedly, his lips only a breath away. "I have to leave the territory. I may never be able to return."

"Why?"

Jean closed his eyes and his brow creased in pain. "I'm in trouble with the authorities."

"What happened?" Gabrielle insisted.

Leaning back and sliding a hand through his wavy hair, Jean appeared ready to talk. At last they were back to being friends, sharing secrets.

"You must promise me, Gabrielle, not to wait for me," he said instead. "I may never return. You must seek out other men, marry someone who will be good to you and take care of you."

"I don't want to marry another man," she interrupted. "Tell me what you have done."

"There are better men than me," he insisted. "I have nothing to offer you, even if there wasn't a price on my head."

Gabrielle leaned forward so that their foreheads almost touched in the cramped cabin. She placed a hand on his cheek and breathed in his scent, fearful that he might disappear at any moment.

"I don't care what you have done," she whispered, tears beginning in her eyes. "I love you. I love the sea. How could there be a better man?"

Jean took possession of her hand and kissed her palm. "I can't bear the thought of you wasting your life waiting for me."

"My mother is not wasting her life," Gabrielle said, her voice rising once more.

"Your mother is a different story."

There it was again, that paternal tone Gabrielle knew he took with his crew or anyone else who crossed his path. Jean Bouclaire, she was sure, could move mountains with only a look or a stern command. But he couldn't move her.

"What have you done?" she asked again. Jean refused to answer, which only infuriated Gabrielle more. "Why won't you let me into your life?" she whispered heatedly.

Something in her words lit a spark in his eyes. He stared at her as if an arrow had pierced his heart. What wasn't he telling her? What was this trouble that would force someone from the territory? What about Delphine?

"Jean," she said, caressing his rugged cheek. "Tell me."

The hesitant look that flickered across his countenance disappeared, replaced by the usual harsh facade. "For God's sake, Gabi, I'm a smuggler who makes his living off contraband. It's a dangerous life, can't you see that? You have to forget about me and move on."

Gabrielle pulled her hand from his and placed it in her lap. "Impossible," she said, her chin lifted defiantly, although her insides were trembling.

Again, Jean pulled his hands through his hair. This was not the answer he was hoping for, but Gabrielle didn't care to ease his worries. She wanted to be with him. Always.

"If I take you with me," he said, "what then? Are you willing to leave your mother now, alone with no family beside her?"

Guilt consumed Gabrielle. For a moment, she'd forgotten about her mother, forgotten about her promise to her father to always look after her. Of course, she could never leave Marianne. When would she ever realize that her dreams of the sea were selfish desires?

Jean must have realized the pain he inflicted, for he inched closer and pressed her head to his, kissing her forehead and caressing her hair. For a moment, Gabrielle thought he might confess his love, but he remained silent, holding her close.

The rain began to taper off and voices were heard coming closer. Jean straightened, then reached into his waistcoat pocket and removed a handkerchief, hers if she wasn't mistaken.

"You found it," Gabrielle said, taking the opportunity to wipe the tears from her cheeks. "I thought I lost it."

"You did," Jean said softly. "I don't plan on giving it back."

Gabrielle tried to meet his eyes, to understand his meaning, but her focus moved to the shiny object Jean was pulling from the handkerchief. Before she could digest what the object was, he took her hand and placed the emerald-studded ring on her right hand.

"I bought this for you in Hispaniola," he said. "I was hoping to give it to you under happier circumstances."

Gabrielle stared at the elegant ring glistening in the small ray of sunshine now beaming into the cabin. The stone complemented her hand well, large enough to produce a sparkle, but not too overbearing to be excessive. Tears gathered again in her eyes. "It's beautiful," she whispered. "I will treasure it forever."

Meeting his eyes once more, she added, "But why do you have a price on your head?"

Jean reached out and took her ringed hand, caressing the top with his thumb. When he squeezed lovingly, Gabrielle felt the world tilt.

Suddenly, she wasn't in the cabin of a small boat. She was sailing on a schooner, the wind in her hair, the stars above her head. It was just like the dreams she had had for years, where she stood at the helm of a darkened ship, a strange, faceless man at her back. This time, she could actually feel the tilt of the boat, the motion of the waves beneath her feet, and the man at her back was placing his hands at her waist and pulling her backward so that she could feel his enormous presence, rest her head in the crook of his neck. When her hand, still sporting the beautiful ring, reached back to steady herself, it landed on a solid thigh. A wave of bliss ran through her, knowing at last who the man in her dreams was, knowing at last that happiness was possible.

Then the ship disappeared. Gabrielle hovered over the shoulder of a young girl dressed in a bright blue gown and white cap talking excitedly to a man in a garden. The girl resembled Jean in many ways, including a large dimple in her right cheek. In her hands was Gabrielle's cross and the letter she was reading sounded like Gabrielle's words. But how could that be, Gabrielle wondered, when she hadn't written them yet?

Her conscious mind started to protest that nothing

was making sense. The vision began to clear, but not
before she sensed something unusual in the man by
the girl's side. A powerful force rose inside her, forcing her to look into the man's face. But someone was
calling her name and the vision faded away.

"Gabrielle."

It was Jean's voice, urgent and fearful. Gabrielle
opened her eyes to find herself lying on the cabin's
bed, Jean's worried face above her and the others
gazing in from deck.

"Is she all right?" Juliette asked excitedly.

"Gabi," Jean whispered. "Speak to me."

What had just happened? Gabrielle wondered. One
minute he had given her a ring and the next . . .
Gabrielle raised her hand to make sure the ring
hadn't been a dream too. The emerald glistened now
that the sun shone brightly overhead.

"What happened?" she asked Jean.

"We were talking and I lost you."

Gabrielle remembered the ship, remembered how
vivid the wind had felt in her hair. "Lost me where?"

"You fainted," Antoine said from above. "You've
been out for several minutes."

Gabrielle gazed up at Jean, noticing the curls at his
collar, his bushy eyebrows, and his high cheekbones.
"Your daughter looks like you. She has your dimple."

Jean frowned, no doubt worried that she was as
crazy as her mother was rumored to be. Gabrielle
attempted a smile to ease his concerns. "She wears
her hair long, tied back in a ribbon, with a white cap
atop her hair," she continued. "She prefers a blue
dress with tiny white flowers, her favorite because you
gave it to her."

"What is she talking about?" Charles interrupted.

"How do you know this?" Jean asked.

"A two-masted schooner," Gabrielle whispered, so no one else would hear. "Shallow and small, but a fast ship. Sharp lines, armed with only swivels. Your best friend helps you sail it." Gabrielle smiled, recalling the sound of the wind inflating the massive sails above her head. "She's a beauty, so sleek."

She was scaring Jean, she could read it in his eyes. "Antoine," he called out. "Is the carriage ready?"

"*Oui*," Antoine answered.

"Can you sit up?" he asked her.

Gabrielle raised herself on her elbows and found that the strength had left her body along with the images. "What is the matter with me?" she asked Jean. "I am so tired."

He placed a steadying hand at her back and raised a glass of wine to her lips. "Drink this. Then I'm going to take you home."

Gabrielle wanted to ask how, since they all had come by boat, but she was too exhausted to speak. She barely found the energy to sip the wine. When Jean removed the cup, she felt her shawl being placed about her shoulders and his hands reaching beneath her knees to carry her up to the deck.

When they'd reached the others, she was greeted by three pairs of worried eyes. Poor Charles seemed to fret the most, reiterating the fact that he really did care for her. Gabrielle thought to consider this, to find some words to comfort him, but she couldn't find the strength to speak.

"I'm taking her home," Jean said, stepping from the boat to the bank.

"We'll meet up later," she heard Antoine answer.

"But the boat?" Gabrielle whispered.

Jean gently placed her inside Antoine's covered carriage, manned by Silvestre at the reins and containing a wide variety of food. Now she understood. Jean and Antoine had arranged for the carriage to be brought to the spot so they would be covered when it rained. That way, Jean would have a chance to be alone with Gabrielle.

"You sly fox," she managed, trying to keep her eyes open.

Jean joined her on the seat and Gabrielle felt the carriage lurch into action. He wrapped his arms about her shoulders and pulled her into the safety of his chest. Despite the comfort of being in Jean's embrace, the vision and her lack of strength scared her.

"What has happened to me?" she repeated.

Jean kissed her forehead and held her tight. "I don't know, *mon amour.*"

Gabrielle thought of the girl, Jean's mirror image, of the cross in her hands. Had Jean given Gabrielle's cross to his daughter? Her hand on his chest, Gabrielle lowered her fingers down his breastbone, searching for the pendant beneath his shirt.

"It's still there." Jean slipped his fingers beneath his shirt's collar and withdrew the cross hanging from a strip of leather. "I've never taken it off."

At that moment, Gabrielle knew he loved her. All her doubts disappeared. Deep inside his waistcoat pocket was the handkerchief he would never relinquish, more proof that his heart belonged to her.

Her strength leaving her, she rested her head

against his chest and closed her eyes. "Oh Jean, what are we to do?"

Jean watched Gabrielle slip into slumber, then kissed the forehead that was more tanned than proper society allowed. He pulled her thick braid loose and ran his fingers through her hair, savoring the earthy smell of her, enjoying the perfect fit their bodies made.

Before he forced his rational mind to intervene, he imagined them like this, every day, in the bed he had purchased just for her. He thought of the many ways he could make Gabrielle happy, beginning with her luscious lips that begged to be kissed. He thought of the places they could travel, the adventures they could share. He thought of waking every morning aboard his ship with Gabrielle, making love before dawn, the sea spray blowing in through the portholes to cool their heated bodies.

And Delphine. God, how he missed his daughter. They were so much alike, these women who wouldn't let him go without a fight. Gabrielle had repeated the exact words Delphine had spoken the day before the duel, stilling his heart with her entreaty.

"Why won't you let me into your life?"

If only he could wrap them both up and carry them away with him, but the idea was ludicrous. As he did the morning after the duel, he would steal away at first light and head back to sea and his waiting ship. Gabrielle and Delphine would forget about him in time, find other men to share their lives.

For one last time, Jean wrapped his arms about his beloved and inhaled her essence, branded to memory the feel of her soft body to his. For one last time, Jean enjoyed the prospect of love.

"What do you mean he's gone?"

Dawn had not yet kissed the horizon when Gabrielle bolted awake. She clutched her head in pain, but it didn't stop her from leaping out of bed.

"Gabi, slow down," her mother warned. "You've had quite a shock."

Marianne wasn't surprised that her daughter had experienced a vision; of all her daughters, Gabrielle was the most sensitive. It did alarm her, however, that her vision included Jean's child and his ship when Jean had no intention of staying at the Attakapas Poste.

"He can't leave," Gabrielle said as she hastily dressed. "He can't just deposit me here and sail away."

"He didn't 'deposit' you anywhere." Marianne pushed her daughter's hands aside and fixed the buttons of her shirt fastened in the wrong places. "He never left your side all night."

Gabrielle paused at the news, tears glistening in her eyes. "Maman, what am I to do?"

Marianne wished with all her heart she had the answers. If anyone understood the pain of a man leaving with the possibility of never seeing him again, it was she. But there were no answers. Only waiting and hoping.

"We are women," she said to her daughter. "We have little choice in life when it comes to love."

Her answer was the last thing Gabrielle wanted to

hear. She began pacing the floor, one hand still holding on to her pounding head, the other curled into a fist at her side. They may share visions, but Marianne knew her daughter was not the waiting type.

"The headache will pass," Marianne said. "The heartache will not. But perhaps you will someday learn to love another."

When Gabrielle's eyes turned toward Marianne, she knew her daughter would never be happy without Jean. She recognized the emotion glaring back at her. Marianne, herself, had had numerous offers of marriage since the exile, but her heart belonged to Joseph and no other. She would die a widow if need be, but she would never give her love to another man.

Yet she couldn't bear the thought of her daughter doing the same.

"Let him go, Gabrielle," she whispered, taking her daughter's fist and releasing her fingers one by one.

Tears gathered in Gabrielle's eyes and poured down her cheeks. "I can't."

A knock sounded on the front door and Gabrielle quickly wiped the tears away. "Who can that be at this hour?"

Marianne heard the hope in her voice, knew she was wishing Jean had returned. "It's Mathurin Dugas, the widow Dugas's oldest child," Marianne said softly. "The widow had a baby last night and I promised to help with the younger children."

Gabrielle nodded, disappointment clouding her features. "I won't be gone long," Marianne continued. "Two, three days at most."

Gabrielle straightened, lifting her chin. "Of course, Maman. I'll be fine."

The knock sounded again, but Marianne couldn't bear to leave her daughter in such a delicate emotional state. "I can ask Juliette . . . "

"No, Maman," Gabrielle said, her voice taking on a more even tone. "Don't worry about me. I will be fine."

"Raymond is next door and willing to help in any way. All you have to do is ask."

"I know, Maman."

"The Vincents said you are welcome to dinner anytime."

Gabrielle squeezed her mother's hand. "I will be fine. It will do me good to be alone for a while. Maybe I will go down to the tree and wait for Papa."

If the sadness reflecting in her daughter's eyes wasn't enough to cause her pain, the thought of Gabrielle waiting for Joseph nearly crushed her. There had been so much heartache in their splintered family, but the past few months of waiting for love to appear around the bayou's bend was killing the two of them for sure. How much more could either of them endure?

"You know where to find me." Marianne paused and swallowed, but she failed to keep her own tears from falling.

The women embraced tightly, grateful that at least they had each other. When the third knock came at the door, Marianne patted Gabrielle on the cheek, picked up her satchel and basket of food, and headed for the front door.

"I made coffee and breakfast," she said. "There is plenty of fruit in the pantry."

Gabrielle offered a smile. "I know I'm not much of a cook, Maman, but I will survive two days."

Marianne nodded, but hesitated on the threshold. She hated leaving her daughter carrying so much pain. Then a thought came to her. "I completely forgot. A letter came from Rose and Emilie. It's on the kitchen table."

Gabrielle instantly brightened. "Good news, I hope."

"No more sickness, but the baby moves so much she has difficulty eating and sleeping." A light appeared in Gabrielle's eyes and Marianne felt her own spirits rise. "Just like you. Never would stop moving."

She shouldn't have said it; the remark only reminded Gabrielle of her endless desire for adventure. Every since her daughter was old enough to walk, she had longed for the sea, begging Felicité's father to take her on his fishing excursions.

"There's another letter too," Marianne added. "From New Orleans without a return address."

"Madame Gallant," came a young, nervous voice from the front door, making them both smile. It was clear Mathurin Dugas was anxious for Marianne's help.

"Go," Gabrielle said. "Madame Dugas is probably beside herself by now."

Marianne hesitated one last moment, then turned and joined the boy on the porch. When the front door closed, Gabrielle felt the blackness swallow her up. Daylight was approaching, a pink glow permeating the early morning gloom, but nothing could relieve the malaise strangling her heart.

She made her way into the room that separated the two bedrooms, a common room for entertaining and eating that housed a central fireplace. Gabrielle sat down at the table and opened her sister's letter. It comforted her heart to hear her sisters in good spirits, to know they were safe and happy, but she missed them dearly. Her beloved sisters and their husbands were four others they would have to wait for.

Gabrielle then picked up the other letter, sealed with elegant designs surrounding the letter D. When she ripped it open, the day suddenly arrived. Like the sunlight breaking the horizon, her heart felt infinitely better.

Chapter Six

Thank God for work, Jean thought as he loaded his *radeau* with supplies. He needed fresh fruit and meats for the long journey, and Antoine was happy to fill his request.

"Odd, me selling you something," Antoine said, handing him a crate of oranges. "Can I interest you in some liquor as well?"

Rum was never in short supply where he sailed, but a bottle of brandy for the trip down Bayou Teche would come in handy, considering his dark mood. *"Oui, merci,"* Jean said.

As Jean tied down the last box of supplies, a shadow fell upon him. Antoine couldn't have made it to the house and back in such a short time, so he drew his blade and turned. In the early morning sunlight, looking as lovely as the first day they met, stood Gabrielle, her dark hair free from its usual braid and hanging loose around her shoulders. She was a natural beauty, a sight to behold, but she wasn't what Jean wanted to see that horrid morning.

"Gabrielle, don't," Jean whispered. "Don't make this harder than it has to be."

Antoine appeared at the bank, a bottle of brandy under each arm. To his credit, he said nothing as he approached them, although Jean knew his friend comprehended everything.

"*Bonjour,* Antoine," Gabrielle said without a trace of emotion. Jean would always be amazed at the woman's strength.

"*Bonjour,* Gabi," Antoine replied. "Are you feeling better this morning? You really gave us a scare yesterday."

"I am much better, thank you."

"Come up to the house, then. I know Juliette would love to have you join us for breakfast."

"*Non, merci,*" Gabrielle answered, sending Jean a sideward glance. "I cannot stay long."

Jean returned his sword to his scabbard. What was she up to? Something wasn't ringing true.

"I just wanted to let the captain know that his daughter has written me a letter," Gabrielle said, a sly sparkle in her eye. "If he's interested, the letter's at my house."

His body tensed, a bolt of anxiety short of panic filling his chest. "What did Phiney say?" he demanded. "Is she well?"

But Gabrielle stubbornly refused to reply, simply smiled, bid Antoine good-day, and strolled back toward her house.

"Damn it, Gabrielle," Jean shouted after her. "What did Phiney say?"

Antoine watched her go with an appreciative glance. Gabrielle wasn't the only one enjoying herself at his expense that morning.

"Women are the most insufferable creatures on the face of the earth," Jean told him, the tension refusing to leave his body.

Antoine's playful smile remained. "Yes, they are, my friend. But I suspect that one is worth it."

Yes, she was worth it, but God help him if he walked back into that house. He had already spent one extra day at the Poste. His ship and crew were waiting. And if word got out that he was in the Attakapas, officials would be rounded up for his arrest.

Jean let a few choice words fly, then grabbed his coat and jumped to shore. "Watch my boat for me, will you, Antoine?"

His friend nodded and laughter followed him up the path toward Gabrielle's house.

Gabrielle placed the letter on the table, counted to ten, then headed for the kitchen. She met Jean at the back door, his jaw as tense as it had been at the bayou. "It's on the table," she told him. "I'll make some coffee."

A fury shone in his eyes, a look that expressed his frustration at not being able to leave. She almost regretted her selfish decision to keep him at the Poste. Almost.

To match his foul mood, the sky darkened and bellowed thunder, making her shiver with each thunderclap. Gabrielle pulled her shawl about her ears and headed for the kitchen. Anything to escape those piercing black eyes.

She took her time dripping the coffee and arranging a tray full of breads, allowing Jean time to read the several pages Delphine had written. Delphine had explained everything, down to the vase her slave almost dropped when Jean accepted the upstart man's duel. She talked of her mother and how Louise Delaronde had regretted Delphine's birth. How her mother had collapsed when she heard of Marcel Prevost's death and that she had taken to her bed and never risen again. How every day the young girl lived in loneliness and misery, longing for her father's return.

Poor Delphine. She penned an entire page speaking of Jean, how she missed his scratchy mustache and enormous arms, how she would give up everything to run away with him. The girl had expressed herself to the right person; if anyone could sympathize, Gabrielle could. If only Jean would take her to New Orleans and they could carry Delphine away with them, sailing off to the Caribbean, leaving their worries behind.

Gabrielle leaned her head against the wooden post and sighed. The notion was impossible. It was those very ideas that had separated her family.

Who was she fooling? she thought as she carried the tray into the house. Jean had to leave and she had to remain with her mother. There was nothing more to say, nothing more to think about. One last moment together and she would say goodbye. She had to face facts, watch him walk out the door. But for the life of her, she couldn't bear the thought of it.

She quietly entered the house and placed the tray on the table. "I'm afraid we're out of sugar."

Jean stood by the front window, gazing out on the darkened horizon. One arm leaned against the window frame, the letter clutched between his fingers, the other hand pressed against his lips in thought. From the back she could sense the tension between his shoulders, the rigidness of his jaw. The way Delphine spoke of their relationship, Gabrielle knew he loved her very much. And that the separation was destroying them both.

Gabrielle slipped her arms about his waist and laid her cheek against his broad back. Jean instantly covered one of her hands with his and squeezed tightly. She wanted desperately to relieve his suffering.

"There's a dance we Acadians like to do," she said. "We pass around a hot potato and eliminate people from the circle when they drop it. The person who holds on to the potato longest wins."

She paused, listened to the thunder drawing nearer, felt the wind blowing the petticoat around her ankles. "We have an expression for the dance," Gabrielle continued. "We say, *lâche pas la patate,* don't drop the potato. It means never give up."

Jean inhaled and straightened. He turned and faced her, and Gabrielle placed a comforting hand on his cheek. *"Lâche pas la patate,* Jean," she whispered.

So much hurt shone back from those fathomless eyes, and Gabrielle wondered if her own father wore the same painful expression, wherever he was. Too many separations, Gabrielle thought, caressing Jean's cheek. It wasn't fair.

"I have to go," Jean whispered. "My men are waiting."

Gabrielle swore she could feel her heart breaking. He stood there, one hand on her shoulder, the other still clutching the only remnants he possessed of his daughter. And she, in turn, held his face in her hand, leaning into the warmth of his chest. He was so near and so real. How could she let him go?

Lightning flashed around them and the sky answered furiously. The storm had arrived in all its fury.

"Ça grimace," Gabrielle said, repeating her father's favorite exclamation that the sky was frowning. "I think God heard my prayers."

As if he suddenly realized the storm had descended and traveling was impossible, Jean cupped his hand around her chin and, with the other at her waist, pulled her close. Before she had time to breathe, his lips were upon hers. They were anything but polite— insistent, hungry, demanding. She parted her own, eager for the communion.

Gabrielle wrapped her arms about his neck and pulled closer. She threaded her hands through his thick hair while his tongue savored the inside of her mouth. His hand moved below her waist and explored the curves of her hips, at the same time pulling her tighter against his solid body.

Gabrielle leaned her head back and allowed Jean to leave a trail of kisses down her neck. She could feel his desire, sense the heat of his passion burning in his veins. Or was it her own passion that singed her skin, demanded satisfaction?

"You could leave at sunrise," Gabrielle whispered.

A wild thunderclap shook the house and Jean sighed and pulled away. He was thinking the same thing; Gabrielle saw the hunger burning in his dark eyes. Then Jean frowned and glanced around the house, releasing his grip of her. "Where's your mother?" he asked.

"Widow Dugas's baby came. Maman went to help with the other children. She won't be home for days."

Jean paused and Gabrielle feared he might have second thoughts about leaving. Then the rain pounded against the roof and Gabrielle sent up thanks for the second time that morning. How could he possibly leave in such weather? When a burst of rain flew in through the window, they both bolted into action.

The weather, despite the drought, remained cold in the Louisiana prairies. Not the harsh, bitter cold that Gabrielle had been used to in Canada, but a milder, humid cold that seemed to sneak in through the floorboards and permeate a person's bones. Marianne had insisted on keeping the front window and the back door open for ventilation, but most of the house was closed up for warmth. Jean had only to secure the back door and Gabrielle the window before they faced each other once more.

"Shall I start a fire?" Jean asked.

The relief that flooded her senses was so intense that Gabrielle placed a hand on her chest to steady her breathing. He did plan to stay. Or maybe it was the promise of what lay ahead that took her breath away.

"It's not necessary," Gabrielle answered, thinking of the heat they could produce on their own.

Jean covered the distance between them, but he

stood at arm's length. "This is not something to take lightly, *mon amour,*" he said. "I have something that will keep us from conceiving a child, but . . ."

Gabrielle's heart quickened at the thought of their lovemaking, of finally being able to be close to the man she loved. "Then stay," she insisted.

For a moment, desire flickered in his eyes, then his familiar paternal look replaced it.

Gabrielle knew what he was thinking. "I want this," she explained, her voice slightly breaking. "I love you and I want to be close to you. If you're going to sail out of my life forever, then give me this one day. Stop worrying about my welfare for a moment and consider my happiness."

Jean stepped closer, brushing the hair from her forehead. "And tomorrow?"

Finally he was close enough to touch. Gabrielle grabbed his lapel and held tight. "Tomorrow is tomorrow. We won't speak of it until the sun rises."

Jean said nothing, kept gazing at her as if he wavered between protector and ravager. He dropped his hand from her face and Gabrielle feared he would make excuses and leave. Instead, he leaned down, placed a hand beneath her knees and back, and raised her up into his chest. Taking only a few strides, he reached her bedroom and kicked the door closed. With the curtains drawn and the storm bellowing outside, the room lay in semidarkness. Jean laid her on the bed, then quickly pulled off his leather boots and joined her.

Gabrielle sat up, her eyes adjusting to the dim room. His enormous presence wasn't difficult to assimilate.

She heard him removing his coat and throwing it aside, knocking over a chair in the process.

"Oops," he said, and her beloved dimple appeared. "Shall I light a candle?"

Gabrielle wasn't worried about what lay ahead, but she appreciated the darkness the storm allowed. She had never exposed much of herself, including her emotions, to anyone. "Later," she whispered.

Two large hands encompassed her face and his lips found hers. Within seconds she was pulled into his embrace, her hands wrapping around his strong shoulders and her body pressed hard against his chest. His mustache tickled her skin every place it touched. When his lips descended down her neckline to the opening of her chemise, Gabrielle pulled her fingers through his hair and leaned back.

"Oh Gabi," Jean whispered in appreciation as his lips dipped into the valley between her breasts.

He began to unbutton her vest, then her underlying bodice, and before she had time to realize what was transpiring the garments had been removed and cast toward the chair. Again, there followed the sound of something crashing to the floor.

Gabrielle laughed, partly out of nervousness. "Are you trying to destroy my room?"

The dimple appeared again, accented by two sparkling dark eyes. Jean pulled his shirt over his head and tossed it carefully toward the other garments, but this time it quietly snagged on the leg of the upturned chair. "Three's the charm," he said with a grin.

Gabrielle would have joined him in the joke, but her eyes were too busy exploring the virile male chest before her. His broad, tanned body glistened despite the dim light, interrupted by a sea of dark hair and two honey-colored nipples. Taut muscles, acquired from years of life at sea, stretched across his chest and arms, then tapered down to a flat belly and a line of hair that ended at the top of his breeches. Gabrielle swallowed. She had never seen anything so magnificent in her life. A wild, sensuous bolt of energy passed through her, causing a shiver to run up her spine.

"Are you cold, my love?" Jean asked her, rubbing her arms.

She wanted to laugh, but the truth was her thoughts scared her. Her sister Emilie had always warned her she thought too much like a man, wanted things that life didn't offer women. Now she was feeling emotions like a wanton woman. But Emilie had found passion in life. Was it wrong to feel this way?

"What are you thinking?" Jean asked her, caressing her neck and bare shoulders.

What would he think if he knew her body ached for their union, her skin burned at the sight of him? They had always shared everything, but would Jean accept a woman with such lurking, heightened passions?

She decided to be honest. "I want you," Gabrielle whispered. "I want to touch you, but I'm afraid."

Jean took her hand and placed it over his heart, while pulling her closer. "Why are you afraid?"

They were so close, Gabrielle could feel his breath on her cheek. "I thought only men were supposed to feel this way."

Jean grazed his lips over hers, then began nipping

at the skin of her neck while he untied the ribbon of her chemise. "No, *mon amour*. We're supposed to feel this way *together*."

With her chemise loosened, he slipped the garment from her shoulders, letting it fall to her waist. Then his large hand covered a breast, stroking the skin, teasing the nipple. Slowly, he lowered her to the bed and his lips replaced his hands at her breast, his teeth gently biting, his tongue savoring.

A crack of thunder sounded overhead, resonating with the sensations raging through her. Of their own accord, her hips lifted toward his as if aching for their joining.

After what seemed like an eternity of heaven, Jean left her breasts and began removing her stockings, untying them at her thigh and kissing every inch of her legs until the stockings, too, were cast aside. Next came her skirt and petticoat and the chemise gathered at her waist. Within seconds, she was completely naked.

Now, Gabrielle did feel a chill—more from nervousness than cold, she was sure—and she clenched her jaw to keep it from chattering. Jean pulled a blanket around her as he covered her body with his, but it was the warmth of his chest that took the chill away.

His hands explored every curve of her body, while his amazing lips followed. When they returned to her breasts, now aching for his touch, his hand lowered into her femininity and began caressing. Something he touched sent a spark through her and Gabrielle swore she had ignited like the lightning flashing across the sky. Her back arched and a wave of euphoria passed through her. She heard someone moan as the sensation heightened and consumed her and wondered if it was she.

When the feeling waned, Gabrielle opened her eyes and tried to resume a steady breath. Jean kissed his way up to her lips, then brushed the hair off her face, gazing down at her with desire still lingering in the depths of his eyes.

"You see," he said heatedly, "passion isn't just for men."

Gabrielle comprehended his message, but something was missing here. Despite the blissful feeling still permeating her senses, deep reaches of her body ached for something more. "And what of your passion?" she asked.

Jean's eyes twinkled as he slid his thumb across her bruised lips. "All in good time. We mustn't rush things."

Gabrielle couldn't help herself; she wasn't a patient person. She took his thumb between her teeth and ran her tongue against its tip. Her hands slid down his back and over his rock-hard bottom, pulling him tightly against her. "I'm tired of waiting," she said before she raised her lips to his once more.

They soon became a tangle of wild caresses and kisses, his hands and lips retreating to her breasts and hers along the ridges of his chest. Feeling bold, Gabrielle leaned forward and took one of his nipples between her lips, savoring its tautness with her tongue. Jean moaned loudly and bolted upright.

She had gone too far, Gabrielle thought, fearing Jean would be shocked at her decadent actions. Instead, he sat up, turned, unbuttoned his breeches and removed them discreetly.

Curiosity got the better of her; she peered over his shoulder, then gasped and placed a cheek against his back. "It's so big," she whispered. "How will it be possible?"

Jean turned and took her face in his hands. "We don't have to go through with this. If you're having second thoughts . . . "

"No," Gabrielle answered. She couldn't back down now. She wanted this to happen. "It's just that it's so large."

That old paternal look returned and Gabrielle regretted her comments. He would worry about hurting her. "It always hurts the first time, doesn't it?" she asked him.

Jean grinned nervously. "I don't know. I've never slept with a virgin before."

Gabrielle wasn't jealous; she suspected there were plenty of women before her. But she couldn't help asking, "What kind of women did you sleep with?"

Jean began kissing her again, tugging at her bottom lip with his teeth, his hands back on the soft curves of her breasts. "None that hold a candle to you."

They lay back down, Jean gently parting her legs and slipping his body between. He tamed his wild affections, offering delicate kisses and soft strokes up and down her body until slowly, smoothly, he entered. Gabrielle felt the painful intrusion, but forced herself to concentrate instead on the magic of their union. As Jean pushed deeper, so came the sensations that had ravaged her body earlier. With each thrust, she felt pleasure building as if she were sailing on the ocean and each incoming wave moved higher, sending the ship upward toward the stars.

"Oh Gabi," Jean uttered so seductively, Gabrielle felt her skin tingle all the way to her toes.

She savored the feel of his back, meeting his lips eagerly as they danced to a mutual rhythm. When Jean slipped his hands behind her bottom and thrust deeper, their dark world burst into sunlight. Gabrielle raised her arms about her head and grabbed the headboard, moaning loudly while the most glorious feeling enveloped her, as if she had become one with the heavens.

Jean called out her name once more in ecstasy, then they both collapsed into each other's arms. They lay together as one, still kissing, still caressing, until sleep finally overtook them.

Chapter Seven

By afternoon, rain still beat at the windows and a harsh wind demanded entrance to the bare cypress walls of the house. Another storm was traveling through and its thunder woke Jean from his peaceful slumber.

Gazing down on the dark-haired beauty sleeping on his chest, Jean wished he could remain in that position forever. Never had he known such complete joy with a woman; never had he experienced such fulfillment.

He gently pushed the hair from her forehead and planted a kiss in its place. Then he traced the outline of her brows with his lips, the sweet curve of her nose, the high rise of her cheeks. Pausing at her hairline, he breathed in her scent, wondering if he would remember these details in the lonely months ahead.

"Are you awake?" he heard a soft voice speak.

"No," he answered playfully.

Gabrielle placed a hand on his chest and leaned

her chin on top. She grinned at him as her eyes sparkled. "I'm starving," she said.

Now that he thought of it, he was ravenous. "Didn't you bring something into the other room earlier?"

Gabrielle sat up in bed, clutching the sheet to her chest. Even though the storm continued, the room had become much brighter. "I'll go get the tray and make a fresh pot of coffee if you promise not to look."

A wide grin spread across his cheeks, but he tried to appear sincere. "I promise."

Gabrielle slipped from the sheets and leaned over to retrieve her chemise, allowing Jean quite an eyeful. She pulled the chemise over her head and let it fall to her knees, but she realized Jean was staring. "Liar," she admonished him.

Jean laughed. "Rule number one, Gabrielle. Never trust a pirate."

Pulling on her robe, Gabrielle sent him a haughty look. "Rule number two, Jean. Never upset the woman who feeds you."

When she left the room, the air seemed ten times heavier, the gloom twice as acute. Jean pulled on his breeches and shirt, pushing from his mind the painful thoughts of what was to come. He would not think of the morning and their imminent separation. He would relish the present, breathing in each moment as precious.

He entered the main room and began a fire, noticing a dramatic chill to the house. The storm had brought colder weather with it, making him wish he could stay and help insulate the new homestead. Rose's wealthy American husband had insisted on building a new house for them on the family's land grant, in addition to the several outbuildings. As Jean looked around the new home, he was impressed with the spaciousness of the design and the comfortable furnishings. But there were still so many improvements to be made, enhancements that only a man about the house could offer.

A gust of air followed Gabrielle as she entered through the back door and Jean immediately noticed a lightness to her step. Gone was the sadness that lingered in her eyes or the pensive countenance that made most people believe Gabrielle to be a shy, passionless woman. Jean knew that to be far from reality, but he knew her secret before that morning.

Gabrielle placed the coffee on the floor between them and poured them both a cup. Jean ripped apart pieces of bread and loaded them down with strawberry preserves. They traded items and nestled shoulder to shoulder in front of the fire.

"There's something I have to know," Gabrielle asked between bites.

"What is it?"

"You said there was a way to keep us from conceiving a child. What . . . " She hesitated.

"Sheep intestines," he replied

Gabrielle nearly choked on her coffee. "I beg your pardon?"

Condoms weren't the most romantic thing to discuss after lovemaking, but Gabrielle had asked. "It's an old pirate secret. It's a long sail to the West Indies and men tend to be quite randy at port. They're worn to keep from acquiring diseases from, well, less respectable ladies."

He pulled an odd-looking sheath from his pocket

and showed it to her. Gabrielle glanced at it quickly then looked down, intently studying the insides of her coffee cup. "Do pirates carry them wherever they go?"

Jean caught her meaning instantly. "You're wondering if there are other women, if this is why I carry them around with me," he said.

She said nothing, but Jean knew what she was thinking. Her question had been a good one, actually, since he had convinced himself he was visiting the Poste to inquire as to her health and nothing more. But other women? Gabrielle commanded his heart and soul. "I assure you, Gabi, I have not so much as looked at another women since I met you."

"Then why . . . ?" Gabrielle frowned, staring back at the black coffee. "Never mind. I shouldn't have asked."

"Because I'm a fool," he whispered, caressing the long strands of hair flowing past her shoulder. "I swore that I was going to visit the Attakapas, make sure you were safe, and head out to sea. Even though my logical mind convinced me of this, my heart was hoping I would see you one last time. I have to admit, I was wishing this would happen, that we would find some time to be alone."

Gabrielle smiled sweetly. "You love me, don't you?"

A tightness began in his chest and spread, cutting off his air. He was never good with words. He could only stare at her, his mind fumbling over what to do and say next.

Instead of being angry at his silence, Gabrielle placed a hand on his unshaven cheek and grinned. "You don't have to say it," she said. "Delphine said you weren't much for words of affection. A man of action, I think she called you."

The tightness intensified when he thought of his precious little girl, whom he might never see again. A man of action? Right now he was powerless to protect the one person who needed him most. "Write to Phiney," he pleaded. "Please write to her and make sure she is well and safe."

"Of course I will," Gabrielle answered.

"She's different," Jean explained. "She's not like other girls. She's not happy with friends her age, nor interested in boys and gowns and dances. She wants to don breeches and sail away with me."

At this, Gabrielle laughed. "I understand completely. We will have lots to talk about."

Jean matched her smile. "I thought a girl was supposed to fall for a man like her father, not the other way around."

Gabrielle slid her hands up the front of his shirt and clutched the fabric, raising her lips to his. "Are you saying you're falling for me, Captain Bouclaire?"

Again, Jean said nothing, but he wasted no time snaking arms about her waist and pulling her into his lap while his lips devoured hers. Yes, he was definitely a man of action.

The coffee and bread temporarily forgotten, the two began a sensual exploration of each other's bodies. Gabrielle couldn't believe that the sensations she had experienced only hours before could return so ferociously.

"Do you want to do it again?" she whispered as his mustache grazed the skin between her throat and the swell of her breast.

Jean pulled back and tried to resume a steady breath, but it was clear he desperately wanted to continue. "No, *chérie*. It's best not to overdo it the first time."

There it was again, that irritating paternal need to protect her. "Jean," Gabrielle said. "There is something I have to tell you."

His eyes shot up, curious.

"You were not my first pirate."

An enormous grin erupted, accented by the trademark dimple. Damned if he wasn't the handsomest man she knew.

What was she doing? she thought madly. What would her mother think hearing her use such foul language? It's only in your mind, she reminded herself. But so were all the other forbidden thoughts, the constant desires raking her with guilt.

"What is it?" Jean took her hand and squeezed, forcing her to meet his eyes. "One minute you were laughing and now this. What caused the shadow to fall upon your heart this time?"

"I have done something terrible," Gabrielle whispered, feeling the pain choke her heart.

Jean wrapped an arm about her shoulder, his other hand still gripping hers tightly. "What could you have possibly done, *ma petite*?"

Gabrielle swallowed hard, reminded once again that she was the cause of her family's ruin. "I'm the reason my family was separated."

Jean removed his arm and turned to face her, his brow creased. "Why on earth would you think that?"

Gabrielle thought back on that horrid day on the beach, where families were waiting to be hauled away from their homes. Marianne and her sisters waited by the water's edge for Joseph to arrive, waiting for the men of the village to be released from the church. When Joseph was finally spotted on the bluff above, when they had waved to him from their place on the beach, Gabrielle had felt secure that everything was going to be all right.

"There were ships," Gabrielle explained. "Lots of them. Papa told me not to go near the water, to stay away from the English and their ships, but I wanted a better look. Maman got worried when I disappeared. She left her place on the beach with Emilie and Rose in tow until she found me. When we looked back, Papa was gone. Then they forced us onto a frigate, sent us off to Maryland, and we never saw him again."

Jean said nothing, simply stared. She couldn't imagine what he was thinking. "You must be fooling me," he finally said.

If the guilt wasn't destroying her now, Jean's condemnation surely would. "No."

Jean leaned close, grabbed her arms, and looked at her like a father about to give a lecture. "You are not responsible for your family's separation," he said sternly. "That's the most ridiculous thing I've ever heard."

Suddenly, Gabrielle felt her cheeks burn with anger. How could he possibly understand? "You weren't there."

"No, I wasn't there," he continued in his authoritative tone. "But a young girl—what, six or seven?—in the midst of chaos is hardly to blame for losing her father."

"If I had stayed put as my father told me to . . ."

"He still would have lost you."

No. Gabrielle thought. They would have seen each other, been able to reunite somehow. "I don't believe that."

Jean placed both hands on her cheeks and forced her eyes to his. "Gabi, you are not alone. There are so many Acadian families who were separated. The English sent you all over the Eastern Seaboard and the Caribbean. I have met Acadians in Santa Domingo who were more than likely your neighbors."

"Still . . ."

"There is a man on my ship who lost his entire family at Grand Pré. He sails with me because he has no one left. His wife and children died in another colony."

She wanted to believe it, wanted to relieve the aching at her heart. Marianne had told her time and again she was not responsible for the family's disunion, but something in the pit of her belly declared otherwise. Even that morning, knowing that her mother would continue to need her by her side, Gabrielle wanted to close her eyes to her family and sail away with Jean. Which proved her desires were selfish ones.

"The last thing Papa said to me was leave the ships alone," Gabrielle said softly, tears falling down her cheeks and onto Jean's hands. "He said take care of my mother and stay away from the water."

Jean sighed and pulled her close, resting her head on his chest and caressing her hair. "You didn't do it," he insisted. "I can't make the pain go away or bring your father back, but I know you aren't the cause of your family's separation."

"But I want to be with you."

Jean brushed her tears away with the tip of a finger. "And you think because you want to leave your mother and sail away with me, that it proves you're a bad person?"

"I shouldn't even be thinking it."

Jean laughed nervously. "You shouldn't be sharing your bed with me."

Gabrielle leaned her head back so she could see his eyes. "I don't regret what we shared."

He gazed at her so intensely Gabrielle felt goosebumps travel up her arms. "Why shouldn't we wish for happiness?" he whispered sadly. "Even seafarers deserve to be happy, *n'est-ce pas?*"

He kissed her then, a gentle reminder that he wanted her by his side just as much. Maybe Jean was right, Gabrielle thought, relaxing against him. Perhaps things were more complicated than she imagined. She still doubted her innocence, but it relieved her heart being able to share her pain.

He kissed her again, deeper this time, wrapping his arms around her back and sliding each leg around his waist. Suddenly, a hunger overtook them and their kisses intensified as their bodies pressed closer.

"Are you sure you don't want to do it again?" Gabrielle asked when his lips headed for her neckline.

She heard a sigh at her throat, then his head became level with hers. "I'm positive I *want* to do it again. That's not the point."

Gabrielle leaned her head to the right and began biting the skin underneath his chin. "No more sheep intestines?"

Jean's large hand found a breast and squeezed,

then he passed a thumb over an erect nipple. "I have another," he whispered.

A wild, delicious shiver ran through her and she eagerly raised her mouth to his. Their tongues danced madly while their hands savored the feel of each other's bodies. Gabrielle crossed her ankles behind Jean's back and felt every inch of his arousal at her hips. They both moaned at the contact, then laughed at their mutual exclamations.

"I think we should move to the bedroom," Jean said.

He attempted to rise, carrying her wrapped about him, but the effort was too much for him rising from a seated position on the floor. Jean stumbled backward, landing against a pillow propped up beside the fireplace. Gabrielle remained with her legs hugging his waist, although not locked at the ankles, but this time she was on top of him, her hair falling across his chest.

"This spot is good, too," Jean said with a grin, and began to untie her robe. He pulled the lace ribbons apart, then pushed the fabric off her shoulders to the floor. He began to pull her chemise upward, but Gabrielle caught his hands.

"I want to see you, *chérie*," Jean said.

The fire sent waves of crimson gold flitting across his midnight hair and flames reflected in his eyes. Gabrielle brazenly sat atop him like riding a horse, feeling his manhood pressed hot against her, yet she was almost shaking at the thought of being naked.

Jean leaned forward and removed his shirt, then took her hands and placed them on his chest. While she buried her fingers in the dark hair over his heart and enjoyed the thick bands of muscles that extended down from his shoulders, he pulled her chemise up above her knees and caressed the soft skin beneath them.

That slow, deft movement erased her trepidations, melted her resolve, and she sighed, thinking of what was to come. Jean slowly moved the chemise up her sides to free her legs, caressing her skin with the simple, seductive touch of a fingertip. When he reached her breasts and began a loop around each nipple until he caught them between his thumbs and forefingers, Gabrielle leaned back and raised her arms in surrender. She closed her eyes to savor his touch and heard the undergarment hit the chair on the far side of the room.

She would have laughed had he not placed his hands at the small of her back and raised her forward so his lips could devour a breast, rolling the nipple gently between his teeth. Gabrielle gasped and clutched at his hair. With his free hand, he slid a finger inside her and caressed the spot that had sent her spiraling into ecstasy hours before.

The heated sensations returned, pouring like waves over her, but she didn't want to travel there alone this time. "Jean," she pleaded. "Come with me."

Jean released her, letting her sit back down in his lap. He raised his head but his eyes were busy examining her naked form, touching her breasts, trailing fingers down to her navel then along the top of a thigh.

"I want you . . ."

He appeared ready to admit something profound, but paused, thinking better of it. Why, Gabrielle wondered, did God have to make men so tight-lipped about their emotions?

"Man of action," she whispered, "it's not fair that I'm completely naked and you're not."

A sly sparkle appeared in his eye as the dimple deepened in his cheek. "That can be remedied."

He pushed her upward again, this time to her knees, enough to pull his breeches free. Gabrielle was stunned to think Jean wanted her to ride him like a bull, but something decadent inside her thrilled at the thought of it as well. He quickly relieved himself of the breeches, but before he discarded them to the other side of the room, he pulled something from the pocket.

How could she have been embarrassed at being naked when his manhood stood poised between them like a sentry and he held a sheep's innards in his hand? Gabrielle tried to force her gaze away, but curiosity got the better of her.

"Put it on me," he whispered.

Gabrielle gasped. "You want me to put that thing on that."

Jean laughed at her discomfort, then took her hand and coaxed her to slide the object over his engorged manhood. She had to admit, she had wanted to touch it. It was an amazing thing, this appendage of a male's anatomy, a lightning rod that could send bolts of energy through her. And it felt just as interesting between her fingers.

This time, Jean gasped, closed his eyes, and winced.

"Oh my God," Gabrielle said, retrieving her hand. "I've hurt you."

A smile appeared, but he still looked as if he were

in pain. "You haven't hurt me, I assure you. You'll only hurt me if you don't continue."

It didn't make sense to Gabrielle, but she did as she was told. She slid the object down the shaft, amazed when she was finished that such an action was causing her heart to quicken and her feminine core to ignite. She suddenly wanted him deep inside her.

Jean opened his eyes and seemed to read her mind. He ran his hands up along her thighs to her hips, then raised her slowly while his eyes never left hers. Gabrielle lifted herself up, placing her hands on his shoulders and letting her hair drape over them both. Then their lips met. And he lowered her down.

She was still tender from their first joining, but she wasn't afraid this time, which made it ten times more pleasurable. His hands remained on her hips to ensure that the union proceeded slowly, letting her drop only small increments at a time. Dear Jean, she thought, caressing his scraggly face, always concerned for her welfare.

When the union was complete, Jean let out a deep sigh and Gabrielle felt its impact rush through her. He didn't need words; she knew exactly what he meant. Their bodies began to dance, building a wild desire through her that intensified with each thrust. When Jean reached up to cup her breasts, Gabrielle closed her eyes and savored the ride. They reached their destination together, blanketed in the fire's glow.

Gabrielle felt dawn approaching before she opened her eyes. She sensed it in the dense air that lingered in her bedroom, that deadly quiet just before sunrise. She slid her hand sideways and found the bed empty, no sign of Jean except for his scent on her pillow. She bolted upright, and his arms grabbed her.

"I'm right here," he said.

He was seated on the edge of the bed, fully clothed, pulling on his boots. "Were you going to leave without saying goodbye?" Gabrielle asked, trying to keep the panic from her voice.

"No, my love," he said, kissing her. "I've only just risen."

"What time is it?" she asked, fearing the worst.

Jean paused and Gabrielle could feel the beating of his heart through his shirt. "It's time," he answered.

Gabrielle nodded, refusing to think about it. The pain of that thought was too much to bear. "I will go and make coffee."

This time, dressing in front of Jean seemed perfectly natural. Gone was the embarrassment, the awkwardness of their lovemaking. He had led her across a threshold, his imprint laid upon her heart. A heart that only belonged to him and always would.

She traveled to the kitchen in the cool morning air, suddenly feeling the emptiness of being alone. How was she going to face never seeing him again? Dear God, how did her mother do it after knowing such intricacies of love?

"Can I help?"

Two enormous arms reached over her and pumped the water from the well, then transferred it to the coffeepot. Gabrielle closed her eyes, relishing the comfort of his presence. She wasn't ready to be alone. "You already have," she said.

The two worked together, then brought the food and coffee into the house, taking care not to be seen by the neighbors. The darkness was getting lighter, although the sun had not yet pierced the horizon.

They sat at the table, drinking in silence, each trying hard not to meet the other's eyes. Gabrielle knew if she gazed into those dark, loving eyes, the separation would be ten times more painful. Better to prepare herself, not make it harder with affections, she thought, but she ached for the comfort of his touch.

A soft glow permeated the room and Gabrielle bit the insides of her mouth to keep from crying. "I never thought I'd detest the sight of dawn."

Jean quietly stood, pulled on his coat, then appeared by her side. He offered his hand and Gabrielle's tears poured free. She had to be brave. Her mother had faced worse. Jean had lost a daughter. Be strong, she commanded herself.

Gabrielle accepted his hand and stood, and Jean immediately pulled her into his embrace. He held her tightly, breathing in the scent of her hair, savoring the feel of her body pressed against him. She, in turn, threaded her fingers into his black, curly hair, enjoying the warmth of his chest for the last time.

"Lâche pas la patate, Gabrielle," he whispered.

Before she had time to comprehend his words, Jean released her and walked out the door, a cold burst of air replacing the warmth of his arms.

Gabrielle felt the blood leave her body, her energy wane. Her head pounded from the realization that he had gone, that she would never see him again. Her body felt empty, defeated, her heart shattered.

She reached for the back of a chair to steady herself, but it offered little relief. She needed to sit down.

No, she commanded herself, as a darkness enveloped her despite the onset of dawn. She wasn't ready to give up.

Gabrielle retrieved her writing box and sat at the desk where Delphine's letter remained. She pulled out her parchment and quill and began to write to the one person who would understand her pain, the one person who knew what it was like to lose the love of Jean Bouclaire.

She inhaled deeply in an effort to dispel the grief choking her heart, then she dipped her quill into the ink and with a shaking hand began to write.

"My dearest Delphine. There is so much to tell."

Chapter Eight

The bell sounded like a death toll, but Delphine refused to acknowledge it.

"She's calling you again," Carmeline said. "Delphine, why don't you answer her?"

The house was ominously quiet, its solitude interrupted only by the occasional outburst of Mardi Gras celebrations in the street.

And the occasional ringing of a bell.

"There she goes again," Carmeline said. "She's your mother, Phiney. Go to her."

Since the morning of the news that Marcel was dead and Jean declared an outlaw, Louise Delaronde had taken to her bed and refused to rise. On that same morning, Delphine stopped speaking to her mother. And even though the doctor had visited three times that week, she didn't wish to now.

The bell rang again, this time followed by her mother crying her name. For the sake of the servants' sanity, if not her own, Delphine sighed in defeat and began up the stairs.

Her mother was always playing sick when she needed attention, and she needed attention now. Marcel's death not only had ruined her chances for love and prosperity and discontinued Jean's support, but had created a new scandal for the family. Louise was no longer welcome at the opera, theater, or other social gatherings, and no one would come again to call. Taking to her bed was the typical reaction of her melodramatic mother. She was hoping to be declared innocent because of her frail health, hoping her friends would forgive her indiscretion and arrive with teas and cakes to nurse her.

But the only one to call had been the doctor.

Delphine turned the corner into her mother's bedroom and grabbed the dreadful bell from her mother's hands.

"Where have you been?" her mother asked. "I have been ringing for you all morning."

Delphine had to admit that her mother looked deathly pale. Her eyes were bloodshot, her lips cracked and swollen. Her breathing was ragged and she was much too thin. But Delphine's hurt lay deep, and she found it hard to speak to the woman who had caused it.

"Why won't you speak to me?" Louise pleaded, her voice also exhibiting true sickness. "I'm not much for this world. I need you."

Delphine pushed aside whatever sympathy she was feeling when her mother spoke the last words. "How could you possibly need me, Maman, when I'm only a regretful mistake you made one night? Or is it because I happen to be the only one left?"

Louise tried to rise on her elbows, but her strength failed her. "I didn't mean it," she said with tears in her eyes. "I love you. I have always loved you. Don't you know that?"

"You have a strange way of showing it." Tears gathered in her own eyes and she looked away to fight them off.

"I wanted a good marriage," Louise whispered. "That's why I left France and came to this horrid place."

Delphine crossed her arms and looked her in the eye. "You could have married my father."

Louise fell back against her pillow and closed her eyes. "You think it's that simple. We're the last two people who should be married to one another. We would have ended up hating each other."

For once, her mother spoke truth. They were worlds apart in so many ways. But if Jean was willing to accept his responsibility, why couldn't she?

"You spent my education money on clothes," Delphine said, trying to keep her anger inside. "You brought that despicable man into this house to educate me, that disgusting creature who tried to put his hand up my dress."

Her mother said nothing, allowing Delphine a chance to let her feelings flow. The anger burned up her spine and spilled forth like a brush fire. "We've had to sell half the household's furnishings to keep you in lace and ruffles while we haven't had enough to eat."

"There was a reason for that. I was trying to improve our situation."

Now, Delphine's anger rose to her brow, making her head pound. "You made my own father arrive at night at the back door like some hired hand while you entertained men in our parlor who weren't fit to clean his boots."

Again, her mother said nothing, but tears flowed down her cheeks. "Don't hate me," she finally whispered. "I was only trying to better our lives. I really do love you."

Delphine's own tears poured forth, despite the fury still pumping through her veins. "I don't hate you, Maman."

"I'm sorry."

Now, Delphine became worried. Gone was the defensiveness in her mother's voice, the insistence of pleading her case. Her tone had turned distant and cold, making her realize this was more than a chance at gaining attention.

Louise held out her hand and Delphine accepted it, finding her cold fingers limp and unresponsive. Her mother turned her head as if every movement caused her pain. "You've grown," she whispered, rubbing the top of Delphine's hand and noticing her sleeves not meeting her wrists.

"I've grown over an inch since Christmas," Delphine answered, watching her mother carefully, noticing the amount of strength it took her just to swallow.

"You've filled out your gowns, too," her mother said slowly, attempting a smile. Then her eyelids fluttered and closed and her hand grew still.

An intense fear invaded Delphine, but her mother's eyes opened again. She breathed a sigh of relief until her mother's eyes met hers once more and death shone back.

"If anything happens to me," her mother said, "I want you to go to Paris, find your father, the count."

"No," Delphine commanded, a fresh set of tears falling. "I don't want to go to France."

"He owns this house," Louise continued. "You must get word to him. He will take care of you. He must."

Delphine shook her head stubbornly. "No. I won't leave Louisiana."

Louise let her daughter's hand go and exhaled deeply. "I must sleep now. We will talk more in the morning."

"Maman?" Delphine felt a panic rise in her chest. There was still so much to say, so much between them to be resolved, but Louise had drifted off into slumber.

Delphine felt two hands on her shoulders leading her away from the bed, but she resisted, unsure of what to think next. What was happening? Her mother couldn't be that sick. She couldn't.

"She's pretending, right?" she asked Carmeline.

"Come now, chile," Carmeline answered softly. "Let's go have our breakfast."

They made their way down the stairs, but food was the last thing Delphine wanted. She needed her friend, a strong male voice offering comfort and protection. "I'm going to the Convent," she told Carmeline.

"Pray for your *maman*," Carmeline said, tears pouring down her cheeks.

"It's not that bad."

If Delphine said it out loud, she could make it true, but the look in Carmeline's eyes told her otherwise and the shiver that ran through Delphine was hard to dismiss. "It's not that bad," she repeated with less confidence, then left the house.

Delphine wrapped her shawl about her as she made her way through the festive streets of New Orleans. Residents were dressed gaily, laughing and enjoying the rites of Mardi Gras, the day before Ash Wednesday and the beginning of Lent. With the prospect of forty days of sacrifice ahead of them, New Orleans residents reveled in the day, eating and drinking their fill.

The annual festivities failed to lift her solemn mood. Delphine wished she had a Carnival mask to hide the tears streaking her face or a handkerchief to blow her nose. She used her sleeve when she found no one watching, reminded again that she badly needed new clothes. To top all that had happened in the past two months, Delphine had sprouted breasts and grown taller. Not only did her sleeves not meet her wrists but her shoes poked out from the bottom of her skirts, a bold exclamation of her dire financial situation. Yet another reason for the residents of New Orleans to label her "poor Delphine Delaronde" behind their fans and shun her from their presence.

"What's the matter with you today?" Sister Marguerite asked gruffly when she arrived at the Ursuline Convent. Most of the Ursuline nuns were generous and kind, but as with the rest of her luck, Delphine had been assigned to the meanest of the bunch.

"You're a sight to behold," Sister Marguerite continued, handing her a handkerchief. "Blow your nose."

"My mother is ill," Delphine said, blowing her nose hard.

"So what are you doing here? Dear me, child, but you are the most insufferable girl. You should be home taking care of your mother, making her realize the sins of her past before it's too late."

Delphine wanted to run back home, to escape the dreadful woman and her insistence that she was a product of sin born from an indecent union, but she had to see her friend. Lately, he was the only person who could get her through each day. "I have to see Monsieur LeBlanc."

Marguerite blocked her way, staring at her hard. "He hasn't slept well in weeks. He's not well. I won't have you upsetting him."

Delphine wanted to argue, to give the woman a piece of her mind, but she had to see Parrain and her defiance might cost her that chance. "I won't upset him," she said as calmly as she could.

Sister Marguerite continued her scrutiny. "You should examine your life, Delphine, when you talk to Monsieur LeBlanc, realize that there are people who suffer more than you."

Guilt, so easily inflicted from Sister Marguerite, replaced her need to be comforted and she wondered if she should burden Parrain with her problems. He had enough of his own, to be sure. Monsieur LeBlanc had arrived at the Convent months before on the

verge of death, insisting that he was on his way into
the territory to find his family. In his fevered delirium
one night he tried to leave the Convent, fell, and
suffered a head injury. Since then he had been unable
to remember his identity and why he was in New
Orleans. From his dialect and accent, they assumed
he was Acadian, traveling to Louisiana in search of
his loved ones. They named him René LeBlanc, one
of the most common Acadian names.

"I promise I will not upset him," Delphine repeated.

The nun relented and Delphine bolted past the
gate into the courtyard. She couldn't get to the infirmary fast enough. She found Monsieur LeBlanc, or
Parrain as he insisted on being called, in the garden
just outside the infirmary's doors. Gazing over to the
older man with warm, expressive eyes, she wished he
was her *parrain,* or godfather. She needed a strong
family member by her side now, but she remembered
the nun's warning.

"Phiney," he said, greeting her with a kiss to both
cheeks.

Although she resolved not to cry or burden him
with her problems, the tears busted loose at their
greeting. Parrain pulled an arm about her shoulders
and held her tightly. "What is it, *'ti-monde?*"

He led her to a garden bench and they sat down,
Parrain still holding her close. "Is it your father? Have
you heard news?"

Thoughts of Jean brought forth another round of
tears, and Delphine buried her face into Parrain's
shirt the way she used to seek comfort with her father.
And like Jean, Parrain brushed the curls from her

forehead and soothed her brow. Whatever family he belonged to, he must have been a wonderful father, she thought. So kind and caring, with loving brown eyes.

"What happened?" he asked. "Tell me."

Delphine straightened and wiped the tears away. "My mother is very ill. I thought she was trying to get attention, but I think she may be dying."

"Oh, *'ti-monde,*" he whispered, placing a paternal hand on her shoulder. "What can I do to help?"

Delphine thought of Sister Marguerite's message at the gate. "You have enough to worry about. I don't want you to worry about me too."

At this, Parrain tightened his arm about her. "Just because a person has problems doesn't mean he has no room in his heart to help those with theirs."

Delphine glanced up at the middle-aged man, a soft-spoken, confident man she had latched on to the first day she started volunteer work at the Convent. Next to her father, he was the kindest of men.

"Have you remembered anything more?" she asked him.

A darkness clouded his eyes and he looked away. "I see images in my dreams but I can't put them together. I suffer from terrible headaches when they come, but nothing makes sense."

"It must be horrible not knowing who you are."

Parrain sighed but the darkness failed to lift. "The worst thing, Delphine, is knowing that I should be somewhere, that I'm needed, but I can't put the pieces of the puzzle in place."

Delphine took his hand and squeezed. "It will come to you. I know it."

Parrain looked back at her and attempted a smile. "Things will look brighter soon for you too. Take comfort in that. And know that I'm here if you ever need me. Anytime."

She nodded, glad to have the friendship, but she doubted her life would improve. Ever since the duel, every day was a trip farther and farther into misery and debt.

"I almost forgot," Parrain said, brightening. "I have a surprise for you."

He pulled a letter out of his pocket and handed it to her. "It may be news from your father, although I don't know why it was sent here."

A wave of euphoria spread through her and she almost stopped breathing. "It's from the Attakapas Poste," she said smiling broadly. "It's from Gabrielle."

"Gabrielle?"

For a moment, the darkness returned to Parrain's eyes. Or perhaps she was imagining things. "Gabrielle is my father's fiancée. She lives on the frontier. I asked her to write to me here because my mother used to hide letters my father sent to me."

Parrain's eyes cleared and he nodded. "Read," he encouraged her.

Delphine ripped open the letter. She couldn't absorb Gabrielle's words fast enough. *"My dearest Delphine,"* she began, then turned to Parrain. "She called me dearest."

"Which is what you are. Read."

"My dearest Delphine," she began again. *"There is so much to tell. First, I cannot express how happy I*

*was to see your letter and to finally meet the woman
I have heard so much about. I can tell by your hand
you are every bit the remarkable woman your father
says you are. He speaks of you constantly, always so
proud of his darling Phiney."*

Delphine paused to swallow the lump gathering in
her throat. She felt Parrain's hand on hers and drew
comfort from it. "Go on," he whispered.

Delphine blew her nose and continued. *"Your
father has just left my side after risking his life to visit
me one last time. He is well, although if health could
be determined by the state of one's heart, I would say
Jean is in poor spirits. He misses you terribly, and our
separation was not an easy one. Writing you this letter
gives me strength because I know you will understand
how it feels to lose someone dear to you. In our case,
that man is one and the same,* n'est-ce pas?"

Parrain stood and gazed out at the courtyard's walls
dotted with images of the coming spring. January's
camellias had come and gone, now replaced by bud-
ding pink azaleas. Soon, the weather would turn warm
and sunny, and spring flowers would burst into bloom
everywhere. The laughter of people outside the sanc-
tuary mirrored that fact, yet Delphine knew that
spring held no promise for the two of them and
Gabrielle.

"There has been no word of my father," Delphine
continued reading. *"Every day my mother waits by
the bayou and every day he does not arrive. My mother*

never gives up hope that he shall return, but now that Jean has gone, I wonder if I will have the strength to carry on, waiting for the men to wander back into our lives. Patience has never been my virtue. And I fear for my father so very much. Thirteen years is so long to be separated and Maryland is such a long journey from Louisiana."

At this, Parrain turned slightly. "She is Acadian?"

"*Oui*, Parrain."

He began to rub his forehead furiously and Delphine knew he was having flashes of memory. "Anything?" she asked.

Parrain shook his head. "Continue reading, my dear. Don't worry about me."

Delphine did worry, but she finished reading the letter. *"Please write to me, dearest Phiney, and I will continue to write to you. I need to know you are well. I am here if you ever need me. Anytime.*

"Your friend, Gabrielle Gallant."

Something slid from the envelope and fell into Delphine's lap. "Oh look, it's a cross like the one Papa wears."

She grasped the oak cross between her fingers and ran an appreciative thumb over the smooth wood, but a feeling of dread passed over her. She looked up to find Parrain wincing from the pain in his head, a look of alarm in his eyes.

"Parrain," Delphine said, rising. "What is it?"

"Gabrielle," he whispered. "She has sisters, Rose and Emilie."

Delphine nodded. "Yes. How did you know?"

"Her mother," he whispered as if each word caused him pain. "Her name is Marianne."

Delphine swallowed and nodded. "Yes," she whispered back.

Parrain grabbed her hand and stared at its contents, then withdrew a pendant from underneath his shirt. Lying on a string of leather was an identical cross carved of oak.

"A preacher in Maryland gave this to me," he said. "I remember now. He said Gabrielle made them to help support the family when they lived there."

Delphine met his eyes once more, eyes tormented from the pounding in his head and the heartache from years of separation. *"Mon dieu,"* she whispered. "You're Joseph Gallant."

Parrain grabbed her arms to steady himself, his hair disheveled and his eyes wild. If she hadn't known him better, she might have been frightened. "They're on my land grant," he said anxiously. "In the Attakapas region."

"Yes," Delphine said. "They're waiting for you."

Parrain's eyes grew wider and his voice quivered. "I have to get out of here."

"Are you sure you're well enough?" Delphine asked, although she knew that no force could keep him from heading west.

"I have to go," he whispered. His worried eyes stared into hers and Delphine nodded. "I have to leave today."

"And where are you going, Monsieur LeBlanc?" Sister Marguerite said as she approached. To Delphine, she sent a scalding look. "What has this child done to upset you?"

Now, it was Delphine who felt panic. "He's not Monsieur LeBlanc. He's Joseph Gallant and he has family on the frontier."

Parrain grabbed his forehead again, then staggered for the door. "I have to get out of here, Sister."

Sister Marguerite snapped her fingers and two men appeared to restrain him. "No," Delphine cried out. "He's Joseph Gallant. You have to let him go. His family is waiting for him."

Parrain instantly pushed them away, but the men were too much for him in his frail health. They held back his aggression and led him into the infirmary. Delphine could hear his shouts of protestations echoing inside.

"Let him go," she cried to Sister Marguerite, tears emerging once again. "He needs to go home. His family is waiting for him."

Sister Marguerite grabbed her elbow, forced her to the courtyard gate, and pushed her into the street. *"You* need to go home," she said. "You have done enough damage for one day."

Before she had time to rebut, the courtyard gate slammed shut, followed by the sound of its locking. Delphine rested her head against its cold iron, her chest heaving from the sobs. Had the world gone crazy? she thought.

Suddenly, she remembered the cross still held tightly between her fingers, and its image gave her strength. She placed Gabrielle's present over her neck, closed her eyes, and asked for guidance.

Jean had mentioned a man once, the family solicitor of Rose's husband. He lived in New Orleans and had been instructed to watch for Joseph's return, to inform the family the moment he found him. Delphine lifted her head and tried to think. What was his name? Where did he live?

Delphine wiped her nose on her sleeve, not caring who saw. Rose had married a man named Coleman Thorpe. If she could find this man's house, she might find help. She had to try.

After inquiring with several soldiers and merchants, Delphine finally found the Thorpe house a few blocks from the Place d'Armes. She knocked on the street entrance and a well-dressed man appeared, gazing at her with apprehension.

"I wish to speak with the man who is Monsieur Thorpe's solicitor," she said, straightening the skirt of her gown and smoothing her tousled curls.

"Why are you looking for this man?" the gentleman asked.

Delphine took a deep breath. "I believe I have found Joseph Gallant."

The man gazed at her intently, then opened the door wider. "Please. Come in."

She followed him into the humid first floor of the house, a place where supplies and food were kept, then climbed a staircase to the more refined second story. He motioned for her to enter what appeared to be a library, a warm, comfortable room with shelves of books and a roaring fire.

"May I get you something?" he asked.

Delphine shook her head, her emotional state still raw from the day's events. The man moved to a table and poured himself a glass of wine. Odd, she thought, she had imparted important news and the man acted as if nothing had transpired.

Suddenly, Delphine worried for her safety. What if this man wasn't who she thought he was? She was standing in his library, unchaperoned. She glanced around the room, plotting her quick escape.

The man moved back to her side and handed her the glass. "Drink," he said. "And sit down. You appear as if you're ready to faint."

Now that she thought about it, Delphine did feel light-headed and weak. "I'm sorry, monsieur," she said, sitting. "I've had a rather shocking day."

The man sat across from her and continued his scrutiny. She must have looked a sight, with her too-tight clothes, runny nose, and bloodshot eyes. Delphine gulped down the wine, hoping it might still her anxiety.

"My name is Michel Bernard," the man said. "I am Coleman Thorpe's solicitor. Are you familiar with this family?"

Delphine nodded, grateful for the calming effect of the wine. "My father," she began, then was reminded of how she was never to speak of Jean as a relative. Delphine paused, wondering how to explain her situation.

"Your father . . . ?" Michel prodded.

What difference did it make now? Delphine thought. The world knew who her father was. If they had doubted it before the duel, they were certain of it now.

"My father is Jean Bouclaire," Delphine said, lifting her head proudly. "He is engaged to Gabrielle Gallant."

Michel nodded. "I have made Captain Bouclaire's acquaintance."

Delphine sighed, feeling the tension leave her body. "I have been helping the nuns at the Ursuline Convent. It was there I met a man named LeBlanc, only that's not his real name. You see, he couldn't remember his name or who he was. He hit his head one night and couldn't recall anything."

"And you believe this man to be Joseph Gallant?" Michel asked.

Delphine reached up and touched her cross. "He wears a cross like this one. It's Gabrielle's. Today, when I received a letter from Gabrielle with this cross inside, he remembered everything, even the names of Rose and Emilie and his wife. I never mentioned them before."

Michel stood, clearly convinced. "Where is he?"

"At the Convent. They won't let him go. They think he's insane."

Michel crossed to a table and began writing something on parchment while Delphine filled him in with details. Michel then called his servant and handed him the letter.

"I am sending a letter right away to Monsieur Thorpe," he told her. "I will go to the Convent immediately and see what I can do."

A relief so intense flooded Delphine's senses she thought she might faint for sure. She took his hand without realizing what she was doing. "Oh, thank you, monsieur."

Michel took the opportunity to raise Delphine from her seat. "Go home, mademoiselle," he said gently.

"I will get word to you as soon as I clear this matter up."

Delphine nodded, thankful for the assistance. Two months before she had insisted to Jean that she was a grown woman ready to take on the world. Now, she wanted nothing more than to crawl back to childhood and escape the endless problems.

Michel walked her home, waiting until she was safely inside the courtyard, then he disappeared down the street toward the Convent. For the first time that day, Delphine felt hope.

When she entered her house, however, hope faded fast. Carmeline stood crying in the hallway, her apron pressed against her eyes, and the doctor lingered at the bottom of the stairs speaking to the priest. When they noticed her arrival, all eyes became sympathetic.

"No," she screamed.

The priest reached her first and placed a comforting hand on her shoulder, but it failed to offer comfort. "I'm sorry, my dear, but your mother has passed on."

Suddenly, there were no more tears, no more pain. Her knees gave way and she felt herself falling to the floor, letting the darkness pull her into a place where nothing could hurt her.

But before she crossed over, she sent up a prayer.

"Papa, come back to me."

Chapter Nine

It was a beautiful spring morning, a brisk breeze blowing from the north after a violent night of thunderstorms while the sun shone bright and warm against Philibert's face. Winter, with its brief visit to the Gulf region, had moved north to linger into April. But here at Isle St. Charles, at the edge of the Gulf of Mexico, the cold days were now only a memory.

Phil gazed out at the whitecaps forming on the high waves that crashed onto the island's beaches. Over the past two weeks he had accumulated a nice stash of contraband. As soon as the wind died down, he would sail up Barataria Pass to sell his merchandise to the plantations outside of New Orleans, maybe even venture into the city. He could feel the coins jingling in his pocket.

The morning had also produced an interesting acquisition, one that wouldn't turn a profit but could be instrumental in other, more valuable ways.

Phil entered Jean's meager house and was greeted by the usual disarray of furniture, filthy eating utensils, and dirty clothes. A dog stood in the corner eating leftovers out of a pot while Jean snored in his hammock, one leg hanging lazily over the side.

"You're a disgrace," Phil said, knocking the hammock with his foot and waking Jean from his alcohol-induced slumber. "When was the last time you bathed, Christmas?"

"Go away," Jean mumbled, turning over.

"I have, my friend, many times. But I'm tired of watching you wallow in self-pity." Phil placed a booted foot at his rear and gave him a good shove, sending Jean to the floor. Jean sat up, ready for a fight but halted and grabbed his head.

"Rum will do that to you," Phil said, bending down to look him in the eye. "Shall I make some coffee?"

Jean's eyes grew harsh. "Go away."

"Not this time, *mon ami.*" Phil straightened, wondering where in hell he could find a clean pot. "Are you planning a suicide by stench and filth?"

Jean rose to his feet and brushed off his breeches, but he still staggered from the effects of the rum. His hair hung wild over his forehead and he needed a shave. But his friend hadn't lost his bravado yet. "Go to hell," he told him.

Phil laughed, grateful for the insult. "Look around you. We are in hell. Although you were supposed to be in the West Indies by now."

Jean staggered to the door and leaned against the side of the frame, squinting at the sun. "I've tried many times," he said. "I can't seem to find the strength to leave the territory."

How well Phil understood. He couldn't leave Phiney behind, and he wasn't related to the bright-eyed girl. "Well, at least the authorities won't find you here. They haven't found our island yet." Clapping his hands, Phil shooed the dog outside. "I doubt they will ever catch up with you," Phil continued. "I think Antoine was right. You can come and go into the Interior and no one will say a word. Especially if you bring that nice case of rum Henri Chevalier picked up in Barbados."

Jean said nothing, remaining like a statue in the door frame. Phil began to throw the pots and plates into a large tub. "Get some water, will you?"

He watched Jean pause at the door, unsure of whether to accept Phil's help or not, then leave the house to gather water at the cistern. Phil felt for his friend. He missed Phiney as much as he did. And then there was Gabrielle, the first woman to claim his friend's heart. It was too much heartache for one person to bear.

Jean returned with a bucket of water and fell into a chair. He said nothing while Phil washed enough utensils to make coffee and some semblance of breakfast.

"Remember Jacques Boutté?" Phil asked. "That spineless weasel who wanted to join our crew?"

Jean nodded, but his gaze never left the drawing on the wall, the one Phiney had created and given him for Christmas.

"The guy who wouldn't take no for an answer no matter how much we explained to him that we didn't hire men for our ship unless we knew them, or they'd served with us."

"Yes, I know the man," Jean said impatiently.

Phil smiled, hoping he was waking Jean from his

misery. "He was here this morning. Came to sell me contraband."

Finally, Jean looked his way, his brow creased. "What on earth would Boutté have to sell you? The man couldn't navigate his way through a bayou."

Phil laughed, withdrew a package from his coat pocket, and threw it on the table. "Mail."

Jean picked up the bundle and examined it. "Mail?"

"Boutté's decided to become a pirate," Phil continued. "He sailed that pitiful excuse for a boat to Balise at the bottom of the Mississippi and fired on the first ship he saw."

"Don't tell me," Jean said, a grin appearing at the corners of his lips. "He fired on a Spanish ship."

Phil leaned in close to emphasize his next words. "He sank her."

At this news, Jean began to smile.

"No one was hurt," Phil explained. "I don't even think it was intentional. The fool sailed for the Spanish schooner, got caught in a river current, and rammed the Spaniards head-on. They took a nasty blow to the bow and went down."

The two men burst out laughing.

"But that's not the best part."

Jean reached into the bucket and began helping with the cleaning. "What else did the idiot do?"

"Tried to plunder the ship," Phil said. "Only she went down so fast the only thing he managed to retrieve was this bundle of mail and a few other items such as women's fabric and a barrel of sugar."

The two laughed at the image. "So now he's a fugitive with the Spanish, who'll be scouring the region for him," Phil continued. "All for a few *piastres'* worth of merchandise."

"I suppose the idiot wants to join us now," Jean said.

Phil scooped the coffee into the pot and set it to dripping. "He's a pirate now, Jean. He thinks he's earned the right."

Jean stared at the bundle in his hands. "You didn't buy this from him, did you?"

Phil threw a long leg over the side of the chair and joined him at the table. "It's mail headed for the postes," he said quietly.

A pair of intense brown eyes met his. "What are you thinking?" Jean asked.

"I'm thinking you could do something noble for the people on the frontier and bring them their mail."

Jean's eyes turned dark. "What is this, a cruel joke?"

Phil placed a cup in front of him and withdrew an apple from his other pocket. "No, my friend. I want to break you from this melancholy."

Jean stood and began pacing. "Nothing can break me from this melancholy. I've lost everything dear to me, or haven't you heard?"

"That's not fair," Phil said. "I was there, remember?"

When Jean didn't answer, Phil comprehended what wasn't being said. "I see," he said softly.

"No, you don't," Jean said, turning and meeting his eyes. "I have never blamed you for anything and I never will."

"But if you would have had a more upstanding

second with you that day, someone whose reputation—"

"Phil, let's not talk about it."

The two men turned their backs to one another, thankful that the subject was closed. Phil didn't want to discuss the reason he was discharged from the French Navy, now or ever.

"I can't go back to the Attakapas," Jean said, breaking the awkward silence. "I can't do that to Gabrielle. She needs to forget about me and move on with her life."

"What about Phiney?"

Jean turned, his eyes cold as night. "What about Phiney?"

Phil opened the bundle and tossed the assortment of letters onto the table. "There could be a letter from her here."

Jean wasted no time approaching the table and searching through the contents. But what he found wasn't a letter from his daughter. He held up a parchment written with a masculine hand, one addressed to Coleman Thorpe, care of the Attakapas Poste.

"Do you know this man?" Phil asked.

"He's Gabrielle's brother-in-law," Jean said. "Thorpe instructed his solicitor in New Orleans to write him with news of Gabrielle's father. Only he's not at the Attakapas. His wife is with child and cannot leave Opelousas."

Phil poured Jean a cup of coffee, knowing he would need it for the journey ahead. "I'll have the crew ready within the hour."

Jean nodded. "Make sure you load the barrel of sugar, too. I know someone who could use it."

* * *

Marianne stared at the placid bayou before her,
wondering how her life had led her to this place.
Even though the years of separation stretched
between Louisiana and Grand Pré, she could still feel
Joseph's hand on her cheek, remember the sound
of his laughter. She recalled the surprised look on her
mother's face when she announced her engagement
and the warning her mother gave not to be hasty in
marriage. But Marianne knew the moment she laid
eyes on Joseph Gallant that she would love him for
eternity.

Thinking of the way Joseph smelled at the end of
the day when he bounded across the threshold and
scooped her into his arms made her heart constrict.
Tears poured forth and her chest heaved with sobs.
What was happening to her, she thought, covering
her mouth and hoping no one was watching. She
hadn't cried in so long, hadn't dwelled on the past
as much as she had these last few months. Maybe the
locals were right. Maybe she was finally losing her
mind.

She pulled a handkerchief from her pocket and
tried to calm herself. She was tired, so incredibly tired.
She longed for the misery to end. If Joseph wasn't
coming back, then let God take her and be done with
it. She couldn't go on like this, couldn't stand the
waiting any longer.

Then there was Gabrielle. Her other daughters
were happily wed, could live on without her, but
Gabrielle needed her now. It had been more than a
month since Jean had visited, and every day seemed

as bad as the day Marianne came home from the Dugas house to find Gabrielle devastatingly sad. She had to remember her middle child, raise her chin, and keep greeting the morning with hope. She had to.

She heard steps behind her and quickly wiped her eyes. Gabrielle appeared, thin and pale as usual, and sat next to her at the base of the oak tree, its moss hanging over them both as if weeping for their loss.

"I didn't expect to see you," Marianne said, trying to keep the pain from her voice. She never wanted her children to see her cry.

"I brought lunch," Gabrielle said.

Was it that late? Marianne thought, gazing up at the sky. So many days the two of them would forget to eat. Marianne raised the fabric from the basket and pulled out two apples and some bread, but neither of them were interested.

"We can't go on like this," Marianne said, replacing the fruit in the basket.

Gabrielle stared off down the bayou. "What choice do we have?"

"What if Emilie and Rose show up?" Marianne asked. "What would they think of us?"

"They're not coming until after the baby's born, Maman," Gabrielle said softly. "Another two months at least."

The two women said nothing, watching the bayou for signs. Then Gabrielle stood, wiped her hands on her skirt, and began pacing. It was always a matter of time before her patience wore thin, usually within ten minutes.

"I can't stand this waiting any longer," Gabrielle

said. "Some days I feel that I will die from the wanting."

Every day Marianne greeted her daughter's nervousness with a long string of calming reassurances, but today she felt just as impatient. Marianne rose and dusted off her dress. "Let's go back to the house," she announced.

Gabrielle looked at her, surprised. "But it's early yet."

"No, it's not," Marianne stated. "I'm tired of waiting, too."

She marched up the embankment toward the house, knowing her daughter followed and was shocked at her actions. Marianne was weary of watching the bayou, weary of hearing the hushed remarks of the Attakapas residents. And she was tired of the defeated look on her brave daughter's face.

"First thing we do is give you a bath," she told Gabrielle when her daughter reached her side. "You've been remiss and quite frankly, dear, you smell."

Gabrielle's eyes grew large. "I do not."

She really didn't, but her current hygiene left something to be desired. Gabrielle usually crawled out of bed hours past breakfast and wouldn't change into proper clothes until almost noon. Sometimes she feigned sickness and remained in bed for days, mostly as an excuse not to accept visitors such as pesky Charles Maase or to decline invitations from Juliette Vincent.

"Darling, your hair is hardly ever combed," Marianne began. "And you don't care what shape your clothes are in." The fear that had been gnawing at her belly returned. "Are you sure you're not with child?"

Gabrielle frowned and passed her on the way to the house. "No, Maman."

It was the same answer she always received, but not exactly the one she wanted. Marianne wished Gabrielle had protested harder, had denied such a union had occurred, but at least she took comfort knowing Gabrielle wasn't left an unwed mother.

While Gabrielle started a fire, Marianne retrieved the tub and heated water inside the fireplace. They filled the tub with the warm water and Gabrielle stepped inside, her body relaxing as the water covered her.

"Feel better?" Marianne asked.

Gabrielle closed her eyes and leaned her head back into the water as Marianne began washing her hair. "We made love, Maman," she said softly. "The night you were at the Dugas house."

A giant sigh escaped Marianne's lips before she had a chance to stop it. Gabrielle rose in the water and turned. "Are you disappointed in me?"

In a sense, she was. Sharing a bed was something precious to be kept for the wedding night. Marianne hadn't waited, but she and Joseph had been promised to one another. Yet when she gazed into Gabrielle's eyes, she didn't feel condemnation. If she had been as young as Gabrielle and known that she and Joseph would be separated in exile, Marianne would have done the same thing.

"No, I'm not disappointed," she said, cupping her daughter's sad face in her hands. "I would have preferred you to be married, but we can't have everything in life, can we?''

Tears slid down Gabrielle's face. "I don't regret it. I will never love another man.''

Marianne leaned forward and kissed her daughter's cheeks, holding her face close to hers. Then she gently pushed her around and continued washing her hair. "How about I braid it tonight?''

"How about you cut it all off?''

Marianne playfully tugged on a strand. "You have beautiful hair. Why do you hate it so much?''

"Because it takes forever to dry,'' Gabrielle said. "It's too long and a bother. I wish I was a man and didn't have to worry about such things as hairpins and braids and petticoats.''

"And waiting for men to come home.''

She shouldn't have said it, but for the first time in her life Marianne felt the same way. At least men were out in the world leading productive lives, earning a living, having something to do with all that time. They didn't have to remain alone by a hearth or the side of a tree, waiting.

Gabrielle reached up and took her mother's hand. "I wish I had been born a man,'' she said. "I would be in New Orleans or the English colonies finding Papa instead of sitting here being a sad, useless daughter to you.''

Marianne squeezed her daughter's hand. "You're not useless. You've been my saving grace.''

Gabrielle wiped her nose with her free hand. "Hardly.''

Marianne sighed. Self-pity was getting them nowhere. "Get up, dear, and dry yourself off. Then go out on the gallery and let your hair dry in the sun while I make us dinner. Shall I kill a chicken and create a chicken fricot? I'll even make *les poutines,* your favorite dessert.''

"Shall I help?"

Marianne laughed. "Absolutely not. You always burn everything. Now get dressed and do as I say.''

Gabrielle nodded, and stepped out of the tub. She pulled on the clothes Marianne had cleaned and left out for her, then headed for the gallery. The spring sun felt warm against her skin, dry and fresh like the summers in Canada. In another month or two it would grow hotter and humid, but for now the weather was perfect.

She sat on the bench that her neighbor Raymond Sonnier had built for them, letting her hair spill over the side of the railing. The sun kissed her nose and cheeks, warming her all the way to her toes.

Maybe Maman was right, she thought. It was time to stop feeling sorry for herself, stop moping around the house in her chemise. Jean wasn't coming back, and Papa might never arrive, but Emilie and Rose would and that was enough to live for, wasn't it?

Gabrielle felt the familiar pain grip her heart and she tried to push it away. How long before Jean's memory ceased to cause her such grief? she wondered. And would she ever forget the way Jean smelled against her pillow or the feel of his hands on her own?

Suddenly, a shadow passed over her face and for a moment Gabrielle imagined it to be a cloud. Then she sensed a presence. When she opened her eyes, she thought Jean stood before her. But that was impossible if he was halfway to the West Indies. She sat up slightly and his image became real. It was Jean.

"Where's your mother?" he asked.

Was she seeing things, becoming as crazy as the locals imagined her mother to be? "Inside the house," she told the apparition.

Jean smiled slightly and held out his hand. When Gabrielle touched it with hers, it felt solid and warm. He raised her to her feet, then slid a hand about her waist, pressing his face to her hair and breathing in her scent. Gabrielle closed her eyes and savored the feel of her body against his chest.

"Jean?" she heard her mother say.

Jean drew back to acknowledge Marianne and it was then Gabrielle knew for sure that he was real. "I have something to tell you both," he said.

"Come in," Marianne said, opening the door.

Jean never let go of Gabrielle's hand, pulling it close to his side in the crook of his elbow. "I have intercepted a letter," he began. "It's a long story, but it's from Coleman's solicitor in New Orleans."

"The man who was supposed to let us know if he spotted Joseph," Marianne added.

"Yes," Jean continued. "But it's addressed to Coleman here, at the Attakapas Poste."

They all gazed at the letter held in Jean's hands as if it was made of gold. "You want us to send it on to Coleman?" Marianne asked.

"No, Maman," Gabrielle said, taking it from Jean's hands. "That would take days."

"You want us to open it?" she asked Jean.

"It's your decision," Jean told her. "But if it's news

of your husband, it would be best to know as soon as possible."

"Of course we'll open it," Gabrielle said.

"But what if it's personal business for Coleman?" Marianne inserted.

"We seal it back up and apologize." Gabrielle examined the letter, her heart beating wildly. "Coleman won't mind."

"She's right," Jean said. "I'm sure Coleman would want it this way."

Gabrielle looked up and their eyes met. Was it possible he was standing in their house, his body inches from hers?

"Then open it," Marianne whispered.

Whatever courage Gabrielle felt before, it left her when she considered the possible reasons for the letter. What if the solicitor imparted bad news? What if Joseph had failed to make it back to the Louisiana Territory?

"You need to know," Jean said, as if reading her thoughts.

Gabrielle gazed up into the brown eyes that haunted her nights and found solace. He was right. They had to know.

She ripped apart the envelope and withdrew a short note. She read the contents quickly, but found her voice had left her body.

"What is it?" her mother asked nervously.

For the first time in months Gabrielle felt a semblance of hope. "He's alive," she said, reaching for her mother's hands. "He's been seen in New Orleans."

Jean took the letter and read it while Gabrielle

embraced her mother and they shed tears of joy. "He'd been injured and lost his memory," Jean added. "The Ursuline Nuns have been taking care of him." He paused and looked back at Gabrielle, shocked at the news as much as she was. "My daughter found him."

Gabrielle felt her mother drop beside her, and she and Jean quickly grabbed her arms and lowered her into a chair. "I'm sorry," she whispered. "I'm afraid I'm a bit overcome."

"Oh, Maman." Gabrielle kneeled before her mother and took her hands and raised them to her cheeks. "I should have known. The vision I had at the boat that day was of Delphine and Papa. I didn't realize it then, but something was telling me he was safe."

The power of that vision returned, and Gabrielle felt its importance in more ways than one. She looked up to Jean. "Strange that it was your daughter who found him," she said softly.

Jean began to pace, as much agitated by the news as relieved. "I will leave immediately for New Orleans," he said. "I will find Joseph and bring him back."

Gabrielle stood and faced him. "I'm going with you."

He rubbed the top of her arms, tenderness lingering in his eyes. "No, *mon amour*. You must stay here. I won't be long, I promise."

Gabrielle shook her head. "No, you can't leave me here."

Jean started to argue, but Marianne stood in between them. "You will need food for the journey, Jean. I will go and get some supplies from the kitchen."

Gabrielle watched her leave the house before she turned back to Jean, her hands planted defensively on her hips.

"No," he said more strongly.

"What happens if they catch and arrest you in New Orleans," she insisted. "I can help."

"You can help me by staying here, safe."

"You don't even know what my father looks like," she continued.

"He looks like you," Jean countered in a harsh tone. "I will not risk your life. The answer is no and that's final."

Gabrielle felt her blood boil. She wasn't about to be left behind again. "You can use that tone with your crew, Captain Bouclaire, but it won't work on me."

Jean leaned in close. "And what about your mother?" he asked. "Are you willing to leave your mother?"

Again, the guilt assaulted her. Gabrielle closed her eyes to alleviate the pain beating at her heart. Of course she couldn't leave her mother. What was she thinking? But she couldn't stand there and watch him walk out that door again. Not after the last heart-wrenching month when every waiting moment without him was agony. She knew she had to relent, to remain with her mother, but her heart spoke the words her mind warned her against. "Please take me with you."

"Jean's right," Marianne said, crossing the threshold with a basket full of supplies. "I need you here with me, Gabrielle."

Gabrielle felt her world ripping in two from the desire beating at her breast and the guilt plaguing her soul. And dear God, her mother had heard every word, her dear mother whose own heart was breaking from thirteen years of separation while she was standing there, arguing with Jean and only considering her own feelings.

She felt Jean reach for her hand, saying something in an effort to comfort her, but Gabrielle felt nothing but darkness overtake her. She couldn't bear to think anymore. She pulled away from his reach and headed for her bedroom, slamming the door behind her.

She lay on the bed, numb from the pain, as night slowly overtook the prairies. She heard Jean and her mother speaking, then the closing of the door, but she forced the images from her mind. She couldn't think of Jean's departure. Her mind couldn't stand any more pain.

Minutes passed before she heard her mother enter her room and place something on the bed at her feet. "Get up, Gabrielle. We have work to do."

She thought to ask what possible work they would be doing now, but Gabrielle was too ashamed to question her mother. She sat up in bed, too guilty to look her in the eye.

"Does Jean have any hiding places on that boat of his?" Marianne asked.

Puzzled, Gabrielle peered at her mother, who was lighting a candle next to the bed. "He has a compartment in his cabin where he keeps his food, why?"

"Do you think you could stow away in it?"

Gabrielle finally looked at the objects on the bed,

a man's shirt and breeches, more than likely Raymond Sonnier's clothes stolen from the line.

When she gazed up at her mother, Marianne held scissors in her hands. "I think it's time you got your wish," her mother said.

Chapter Ten

"I knew Jean wouldn't agree to take you with him."
Marianne said as she cut her daughter's hair. "That's
why I agreed that you should stay."

Gabrielle sat silently, listening to the sheers cut off
her long strands of black hair. Guilt still consumed
her, although her heart raced with the thought of
following Jean.

"I know what you're thinking," Marianne said.
"You're feeling that you should stay here with me."

"It was Papa's last request of me," Gabrielle whispered.

"Nonsense." Marianne handed her a mirror. "He
said to take care of me, not waste away your life in
the process."

Gabrielle stared at her new self in the mirror but
all she comprehended was her mother's last words.
"I'm not ruining my life being with you," she insisted.

Marianne grabbed her daughter's shoulders and
turned her around. "I had a vision," she said sternly,
"that your father came up that bayou. Emilie and

Rose were by my side, but you weren't. Have you ever thought why?"

Gabrielle had, but she shook her head.

"Because you were on the boat bringing him here."

Before Gabrielle had time to digest that information, Marianne tucked her hair behind her ears and pulled the man's hat over her head. "You weren't meant to wait," she said. "You are a woman of action and it's time you took it."

Marianne said nothing more, grabbed a satchel, and headed out the door into the moonless night. Gabrielle followed, listening for her mother's skirts in front of her down the path they knew so well. When the bayou came into view, Gabrielle saw Jean's *radeau* waiting by the bayou's edge.

Marianne grabbed her and held her tight. "For God's sake be careful," she told her, her voice shaking. "I love you so very much."

"I love you, too, Maman," Gabrielle whispered. "I promise I will bring him home."

Gabrielle felt her mother's tears on her cheeks. "Bring yourself home too," Marianne said.

"How can I not, when you envisioned it?" Gabrielle wished she could feel comfort in that thought, but fears assaulted her. Fears over what lay ahead. Fear of her failure to bring her father home.

A noise came from the boat and Marianne pulled back, determined to send her daughter away but hesitant to let her go. "Hide," Marianne finally whispered, and Gabrielle sought refuge in the trees nearest the boat.

"Jean," Marianne announced.

Gabrielle hunched behind a group of cypress trees

while she watched Jean leave the boat and talk to Marianne onshore. She heard her mother speak, then the two of them moved up the embankment out of sight. Gabrielle slipped on board, then entered the cabin. She opened the small compartment where she had watched Jean withdraw food and wine. There was only a semiempty bottle inside, so she placed it on the floor of the cabin and crawled within. The compartment reeked of spoiled cheese and she had to fold her body in two to fit, but Gabrielle was determined to follow Jean to the Gulf.

She heard voices again, then the boat began to move. Her legs cramped and the smell made her nauseous, but Gabrielle closed her eyes and forced sleep upon herself, anything to endure the voyage. After what seemed like hours of discomfort, sleep finally overtook her.

When Gabrielle awoke, the boat was stationary and the air seemed lighter, a small beam of sunlight filtering in through the wall. Gabrielle listened for sounds coming from the exterior of the boat and, finding none, opened the compartment door and crawled into the cabin.

It was obviously day, but something was concealing the light from outside, keeping the cabin dark and murky. Gabrielle slid onto the cabin's floor and tried to sit up, but the pain in her legs was excruciating. She stretched them in an effort to get her blood circulating, but what she needed was fresh air and a place to stand. She had to get out of there.

She made her way to the cabin's entrance and pushed open the door. Palmetto palm branches were scattered everywhere in an effort to hide the boat from trespassers.

"Smart idea, Jean," Gabrielle said to herself. "I always wondered what you did with this boat when you weren't using it."

She gingerly made her way through the camouflage, careful not to upset the palmetto branches or to cause more cramps in her legs. She practically crawled to the bow of the boat, finally standing when her feet hit the mud of the bank.

It felt blissful to stand up straight, to relieve the tension in practically every muscle of her body, but she still ached from the confinement. When she gazed around her to see where she stood, her aches and pains became the least of her worries.

"Where am I?" she asked no one.

Somewhere to the south she felt a breeze, thought she heard the sounds of sea birds, but what lay in front of her were arpents of marshlands. Fighting back the fear of what lived inside the swamps, Gabrielle rallied her courage and headed down what looked like a small, semiconcealed path. The wet ground gave way on several occasions and twice she nearly sprained an ankle in the deep, greenish mud. "No wonder he wears knee-high leather boots," she said to the marsh.

Something large answered her, a sound of twigs cracking, then a deep splash of water. Alligators instantly came to mind and Gabrielle quickened her step. She seemed to be going nowhere, only deeper into the marsh, but the breeze felt stronger on her cheeks and she sensed something in the wind—salt perhaps?

Finally, when she was ready to admit being lost, the woods opened onto a beach. There before her, with the sun setting to the west, was Côte Blanche Bay, the bright waters of the Gulf of Mexico twinkling in the distance, and the most beautiful schooner anchored in between.

Gabrielle knelt on the beach, closed her eyes, and relished the sea wind kissing her face. Oh God, how she missed the sea. She couldn't wait to get on board *La Belle Amie* and sail away to New Orleans, feel the Gulf wind at her back.

"What have we here, a preacher?"

Gabrielle looked up to find two men before her, one without several teeth and the other smelling of hell.

"What you praying for, eh?" the smelly one asked. "Maybe we're the answer."

The men howled with laughter and Gabrielle felt a chill run up her spine as she struggled to her feet. Did they recognize her as a woman? In her long breeches and oversized shirt, she doubted her feminine attributes were showing. And the hat covered her face well.

"I need to speak with Captain Bouclaire," she said in the deepest voice she could muster.

Again, the men laughed. "What for? You expect to serve with him, do you?"

Maybe they considered her an inexperienced boy. She hoped the disguise was working. "I have lots of experience sailing ships," she said. "I wanted to sign up with Bouclaire."

The men laughed again, causing Gabrielle's courage to quickly dissipate. "Bouclaire doesn't hire anyone he doesn't know," Toothless said, gazing at her intently. "He hasn't hired anyone for years."

The smelly one ventured close, too close for Gabrielle's comfort. She wondered again if he suspected her gender. "But if you're looking for work, we can put you to it."

The two laughed, but this time there was something sinister in their voices. "Yeah, boy," Toothless said, "we can teach you a few new tricks."

Gabrielle had no idea what the men were referring to, but she backed up toward the water. "How do I get to Bouclaire's ship?" she asked.

"You can't," Toothless said, an evil look in his eye as he crept toward her. "The only way out there is to swim."

Gabrielle kept inching backward toward the water, but she turned to gauge the distance between shore and the schooner. A hefty swim lay ahead of her, but it could be done. She had swam long distances before.

"Come on now, boy," Smelly said. "It only hurts the first time."

Gabrielle's eyes widened as she looked at both men. What on earth were they referring to? She didn't care; she knew danger when it looked her in the eye. Still creeping backward, she withdrew both shoes and slipped them inside her satchel. Then she tied the satchel around her waist.

"What are you going to do?" Toothless asked with a devilish grin. "Swim?"

Gabrielle pulled off her hat and slipped it inside her belt. "You did say it was the only way out there," she told the men, then turned and dived into the surf.

She swam furiously from the two men, who stood yelling at her from shore. Thankfully, they didn't know how to swim and moved on down the beach. But when she was halfway to the ship, Gabrielle realized the distance was a lot farther than it had appeared. Her legs, still aching from their confinement on the *radeau*, began to cramp and a stabbing pain ripped through her side.

"Just keep going," she instructed herself, forcing her arms to continue stroking toward the ship. Her arms rebelled, echoing the pain in her legs.

Gabrielle refused to give up. She was nearing the ship; she could see the schooner's rope ladder hanging down to greet her. It was only a matter of minutes and she would be there. She could do this, she told herself over and over. She had to do this.

Finally, Gabrielle felt the rope between her fingers. She slid her arms through the bottom rung and let her body go limp. She rested her head against the side of the ship and felt the ebb and fall of the waves as she tried to regain a steady breath. Somewhere in the back of her mind a voice warned her against being caught so she removed the hat from her waist and pulled it onto her head.

After several minutes of rest, Gabrielle began to climb onto the ship. Every muscle screamed out in protest, but she forced herself up. She had to be careful, had to slip on board without anyone spotting her, so she climbed up as quietly as possible.

Just before her head reached the side of the ship, two enormous arms grabbed her shoulders and pulled her over the side. With the same amount of strength, the large man dropped her on deck. The one place in Gabrielle's body that didn't ache was now pounding.

"What have we here?" a booming voice asked.

Gabrielle looked up to find two leather boots planted in front of her, but they weren't Jean's. For a moment she wondered if she had the right ship, but she remembered Delphine's description and knew it had to be the right schooner.

"Get up, rat," the voice commanded.

Gabrielle attempted to stand, but her legs felt like lard.

"I said, get up," the voice said.

Gabrielle grabbed the railing and managed to stand. When she peered up from beneath her hat, she found a man the size of Jean staring back. "Who are you?" he asked.

Now what? she thought madly. "I am looking for work," she managed to mutter.

Several men to her rear began laughing. Gabrielle turned and found most of the crew had gathered around.

"We don't hire rats," the tall man said. "I guess it's going to be a long swim to shore."

"No," Gabrielle almost shouted, knowing she wouldn't survive another swim. "I barely made it here."

"Who asked you to swim out here?" one of the crew members shouted and the others responded in laughter.

The tall man drew closer, his eyes cold and unnerving. "Anyone could have told you we don't hire boys for our ship. We don't hire anyone, for that matter."

"Please," Gabrielle said, hoping her feminine voice

wouldn't emerge along with her panic. "I have to get to New Orleans."

The man stepped back, his eyes narrowing. If Gabrielle wasn't fearful of her life before, she was now. "What makes you think we're heading to New Orleans, rat?"

Why did he keep calling her that? she wondered. *Because no one knows where they're heading, you idiot,* she berated herself. They were smugglers, after all, men with prices on their heads.

"Please, monsieur," Gabrielle said, knowing there was no way out now but to face Jean and his wrath. "I must speak with Captain Bouclaire."

The man released a long knife from his sheath and pressed it against Gabrielle's neck. "We kill spies on this ship," he said menacingly. "Now, unless you want to be tied to the mast and have your insides ripped open, you best tell me where you got that information and who paid you to get on this ship."

Gabrielle felt the cold blade on her skin and suddenly all her aches and pains disappeared. "No one, monsieur," she whispered. "I'm a friend of Jean's."

The man pushed the knife closer against her skin. His eyes were inches away, boring into her soul. "Don't play games with me, rat," he said so intently that Gabrielle shivered.

"I'm telling the truth," she said, hoping her voice wouldn't cause the blade to break her skin. "Ask him."

The tall man moved back, and with a sly grin replaced the knife to his sheaf. "Maurice," he yelled to a crew member. "Fetch the captain."

Maurice acknowledged the order and hurried away.

The tall man placed a hand on the railing and hovered over Gabrielle. "We'll conclude this game, quick enough."

Out of the frying pan into the fire, Gabrielle thought, as she waited for Jean to arrive. A quick knife to the throat might be preferable to what Jean was going to inflict upon her.

Gabrielle bit her lip and stared down at the deck and the collection of shoes and boots before her. Feeling like a man convicted of death and awaiting his hanging, she could only stare at the deck, waiting for the familiar boots to arrive.

And they did.

"What's this?" she heard Jean say.

"This rat," the tall man replied with a laugh, "says he knows you."

"I don't know any boy," Jean replied.

"He thinks we're going to New Orleans," one of the crew members said.

A deadly silence followed, and Gabrielle closed her eyes waiting for the fateful moment.

"What business do you have with us?" Jean asked harshly.

Gabrielle swallowed, afraid to lift her eyes.

"Look at me, boy," Jean commanded.

It was now or never, Gabrielle thought. One more minute and they might fling her over the side. She slowly raised her hand and removed her hat, then she lifted her eyes to Jean's. His eyes grew enormous at the sight of her. "Please don't be mad at me," she said quickly.

A long stream of obscenities passed his lips and Gabrielle waited for his fury to subside. But it appeared his anger had no limits. Finally, Jean grabbed her elbow and pulled her through the crowd of men, all staring at her as if she had lost her mind. He pulled her down below deck and into his cabin, then slammed the door shut.

"What in hell are you thinking?" he yelled at her.

"I want to go with you," she began.

"I thought I made it clear—"

"Yes, you made it perfectly clear," she yelled back, amazed at how quickly her own anger emerged. "You're always making it clear at how my safety is more important than my happiness."

Jean stared at her the same way the men had. "You were almost killed by my own men. Does that mean nothing to you? God knows what might have happened to you had you run into some of the men who work in the port."

Gabrielle thought of the two men on the beach and had to admit Jean had a point. But it still didn't matter. She wanted to be with him, wanted to help him find her father. "You need me," she insisted.

Jean pulled his hands through his hair and began pacing the cabin. "What about your mother? She must be sick with worry."

"This was my mother's idea," Gabrielle said softly.

"And you expect me to believe that?"

Gabrielle met his eyes and lifted her chin. "Who do you think cut my hair?"

Jean planted his hands on his hips and stared at her hard. "You're crazy," he said. "You both are."

Gabrielle threw her wet hat on a nearby chest and gazed out a porthole. "That's old news, Jean. Everyone knows the Gallant women have gone mad."

When a long silence followed, Gabrielle turned back to look at him. He stood there, eyes burning into hers, arms folded against his chest. He frowned and she knew he was grinding his teeth. "Look around you," he said solemnly. "You think my life is some grand adventure. This is what you have thrust yourself into."

Gabrielle gazed around the cabin with its large windows across the stern and the portholes providing a nice breeze. In the center was a mahogany bed covered in what appeared to be silk sheets. It was the wrong thing to do, but Gabrielle couldn't help herself. She grinned at the sight of it, then she turned her appreciative eyes to Jean, letting him know this was just the kind of life she wanted.

"Stubborn woman," he said, shaking his head. "You're going to regret this someday."

Suddenly, an intense fear crossed her heart, a thought she had not considered before. "Will you?" she asked.

Jean placed his hat on his head and moved to leave. "There are some clothes in that chest," he said. "Change. I'll be back within the hour."

He headed for the door, but she didn't have time to ask more questions. The door slammed in her face.

Gabrielle stood in the center of the cabin, her body chilled from the wet clothes and her muscles aching from the swim. She reached up to wipe the hair from her face and was reminded that her long, silky strands now only reached her shoulders. She turned and gazed into the mirror on the wall, shocked at the face looking back.

For a moment, self-doubt flooded her senses and

she wondered if stowing aboard and following Jean to the ends of the earth had been the right thing to do. But she straightened her back and met her reflection with resolve. No, she had to find her father. She had to accompany Jean into New Orleans. She would clean herself up, change into something warm and dry, and make Jean understand.

Inside the chest was an assortment of clothes, making Gabrielle wonder who had visited Jean Bouclaire's cabin. Most of the garments were men's shirts and breeches, but on the bottom lay a woman's gown, petticoat, and cape. Gabrielle pulled the outfit from the chest and placed it on the bed, removing the wet clothes and becoming a woman once more. The gown was a size too small and the buttons wouldn't meet, but the cape allowed her to hide the open part at the back of the dress. Her feet stuck out from the bottom of the skirt, and lacking dry stockings and shoes, she decided to go barefoot. All in all, she felt more like *half* a woman.

Gabrielle spent the remaining time trying to dry her hair and smooth it into an attractive fashion, but the attempt was fruitless. The thick, black hair fell about her shoulders, curling at the ends toward the tilt of her chin. Few boys and no women ever sported such a look.

Voices were heard on deck, then steps leading down to the cabin. A knock sounded at the door but no one waited for an answer. Jean immediately entered the cabin with the tall man and a priest.

"Gabrielle Gallant," Jean brusquely introduced her. "Philibert Bertrand and Father Freleaux."

Gabrielle curtsied, but said nothing. Why had Jean summoned a priest?

"Do you have a Bible?" the priest asked.

Jean moved to the chest, sending Gabrielle a scathing look as he passed, no doubt on account of the ridiculous way she looked. He pulled out an old Bible and handed it to the priest.

"Fine," Father Freleaux said. "Then let's get started."

It was only then, when the priest began the marriage ceremony, that Gabrielle understood Jean's intentions. She gazed up at him wide-eyed for confirmation, but he refused to look at her. When the priest asked for her full name, Jean turned to meet her eyes.

"Is this what you want?" she asked him nervously.

"It doesn't matter what I want, Gabrielle," he said coldly. "Where do you think you're going to sleep tonight? You're alone on a ship full of men. I'll not be the cause of your ruin."

She started to object, that she hadn't planned to force marriage on him, but Jean's eyes softened and he turned back toward the priest. "Go on," he said.

The priest looked at Gabrielle, and for the life of her, she didn't know what to do. Even the tall, awful man who had tried to slit her throat stared at her with contempt. Or at least she thought he did.

"Her name is Gabrielle Gallant," Jean said.

Tears formed in the back of her eyes, but she found her strength and willed them away. "I am Gabrielle Alexis Gallant of Grand Pré, Nova Scotia."

When it was Jean's turn, he announced a long line of aristocratic-sounding names that must have been passed down in his family for generations. He had spoken so little of his family back in France. What would they think of his marriage to a poor Acadian girl with hair no longer than her neckline?

The priest began his usual ceremony, but Jean continually interrupted him to urge him to speed things along. "Tides don't wait," he told the priest.

They exchanged vows, then signed their names in the Bible.

"Where's your ring?" Jean asked her as she marked her name.

Gabrielle reached inside her bodice and pulled out the piece of leather hanging around her neck, the emerald ring dangling from its end next to a wooden cross. She raised it over her head and removed the ring. "I was afraid I would lose it," she said softly.

She went to place it on her right hand, but Jean took the ring from her fingers and placed it on her left hand. During the brief moment their hands touched, Gabrielle gazed up into his eyes. His countenance had altered slightly, but his anger still brewed.

Philibert signed the Bible as a witness, then straightened and offered Gabrielle his hand. "I'd offer to kiss the bride, but under the circumstances, I think a handshake is more appropriate."

Gabrielle accepted his outstretched hand and they shook, but her opinion of the horrid man hadn't changed.

The priest also took her hand in his, but he kissed her gently on both cheeks. "Congratulations, my dear," he said, but she knew he wondered for her happiness, a woman in a boy's haircut on a pirate's ship with a husband who wasn't thrilled to be wedding her.

"Wine?" Philibert suggested.

"Don't be ridiculous," Jean said. "We have to weigh anchor."

Jean opened the door and the two men motioned for Father Freleaux to ascend the stairs. "One of my men will bring you back to shore, Father," Jean said. "Thanks for coming on such short notice."

Father Freleaux turned and glanced at Gabrielle one last time. Then the three men left the cabin, Jean shutting the door behind them.

Chapter Eleven

Jean stood on the quarterdeck and watched the sails billow with a north wind as the ship made its way through the muddy-colored waters of Côte Blanche Bay. His temple still pounded from his anger, but he began to regret his harsh actions in the cabin.

"Any sight of ships?" he asked Phil, who was scanning the horizon with his spyglass.

"Both bays are quiet," Phil answered. "Whoever was inquiring about us didn't get a chance to follow."

As soon as Jean had made it back to the ship that afternoon, Phil had informed him that several men were asking questions onshore. Men were always hoping to join his crew; questions weren't unusual. But these days, Jean had to be careful. By now, everyone knew there was a price on his head.

"Bring her to full sail then," Jean said. "Let's get back to Isle St. Charles as fast as we can."

Phil nodded and began barking commands to the men on deck. Sails unfurled and the schooner picked up speed. For the first time since he'd recognized Gabrielle on deck, Jean exhaled and tried to relax.

"Damned stubborn woman," he mumbled, thinking back on Gabrielle standing in his cabin soaking wet in men's clothes. What was even more surprising was Marianne calling him to shore to hand him a basket of oranges while her daughter stowed away aboard his *radeau*. Maybe the locals were right. Maybe the two of them had gone mad.

Jean heard steps behind him and knew it was Gabrielle. She carefully walked across the deck littered with ropes, cannons, and other supplies, then stopped at the ship's edge and gazed out on the dark, mysterious waters.

He had to admit, she looked amazingly attractive in her chopped haircut. Now that it flowed around her face, she no longer resembled a boy; it accented the soft curves of her cheeks that rounded out like a heart to the point of her chin. Free from its usual constraints, her silky black hair shone in the moonlight, strands blowing free across her forehead.

Oh Gabrielle, he wanted to say. What have you done?

As they neared the pass where the bay opened into the Gulf, the wind shifted slightly and the ship lurched as Jean shifted its course and the men adjusted the sails. Gabrielle turned her face to search the horizon and Jean watched as a gentle smile spread across her face. She closed her eyes and relished the feel of the salty, warm breeze on her cheeks, then her shoulders rose and fell with a heavy sigh. A sigh of contentment, he was sure.

God, why couldn't the woman understand?

"Madame Bouclaire," he called out to her.

Gabrielle didn't answer, her eyes still shut and that adorable grin still playing on her lips. "Gabrielle," he said.

This time, Gabrielle recognized her name and looked back. Her eyes gazed at him cautiously, as if she wondered what new wrath he would inflict upon her.

"Would you like a turn at the helm?" he asked.

The light that illuminated her face could have turned night into day. She grinned and nodded, thought best of her enthusiasm, bit her lip, and tried to compose herself. Jean almost laughed, watching Gabrielle approach the helm, she trying so hard to contain her eagerness.

He stepped back and let Gabrielle take the wheel located in the middle of the quarterdeck. She immediately grasped the wood at its outer rings, so Jean took each hand and placed them closer to the wheel's center. "Not so far apart," he whispered, noting that she smelled as delicious as ever. "If we have to turn quickly, you want to have better control of the ship."

Gabrielle didn't look back at him, simply nodded, more than likely afraid of another outburst. He felt guilty for the rushed marriage, the lack of affection on his part during a ceremony that should have been blissful, but swimming out to his ship in the middle of the night, stowing away on his boat?

"I would wring your neck if you didn't look so adorable in that haircut," he grumbled.

Gabrielle glanced at him briefly, then turned back toward the bow. As they entered the bluer waters of the Gulf, waves rocked the ship and Gabrielle moved the wheel accordingly as the schooner drifted with the oncoming wind. Jean leaned over her and guided her hand at the wheel.

"Watch your sails," he said. "The wind is coming from over your left shoulder and you want to move the ship to always keep the sails full."

"The wind is coming from the port stern," Gabrielle corrected him. "If you would adjust the mainsail and the gaff topsails, we'd go faster."

So she knew the language and she commanded the wheel like a seasoned sailor, Jean observed as the men tightened the sheets of the sails and the ship gained speed. She stood on deck, feet firmly planted apart, not the least bit concerned over the dramatic listing of the ship. But was Gabrielle really prepared for life at sea? He thought not.

"Have you any idea what you have done?" he asked her.

She still wouldn't meet his eyes. "I told you I wouldn't be left behind again," she said. "You need me."

"Need you?" he asked, leaning against the railing of the quarterdeck and crossing his arms. "How do you figure that?"

Gabrielle stared out into the Gulf and the blanket of stars above their heads. "She's fast," she said. "I'll bet her shallow draft lets you sail her into those back, marshy bays."

She was trying to impress him and he had to admit he was, but that didn't change facts. "She's not easy to maneuver in bad weather," he said. "Water comes down the hatchways and wets everything below deck. We sometimes go days without dry clothes and linens. Days."

Gabrielle turned up her chin, knowing a lecture was forthcoming. "Do you have any idea what we eat on this ship?" he continued. "The smells alone—"

"If you're trying to scare me, Jean, you can stop now," she said. "I've been on two sea voyages in my lifetime, one more horrifying than anything you have experienced."

Jean smirked, thinking of the many dangers he had encountered on his trips to the Caribbean. "I doubt that."

Gabrielle looked at him then, her deep-set eyes dark with pain. He instantly regretted his words, remembering that as a child she had been shoved aboard an English vessel in Nova Scotia and hauled into a crowded hold for a long journey to Maryland. He had heard the tales—too many people inside too close quarters, little food, no medicine. Men, women, and children dying daily from disease, malnutrition, and heartache. Jean's lieutenant, Mathurin Hébert, had related his voyage where half of the Acadians had died of smallpox and exposure before reaching shore.

"I'm sorry, Gabrielle," Jean said. "I forgot."

Gabrielle's fingers loosened on the wheel and a finger traced a groove in one of the spokes. "I was raised on the sea, Jean. I won't let you down. I'll do whatever is expected of me."

He instantly erased the distance between them, standing behind her and caressing the exposed skin at her neck. "It's me who's afraid of letting you down, *mon amour.*"

A wave crashed against the bow and the ship dipped. Gabrielle lost her balance for an instant and reached back to steady herself against him. Like the moment in the kitchen so many weeks before, her hand found his leg. A small gasp escaped her lips as her fingers touched his thigh.

It took everything in Jean's power not to pull her into his arms and carry her off to his cabin. He had dreamed of having her aboard his ship, in his bed, standing by his side. Here she was leaning against him, her hands desperately clutching the material of his breeches as if afraid he might once again disappear—was it so wrong to allow her into his life?

"Nothing so far," Phil announced as he approached the couple from the bow. Gabrielle instantly let go of her grip and Jean moved backward to allow space between them.

"Bon," Jean said. "If we come across a Spanish ship, we'll fly the flag. We'll act as if it's business as usual."

"You sail under the Spanish flag?" Gabrielle asked incredulously.

"We sail under our own flag," Phil explained. "We have a letter of marque from the Spaniards to do business in Louisiana and to attack and plunder the English in their name. We fly the flag on those occasions."

"Then you're a pirateer."

"Not exactly, madame," he answered. "We are maritime businessmen, sometimes dealing with pirates and privateers for our merchandise, and we appeal to whatever government helps us to make our money. However, we will fire on the English at any opportunity in the name of Spain, so in that instance, yes, we are pirateers."

Jean watched as Gabrielle studied Phil cautiously,

her eyes growing large when he talked of shooting Englishmen. He must have given her quite a scare before Jean saved her from a hanging. Gabrielle placed a hand at her neck as if making sure it was still intact.

"I pray, madame, that you were not injured in the scuffle earlier," Phil said soberly.

"I am fine, monsieur," she answered, but the fear in her eyes lingered.

What the hell did Phil do? Jean wondered. He felt the blood rise to his face. "Injured?" he asked his partner and quartermaster.

Phil looked guilty and stammered to say something before Gabrielle interrupted. "I hurt myself climbing over the railing," she said.

Jean didn't believe it, but he'd rather not hear the truth. "Which wouldn't have happened had you stayed at the Poste," he bellowed.

Gabrielle grimaced and stubbornly faced the bow again.

"How did you manage to swim from shore?" Phil asked her. "That was quite a distance."

Gabrielle brightened, although Jean could tell she was still afraid of Phil. "I love to swim," she said. "I always have. My father used to call me the tide chaser."

"Tide chaser?" Phil asked, sending her a gentle smile.

Gabrielle began to warm up. "We had enormous tides back home. Whole rivers used to disappear."

"That's hard to imagine."

"That's why I'm a good swimmer," Gabrielle said. "I had to be when the tide came in."

His wife and business partner began a long conversation about the differences between Canadian and Louisiana waters, as if nothing had transpired between them. They talked amiably about sailing, water temperatures, and currents, until Jean could stand it no longer.

"Phil," he almost barked. "Tell Gabrielle that life on board ship is not what she thinks it is. Tell her that it's not about romantic stories of pirates and pirateers, but hard work, rotten food, and disgusting conditions."

Phil considered the statement, then leaned in toward Gabrielle and smiled. "It's a grand adventure," he whispered.

Jean wanted to strangle his partner. The last thing Gabrielle needed was encouragement. "That's not the answer I was hoping for."

"No, I suppose not," Phil answered with a grin, then withdrew a bottle from his coat pocket. "What I'm about to say won't be welcomed either, I'm assuming."

Phil handed Gabrielle the bottle, then took the wheel from her grasp. "Pardon, madame," he said. "But I believe it's time you and your husband retired for the evening."

The thought of retreating below deck with Gabrielle and testing out the wedding bed nearly affected Jean's common sense. Three days he had slept only marginally and fatigue was taking its toll. Before logic resumed its stronghold, Jean imagined making wild love to Gabrielle, then enjoying a glass of brandy and a good night's sleep. But logic did return.

"We have to get through the pass," Jean said.

"We're almost there," Phil returned. "Besides, I can sail this ship through the pass and anywhere else, remember?"

Despite his scandalous discharge from the navy, Phil was one of the finest seaman Jean knew. But Jean always sailed *La Belle Amie*. He stood atop the quarterdeck, ready to say as much, but couldn't find the words to insist otherwise.

"Bonsoir," Phil said.

"The reefs," Jean said, thankful that he remembered the reason why he *had* to sail the ship. "There are shallow spots to avoid. Just past the Atchafalaya, you can get caught inside Four League Bay."

Phil turned his back on the couple and waved his hand as if to dismiss them. Somewhere at the bow of the ship crewmen laughed. Jean felt his temper rise but someone was taking his hand and leading him toward the stairs. When he found Gabrielle staring at him with loving, inviting eyes, he surrendered.

But he had to have the last word. "Wake me at first light," he called back to Phil.

"Aye, aye, Capitaine," Phil replied. "Sleep well. We will live without you."

Jean let Gabrielle lead him below deck, unnerved at the mutiny. He wasn't used to letting others make decisions regarding his ship, even though he commanded the finest crew in the territory. When they reached the bottom step, Jean sighed and opened the door to his cabin, waiting for Gabrielle to walk through.

Soft rays of moonlight danced on the water outside and shot moonbeams through the cabin's portholes and along the windows stretching across the stern.

There was no need for lanterns. He had no trouble making out Gabrielle's sparkling eyes in the moonlight.

He reached for her, cupping her face with his large, callused hands, caressing the tender skin with his thumb. But he still couldn't forget that he had ruined her life.

Gabrielle covered his hand with hers, hoping to hold it in place in case Jean decided to bolt. She placed a hand on his chest and clutched the soft material of his billowing shirt to make sure he wouldn't charge out the door. Jean didn't bolt, but he wasn't happy either, a frown creasing his forehead. Her earlier fears returned.

"Do you regret marrying me?" she whispered.

Her question brought him to life. He straightened and his eyes softened. "Why would you think that?"

"You don't seem happy to be here with me."

Something between a smile and regret crossed his features and he pulled an arm about her waist and drew her close. "Do you see that bed?" he whispered seductively, skimming his lips along the rise of her cheek. "I bought it for you."

Gabrielle leaned her head back, allowing his teasing lips more room. At the same time, she peered toward the beautiful bed. "For me? When?"

"The last time I was in Hispaniola," Jean said against her neck, planting kisses underneath her ear and nipping at her earlobe. "The same place I purchased your ring."

His words took time to register, but when they did, Gabrielle's heart felt infinitely lighter. He *had* wanted to marry her. He *had* been planning on returning to the Attakapas Poste.

"Oh, Jean, if you wanted to marry me then, why not now?" she asked.

Jean sighed and pulled back, taking her hands and holding them against his chest. "It's not what *I* want, Gabrielle. It's what best for you."

"What's best for me is to be with you," she returned.

"A ship with a fugitive at its helm is no place for a woman."

"You want to sacrifice our happiness because I'm a woman?" she asked, her fury rising. "I'm supposed to wither into old age alone because I *might* experience danger on board your ship? I have been sent into exile. I live on the frontier. I could perish at any time, with or without you and the price on your stubborn head."

"What happens, Gabi, when the children come?" Jean returned. "Have you thought of that? Where do we raise our family, among the powder kegs and the spoiling meats?"

She hadn't considered children, but if she could survive an Atlantic crossing at the age of six, then surely they could raise a family aboard a ship of their own making. "We'll make do."

Jean released her hands and they suddenly felt cold. He sat on the edge of the bed, running his hands through his hair. "There was a time when I wanted to partner with your brothers-in-laws, running furs and skins from the frontier to New Orleans or the Caribbean and bringing merchandise back to the postes," he said softly. "Phil was going to take charge of the ship and we could sail when it was convenient for us."

Gabrielle's heart constricted. It was exactly what she had hoped for too. "And now?"

When Jean looked up, the moonlight reflecting off his dark eyes, Gabrielle was shocked at the pain shining back. Only when he had read his daughter's letter in her sitting room had she seen him in such despair. "Now, I have no choice but to flee the territory," he said. "Or spend my days hiding on an island that's little more than a hellhole."

And what about Delphine? she thought. What about his poor little girl who desperately needed her father? Gabrielle knew that need well, had felt it all her life. If it took her last breath, she was going to New Orleans to retrieve both her father and Jean's sad daughter, who wrote letters like poetry.

She knelt before him. This time she took his hands in hers. "I love you and I want to be with you," she said gently. "The rest we will work out together."

He was so tall he had to lean over to gaze into her eyes, but what she saw there she could have sworn was gratitude. For a moment Jean Bouclaire the protector disappeared.

Sliding his hands through her hair, he pushed back the strands hanging about her face. "Did your mother really do this to you?"

Gabrielle cringed, thinking about her boy's haircut. "Is it that hideous?"

Jean's dimple appeared for the first time that night, or was it moonlight playing tricks on her eyes? "It suits you," he said.

Before she had time to note his approval, he reached down and grabbed her elbow, pulling her to her feet. He parted his legs, wrapped his arms about her waist, and drew her into his chest. They were almost eye to eye, Jean sitting on the bed and

Gabrielle standing, and when his thighs tightened around her legs and he pulled her closer, she knew exactly what his intentions were.

He was poised to kiss her, his hands on her face, his eyes studying her so seductively she shivered. But something was holding him back, some nagging worry in the back of his mind about her safety, she was sure. "What am I going to do with you?" he whispered.

Gabrielle leaned forward and brushed her lips against his. "I can think of many things."

Now, she was positive his dimple emerged. An appreciative grin accompanied it before his lips took wild possession of hers and his hands explored the folds of material at her back. As his kiss deepened and his tongue made communion with hers, he reached inside her cape and moved a hand up the side of her gown.

Gabrielle slid her hands through his black curls, then grabbed them tightly while she savored every moment of his savage kisses. When his lips left hers and began to taste every inch of her face and neck, Gabrielle arched her back and let her hands roam across his mammoth shoulders and down the thick muscles of his chest.

Suddenly, Jean's hands found the open spot of her gown and he gazed up at her with a surprised look that almost made her laugh. Until she was reminded of the other woman.

"The woman who frequented your cabin was a size smaller than I am," Gabrielle said with a frown.

Jean's dimple deepened and he untied the cape at her neck and let it fall to the floor. Then he turned Gabrielle around to get a better view of the gaping hole at her back. She had managed a few buttons to keep the dress from falling off her shoulders, but there was plenty of exposed skin. Since her chemise was wet and there were no undergarments in Jean's chest, Gabrielle stood naked beneath the other woman's gown.

"I bought this for Louise," Jean said. "It was a peace offering, but we got into another fight and I decided against giving it to her."

"A fight about what?" Gabrielle couldn't help herself. Even though Jean never had kind words for his daughter's mother, jealousy poured through her.

"Delphine, of course."

Jean unbuttoned the top two buttons and pushed the dress easily off her shoulders. Gabrielle wasn't ready to let the image go of Jean buying presents for another woman, even Louise Delaronde, so she grabbed the front of the gown and held it against her chest. "Did you ever care for—"

"No," Jean said firmly, kissing the skin beneath her shoulder blades and working his way down toward her waist. "If it hadn't been for Delphine, I would have had nothing to do with that woman."

Gabrielle felt Jean loosening the buttons at her waist, his mustache tickling the tender skin at her side as he kissed her. She didn't know what had come over her, thinking such things about Jean and Louise. Gabrielle knew Jean cared for her, saw it constantly in his eyes even when he was furious with her, but he never admitted to love and the lack of those words fed at the fear in her belly.

She turned and faced him, holding the gown tightly against her chest. "You are glad you married me, aren't you, Jean?"

Like so many times before, he said nothing, but his actions spoke volumes. His eyes, laced with desire, never left hers as he kicked off his leather boots. Next, he removed his shirt and tossed it onto the bedpost. Then, still staring deeply into her eyes, he gently tugged the gown from her fingertips and let it fall to the floor. In a second, Gabrielle stood completely naked before him.

He pulled her against him, her nipples brushing against the soft hair at his chest and her belly pressed against his rock-hard erection. Lightning seem to shoot through her as his hands caressed her back and lingered over her bottom.

"The only woman who has ever been near this bed was my daughter," he said, his lips only a breath away. "And we were discussing you at the time."

It wasn't what Gabrielle had hoped for, but it was enough. She wound her arms around his neck and their lips joined long enough for a deep kiss before he pulled her backward onto the bed. She let out a squeal as she tumbled on top of him, but within seconds Jean turned her over onto her back and gazed down into her face. He kissed her gently then, slow and seductive, his tongue exploring the reaches of her mouth, and she felt her insides burn with desire.

When his lips slowly trailed downward, Gabrielle felt her core burst into flame. Jean lingered at her breasts, alternating between his teeth nipping at her nipples and his lips sucking while his mustache brushed against the sensitive skin. She felt her hips arch against his erection, involuntarily begging for a union. A moan emerged from somewhere deep inside her.

"Oh Gabrielle," Jean whispered. "I want you so badly."

Gabrielle reached for the clapet of his breeches and pushed the buttons apart. "I want you, too," she answered.

She knew he was ready to burst from the wanting, moaning when her fingers brushed against his manhood, but he kept massaging her breasts, kept kissing her everywhere. He slid a finger inside her and caressed the point where all light burst forth, sending wild sensations roaring through her. Just when Gabrielle thought she would die from waiting, Jean removed his breeches and entered.

Gabrielle couldn't tell if it was the ship's rolling or the rhythm of their lovemaking, but the motion rocked her very being. Pleasure so intense built inside her until the passion turned into waves and broke upon the shore. She cried out his name as her body arched in ecstasy. Within seconds, Jean joined her, his body shuddering from the release.

When the passion subsided, neither one moved apart. Jean kept kissing her face, holding her tight while Gabrielle's hands relished the feel of his strong body against hers. Finally, Jean released her and moved onto his back, pulling her into his chest in the process.

"Gabrielle," he whispered. "I . . ."

She waited for Jean to finish his thought, but all she could hear was the rapid beating of his heart. After several minutes, Gabrielle knew from the cadence of his breath that Jean had fallen asleep.

"I love you, too," she whispered back.

Chapter Twelve

"Any news of Monsieur LeBlanc?" Delphine asked the nun through the iron gate of the courtyard. It had been weeks since Joseph had remembered his identity, weeks since he'd attacked two of the convent's men and fled the building. If only someone would confirm he had returned to his family, let her know he was alive and well.

"Not today, Delphine," the nun answered.

Delphine wanted the best for Joseph, prayed he had found his way back to the Attakapas. But deep down she longed to see her friend again, wished he remained in the city so she would have someone to talk to, someone to guide her. Or perhaps she wished to follow him into Gabrielle's comforting arms, the other woman who loved her father as much as she did.

"Go home, Delphine," the nun softly said. "Get some rest."

Delphine nodded and headed back toward her home, but rest was out of the question. Ten days. She had ten days. In less than a fortnight she would be homeless.

It wasn't the threat of losing her home that scared her the most; she still had silver to sell and money sent to her from her father by way of Antoine Vincent. Gabrielle, too, had insisted she had a place to come to if she chose to leave the city. She could easily board a ship and head west toward the Attakapas.

But Edouard Prevost, in the name of the governor, had warned against such action. The house and everything in it, including Delphine and the slaves, were placed in probate until news from Count Delaronde arrived. Prevost had given her a month to send word to France, an impossible deadline, or face confiscation by the government. If Count Delaronde's money arrived, she would be sent to live in France and risk never seeing her father again. If word failed to arrive in time, which was more than likely, Delphine would lose everything and be thrown from her home.

She would have wished for the latter had it not been for Carmeline and the other slaves. She couldn't bear thinking of her best friend being sent to the auction block. If only she had the power to set Carmeline free. If only her mother's possessions had passed on to her, she could have salvaged the estate and sent the slaves on their way west to freedom.

Edouard Prevost. What had her mother seen in his insipid son? The horrid father visited every day asking for news. Waiting. Watching. Something in Edouard's eyes when he gazed at her ran Delphine's blood cold. Carmeline said he had ideas about her when he looked that way, but Delphine shuddered to think what they were.

"Where have you been?"

Speak of the devil, Delphine thought when she spotted Edouard standing in her courtyard. Like so many times before, his gaze roamed over her body, lingering at her breasts as he wetted his lips.

"Your mother's clothes suit you well," he said in such a way Delphine wished she could take a bath.

"I haven't received word today, monsieur," she told him flatly, pushing past him toward the house. "Now if you don't mind . . ."

Edouard grabbed her arm and his thumb began to massage an inch of exposed skin below her sleeve. Delphine jerked her arm away. "How dare you touch me in such a fashion?" she exclaimed. "I'm thirteen years old."

"You're every bit a woman," he answered her, stepping too close for polite company. "Just like your whore of a mother."

Delphine slapped his face so hard she could see her handprint on his cheek. Edouard stepped back, shocked at her actions, and placed a handkerchief to his face. "Bitch," he spit out.

"Get out of my house," she commanded him, trying desperately to keep her tears from her voice. "Get out."

Edouard's eyes grew cold. "Ten days. You've got ten days." He inched closer, his eyes boring into hers. "The government will take this house, mademoiselle, but you are mine." He placed his hat upon his head and tugged at the rim. "Your father took my son, but I'll have you, as God is my witness."

He marched from the courtyard into the streets of New Orleans and Delphine faced his retreating form, her chin held high, until he was out of sight. She then reached for the nearby bench and fell into it, the yards of maroon fabric billowing around her like her father's sails when the wind died. How did it all come to this? Delphine wondered, gazing at the frivolous gown that felt as foreign to her as the absence of her mother. In the course of a few months she had matured into a woman tall enough to wear her mother's clothes, her father had been declared an outlaw, she had lost her dear friend, and she was trapped inside the house of a man who wanted nothing to do with her. Now, a stranger who wished for revenge for his son's death was waiting to molest her.

She was helpless and she knew it. There was nothing left to do but pray. Was God listening?

Delphine closed her eyes, feeling the warm spring breeze tease the curls against her forehead, remembering how that felt on the rolling Gulf waters when Jean had taken her sailing. Where was he now? she wondered. Was he thinking of her? Was he close enough to hear her prayers and save her?

A sense of hopelessness poured over her, but she prayed anyway. "Dear God," she began. "Send my father home to me."

A fear so intense invaded his dreams that Jean bolted awake. His breathing was ragged and his heart raced. He could still hear Delphine's pleading screams echoing in his head.

Jean sat up in the bed, trying to calm his nerves. It was the third time he'd had the disturbing dream, only this time there was a sense of urgency to Phiney's appeals. But dreams and visions were things women experienced; he couldn't give credence to the nightmare. Delphine was safe in Louise's care. Antoine was sending her money.

If only he could be sure.

Gabrielle shifted in bed and Jean suddenly remembered he was married. Looking down upon his wife, her young, innocent face resplendent in slumber, Jean was reminded of the many reasons Gabrielle shouldn't be there, the same reasons why he couldn't claim his daughter and carry her off to sea. Yet he couldn't stand the endless nights wondering of Delphine's safety, worrying about how Louise was treating, or more likely mistreating, his precious angel. The agony was ripping his soul in half.

"What is it?" Gabrielle leaned on an elbow and pushed her hair from her eyes, her hand coming up short when she did.

"Bad dream," Jean muttered, which was a gross understatement. "About Phiney."

Gabrielle pulled the sheet to her chest and sat up. She snaked an arm through his and rested her cheek against his upper arm. Jean couldn't help feeling thankful she was there by his side. If anyone knew the pain of separation between a father and daughter, it was Gabrielle.

"We have to get her out of New Orleans," she said.

Gabrielle's words were exactly the thoughts Jean was thinking, but the fears remained. What life could he offer his daughter aboard ship?

"Jean," Gabrielle said, straightening. "You are going to get Delphine, aren't you?"

Jean threw his legs over the side of the bed and

pulled on his breeches. "It's close to daybreak," he said. "Go back to sleep."

Gabrielle fell back against her pillow and sighed. "If you don't, I will."

"She has a mother, Gabrielle," Jean said more for his own reassurance than hers. "I'm sure she's well taken care of."

"You read her letter. She's miserable."

Jean pulled his shirt over his head and slid on his boots. He stood and tucked the shirt into his breeches. "She's thirteen. She's supposed to be miserable. She'll thank me one day when she meets a nice boy, and the last thing she will want then is to be stuck on a ship in the middle of nowhere."

When he met her eyes, Jean knew Gabrielle wasn't buying his story, but he didn't want to talk about it. Remnants of the dream still plagued his soul. He grabbed his hat and headed for the deck.

Gabrielle watched his tall form exit the cabin and heard his heavy footsteps on the stairs. "Stubborn man," she said to no one, but her heart ached for the conflict she knew was raging inside him.

Her stomach growled, reminding her it had been hours since her last meal. She didn't feel like sleeping, so she tossed off the blankets and felt her way through the semidarkness to the spot where her clothes were hung out to dry. She pulled on her chemise, then her Acadian breeches and vest over the man's oversized shirt. When she glanced in the mirror, the shirt hanging from her shoulders, her hair bouncing at her neckline, and her bare feet peeking out from beneath her breeches, she resembled a pirate. All she needed was a gun tucked inside her waistband.

Suddenly, with amazing clarity, she remembered the last time she saw her father. He was returning home from the orchards and fields to their home in Nova Scotia, a smile upon his lips, oblivious to the fact that the English were planning their ruin that very afternoon.

She was playing pirate by the side of the house and had attacked him with her willow branch sword. She had been sour since he'd forbidden her to travel to the water's edge. There were too many soldiers about the town of Grand Pré and Joseph had feared for her safety.

"I don't care if the entire Royal Navy has come to Canada," Joseph had told her. "You are not to go down there. Take care of your *maman* and leave the ships alone."

What would her father think of her now, she wondered, dressed like a pirate and married to a fugitive? Would he still blame her for their separation after all these years?

"Oh, Maman," Gabrielle whispered to her reflection. "I wish you were here."

Her reflection faded slightly and Gabrielle swore she saw her mother sitting by the side of the oak tree, singing Gabrielle's favorite lullaby.

> *Fais dodo*
> *Fais dodo, Gabrielle, mon p'tit,*
> *Fais dodo, t'auras du lolo*
> *Papa est en haut*
> *Qui fait des sabots*
> *Maman est en bas*
> *Qui fait des bas*

"Go to sleep, Gabrielle, my little one," her mother sang. "Go to sleep, you'll have some candy. Papa is upstairs making wooden shoes. Mama is downstairs making stockings."

She could almost see her mother smile, feel her comforting arms about her shoulders. Tears gathered in Gabrielle's eyes, but she fought back the urge to cry.

"I will bring him back to you," she repeated her vow. "I promise you, Maman."

A knock at the door interrupted her thoughts. "*Entrez,*" Gabrielle answered.

Phil entered cautiously, carrying a tray full of food. "Jean said you wouldn't be sleeping."

"Married one day and he already reads my mind."

He didn't look up, but Gabrielle made out the semblance of a smile in the darkness. "I've met a lot of women in my travels, Madame Bouclaire," Phil said. "Jean has met his match in you."

"Unfortunately for him," she said.

He placed the food on the bed and met her eyes. "I'm betting not, madame." With a warm grin, Phil turned to leave.

"Wait," Gabrielle said. "Do I have to eat this here?"

"What did you have in mind?"

Fresh air, sea breezes, the sun breaking the horizon as it reflected shades of crimson and gold off the water. "Can I eat on deck?" she asked. "Would that be breaking some male law of the sea?"

Phil's smile stretched across his face. "I think we males can handle a woman about our ship."

"Good," Gabrielle said, grabbing the tray. "That means more than you know."

Phil took the tray from her hands and they made their way up the dark stairs onto the deck, lighted softly by two lanterns swinging in the sea breeze. Jean acknowledged her while he commanded the ship, but he said nothing when she sat upon the quarter-deck and began enjoying the stale bread and coffee. The men stared until she met their eyes, then they continued on their business. Gabrielle wondered how many women had graced the deck of *La Belle Amie*.

"Don't mind them," Phil whispered in her ear. "They're a little shocked that the captain married, 'tis all."

"And even more shocked, I suppose, that the bride had to swim to his ship for the ceremony," Gabrielle added.

Phil tilted his head back and laughed, making the crew stop and stare once more. Jean barked at them to get back to work, then glanced in her direction.

"Can I offer you something to eat, Captain," Gabrielle asked him.

Jean mouthed the words more than said them, perhaps uncomfortable with the crew watching his wife serve him, but Gabrielle undersood what he wanted. "Black or with cream?" she asked.

This time, Jean laughed. "Cream?"

Of course, Gabrielle thought. What ship would store cream for one's coffee? She poured him a cup of the steaming black liquid, wondering who had dripped the coffee that morning and how, then rose and brought her husband the cup along with some bread. When she handed him his breakfast, he took her hand and raised it to his lips, one hand still plying the wheel and guiding the ship.

Whatever doubts Gabrielle felt concerning his reluctance to speak words of affection, his action that morning erased them. He loved her; she knew he did. He was willing to exhibit his adoration in front of God, Phil, and his entire crew.

"You really need to rest," he told her, his eyes sparkling in the dim light. "It's a long journey."

"How long will it take us to get to New Orleans?" she asked.

Jean sipped his coffee and sighed with pleasure. "A few days to our island, where we will restock our supplies and drop off a few men. Then a day or two into New Orleans up the Barataria Pass. Ten days at the most."

"We won't be sailing up the Mississippi?" Gabrielle asked. It was how she had first entered New Orleans when they'd arrived from Maryland.

"No," Jean said. "The Spanish watch the mouth carefully. If we go up the Pass, we'll be coming into the city by the back door. I'll cross the river and enter the city by night."

"You mean *we'll* enter the city by night." Gabrielle's heart quickened, thinking she might be left behind again.

"Gabrielle, don't argue with me," he whispered. "I know what's best."

So that was his plan, to leave her behind on the ship while he risked his life in New Orleans. "You're crazy if you think I will be left behind. What if you get arrested? Who will be able to help you?"

Jean gritted his teeth, then leaned in close so only she could hear. "I don't wish to speak of this in front of my men. I don't wish to speak of it at all, but particularly not now."

Gabrielle withdrew back to her seat on the quarter-deck and angrily sat down. Her brow pounded from Jean's stubborn refusal of her help and her appetite deserted her. Why couldn't the insufferable man understand?

"Does the breakfast not meet with your approval, madame?" a voice asked her.

Gabrielle looked up to find a middle-aged man standing before her, dressed in Acadian clothes and looking vaguely familiar. She sifted through her mind wondering if Jean had introduced them before, but his face didn't register. Still, he reminded her of something.

"Don't let the captain scare you," he said good-naturedly. "His bark is worse than his bite. As for traveling into New Orleans, he won't be going alone."

It eased Gabrielle's heart knowing Jean would have company should he be discovered, but she still bristled that she wouldn't be one of them.

"You're not eating," the man said. "We're low on stock at present, but is there anything else I can get you?"

"Non, merci," Gabrielle said, picking up the bread. "It's fine. I have a lot on my mind."

The man sat down next to her, studying her intently. "Have we met before, madame?" he asked.

Gabrielle tried not to talk with her mouth full, but she was eager to confirm his suspicions. "I was thinking the same thing," she said, gulping down the bread with a swallow of coffee.

"Maybe I'm thinking of Grace O'Malley," he said with an amiable smile. "She was an infamous Irish pirate known as 'the bold Grania' because she cut her hair like a boy's."

Gabrielle nearly choked on her bread. "Is it that bad?" she asked, wondering if Jean had told her what she wanted to hear the night before.

"It suits your personality," the man replied. "I have a feeling you're not that different from Grace. She owned a fleet of ships and raided the Irish coast. She became so notorious Queen Elizabeth sought out her company."

"She sounds like a menace," Gabrielle said between bites. "I'm not that ferocious, I assure you, despite my appearance on deck last night."

The man leaned back on an elbow. "No, I don't suppose you are. Still, there is something familiar about that smile. You remind me of someone I once knew."

She was about to ask who, when the man stopped her from breaking off another piece of bread. "Don't eat too much at once," he said. "Eat small meals and you'll be less likely to get seasick."

Suddenly, Gabrielle realized she was extremely hungry. When the man removed his hand, she snatched up the bread. "I don't get seasick," she informed him.

The man smiled again. "That's what they all say."

"No," Gabrielle insisted. "I was raised on the water. I've never been seasick in my life."

The man's smile disappeared and he stared at her hard. A shiver ran through Gabrielle as her mind raced to place the face before her. "What is your name, madame?" the man asked.

A bolt of lightning hit when Gabrielle remembered Jean's words the night before. Hébert. There was an Acadian named Mathurin Hébert on board. Could it be the same man who had taught her to sail back home at Grand Pré? She had been too young to know his first name. "Monsieur Hébert?" Gabrielle whispered.

The man's face lit up at the words. "Gabrielle Gallant?" he practically shouted.

Gabrielle was so stunned to meet someone from home she merely nodded.

"Gabrielle Gallant?" Mathurin repeated. "The little elf who used to follow me around, begging me to take her sailing?"

Gabrielle's smile matched his and the two reached for each other's hands. "It is good to see you, Monsieur Hébert."

"Mathurin, my dear," he insisted.

It felt odd to speak the Christian name of a grown man she had admired as a child, but then she was now grown too. So many years had passed between them.

"Your family?" he asked. "Did they fare the exile well?"

"As well as could be expected," she answered. "My mother and sisters are in good health. Rose and Emilie have married and we're expecting the first grandchild soon."

Mathurin's eyes darkened and his smile disappeared. "And your father?"

All the grief of the past thirteen years, all the stress

of their poverty and migration fell heavy about her shoulders. Suddenly, Gabrielle felt seven again, looking to her neighbor for advice. "Oh, Monsieur Hébert," she said. "We were separated at the beach and we haven't seen him since. When we were in Maryland we got word he was in Louisiana, but when we arrived here, we learned he had left the territory for Maryland to find us. Maman and I are living off his land grant at the Attakapas Poste until he returns."

"Have you not heard word?"

"We heard he was ill at the Ursuline Convent in New Orleans."

"That's good news," Mathurin said, brightening. "Not that he is ill, of course."

"I hope we won't be too late," Gabrielle whispered.

Mathurin leaned forward and grasped her hands tightly. "This is why we're going into the city?" he asked.

Gabrielle nodded.

"Then rest assured Jean and I will do everything in our power to get Joseph back to you and your family. You can count on it."

The disappointment of being left behind resurfaced. "But I must come with you."

Mathurin turned and glanced at Jean, who was busy barking orders to adjust the sails. Then he looked back at Gabrielle and frowned. "Eat," he finally said. "I know you don't get seasick, so eat up."

They sat in silence for several moments, Gabrielle wondering what her old friend and neighbor was thinking. Then she remembered Felicité and nearly choked on her food.

"Monsieur Hébert," she began.

"Mathurin," he corrected her.

"Mathurin, what are you doing here?"

He looked surprised at the question and a shiver ran through Gabrielle. Could he not know what had become of his own family?

"Your family," she uttered softly, afraid to venture too far, too fast. "Felicité?"

Mathurin's eyes darkened and he looked away. "I lost them," he whispered. "I followed them to Georgia, but it was too late."

Gabrielle found breathing difficult, thinking of her best friend and the prospect of their reunion. Her heart felt as if it would burst.

"Felicité is alive," Gabrielle said. "She lives in the Attakapas Poste."

Mathurin turned pale and began to tremble. He squeezed her hands tightly, close to causing her pain, but Gabrielle refused to pull them away. "Did you not know this?" she asked.

He shook his head, his eyes reflecting pain and disbelief. "They said my family had died," he whispered.

"Felicité ran away from the place she was sent to," Gabrielle explained. "When she found herself an orphan, or so she thought, she went to live with the Doucets. They took very good care of her, brought her here to Louisiana."

Mathurin's eyes overflowed with emotion and he looked away. "Is she well?"

Again, the pain of separation, the pain Gabrielle knew only too well, flooded her heart. "As well as a child can be without her father."

Mathurin grabbed the material above his heart and

grimaced. He leaned forward as if in pain, and Gabrielle grabbed his arm. "Mathurin, what is it?" she cried.

Immediately, Jean was at her side, his large arms steadying Mathurin and bringing him upright. Still, Mathurin appeared as if he might collapse on the spot.

"What happened?" Jean asked her.

"He just learned his daughter is alive," Gabrielle answered.

"His daughter?" Jean asked softly. "Where?"

"She lives near me at the Poste. Maybe you remember her from the night at the Vincent's party. Felicité Hébert. She walked me to the door when we left."

Jean smiled slightly. "The pretty one making eyes at the stable boy?"

Gabrielle nodded and met his smile, but she felt like crying. Poor Felicité and poor Monsieur Hébert, living so close together yet never knowing the other one lived.

Finally, Mathurin straightened and his eyes cleared. He pulled away from Jean. "I'm fine," he said. "Just a bit of a shock, is all."

Jean kneeled before the older Acadian to get a better look. Gabrielle could tell from his concern they were old friends. "Do you want us to let you off here?" he asked him. "We could sail to shore and give you a boat to get back to the Attakapas."

Mathurin shook his head. *"Non, merci.* I must help you get in and out of New Orleans."

"There are plenty of crew members to help me, Mat," Jean insisted. "You need to find your daughter."

By now, several of the crew had gathered around, including Phil. Mathurin looked up at the tall Frenchman and passed him a knowing look. "No," he repeated. "I will wait for the return trip."

Jean rubbed the stubble growing on his chin and sighed. "I appreciate the concern, old friend, but I don't need *everyone* looking after me."

No one said a word and the silence that ensued sent a chill up Gabrielle's spine. The way Phil and Mathurin were looking at each other made her realize something was amiss.

"It's not that, Jean," Phil finally said. "We're being followed."

Chapter Thirteen

"How long has this been going on?" Jean asked. "Why didn't you wake me?"

Phil folded his arms across his chest and appeared as calm as the waters they were sailing. "There's nothing to worry about. They began trailing us after we entered the Gulf, but we've put some distance between them since."

Jean grabbed the eyeglass from Phil's waist sash and gazed out past the stern. "Where did they come from?"

"They were hiding in the cove off Côte Blanche is my guess," Mathurin said. "They appeared right after midnight."

"They were waiting for us."

Jean's words cut through Gabrielle's heart. Or perhaps it was his tone that made a chill race across her skin. Suddenly, the fear of losing him became all too real.

"What will we do?" she asked.

When Jean's eyes met hers, she felt his fear, but it was for her safety, not his. He began barking orders, sending the crew in all directions to trim the sails and alter the course.

"We are making good time," Phil said to him. "There are few people who can outrun *La Belle Amie*." With a grin he added, "And we have yet to meet them."

"We have to get to the island as soon as possible," Jean said. "We can't even think about them boarding this ship."

Phil placed a hand on Jean's shoulder and squeezed. "She's safe with us, my friend. No harm will come to her."

Phil sent her a wink and a smile on his way to the main mast. The man still unnerved her; she couldn't forget the look in his eyes when he pressed his knife against her neck. But there seemed to be a kinder side to him. If Jean approved of him, counted on him as his partner, then Phil had to be one of the finest of men. And what he said about outrunning the other ship had to be true.

Mathurin tugged at a piece of her hair and gave her a wink as well. "Stay out of trouble, Tide Chaser," he said before moving to the ship's bow.

With the absence of company, Gabrielle felt lonely and out of place. Everyone had a job, knew the urgency of the situation, and each was acting on it. She, in turn, was the cause of their extra worry.

"Gabi," Jean called out to her.

She stood on the quarterdeck and moved to his place at the wheel. For the first time since she'd donned men's clothes and stowed aboard his *radeau*, Gabrielle wondered if she was doing the right thing. She wanted to protect him, to help retrieve her father and Delphine from New Orleans. But would she be a hindrance to this seasoned crew who knew better how to protect their captain than she did?

"Do you see that line of clouds?" Jean asked, pointing in the direction of the ship that trailed them.

Gabrielle turned and looked behind them. The sun had finally risen and a dark, red glow spread across the horizon. The weight of guilt pressing against her heart became ten times more acute. "A storm," she whispered.

"It should hit us by late afternoon, I'm thinking," Jean said. "But that should work in our favor. If the wind comes down from the northwest, we could do a larboard tack as we hug the coast."

"The other ship?" she asked.

"Can't keep up with a schooner like mine in this kind of wind," Jean answered her with a hint of pride.

"Is there anything I can do?" Gabrielle asked.

His dimple appeared and the lantern's light glimmered in his eyes. "As you said last night, I can think of lots of things."

When he turned toward her, Gabrielle could feel the fire burning in her cheeks as she remembered all that had transpired the night before. "I don't think it would be appropriate in front of the men," she whispered.

Jean cleared his throat and looked away, but his dimple remained. "No, I think not."

His flirting failed to relieve the heaviness hanging over her heart, and when Jean looked back, he must have noticed. "Don't worry, Tide Chaser," he said softly.

"Why not?" she answered. "You are."

"I'm allowed," Jean said. "All captains must worry for their crew and passengers. But Phil's right, we'll outrun them, whoever they are. Believe me, I've been in worse scrapes than this."

Despite his words of comfort, Gabrielle still felt like an intruder. "Jean, is there something you want me to do?"

"Yes, actually, there is." Jean gazed up at the sails above him.

"I hope it's not cooking," Gabrielle said. "I'm afraid I'm not very competent in that area."

Jean looked at her with a quizzical expression, but he didn't seem surprised.

"I know," she answered his unspoken thought. "My father said I should have been born a man."

Jean laughed, leaning in close so only she would hear. "I'm thankful you're not."

Gabrielle blushed again, hoping no one was watching. "Is there something you want me to do besides burning the ship down? I can try my hand at cooking since it looks like all you eat is bread and things that don't need heating . . ."

"No," Jean said with a warm smile. "Mathurin is one of the best galley cooks I've met. We'll leave the cooking to him. I have another job for you, but you have to do it my way. No arguments."

Gabrielle's mind rushed to imagine the assignment, but she came up short.

"We tore the spanker gaff," Jean explained. "Are you good with a needle perhaps?"

At this, Gabrielle smiled broadly. "You're in luck," she said. "It happens to be one of the few feminine traits I own."

Jean didn't look at her, but his dimple deepened. "What feminine traits you own, my dear, are enough for me."

When he finally looked her way, so much emotion poured forth from his eyes that Gabrielle shivered. She wondered if Jean would ever say he loved her. Not that it mattered. His eyes were saying it now.

Gabrielle took his large hand and threaded her fingers between his. She brushed up against his sleeve, but discreetly so that no one would notice.

"Tell me what to do, *mon capitaine,*" she said, turning her gaze to the rope ladders leading upward along the mast. "And please say I will finally get to climb the ratlines."

Jean shook his head vehemently at the thought of her climbing skyward toward the yard, but Gabrielle grinned. She knew it was only a matter of time before he relented. After all, she was now mistress of this fine vessel.

The storm rocked the ship endlessly as waves beat against its sides, sending water down into the hold and cabins. Jean had been right about water permeating everything; it seeped in beneath the door and created puddles on the floor. Sometimes so much water poured forth that it lapped up against the cabin's walls and splashed against the bed linens and the clothes raised high atop the trunk.

But it wasn't the actual rain and seawater that caused Gabrielle's discomfort. She had closed the portholes when the storm began and it wasn't long before the cabin became unbearably hot. The water only added to the already humid atmosphere. Although Gabrielle was dry from the rainwater by sitting atop the bed, she was drowning in a sea of perspiration. She hated being confined to her cabin, but she didn't wish to be in the way either. There was still so much to learn and now was not the time.

She had quickly repaired the torn sail, and Jean wasted no time in pushing her below deck to safety. Now she was working on her next project—one of Jean's torn shirts.

She tried to concentrate on the material in her hands, but a trickle of sweat fell across her forehead into her eyes, blurring her vision. Then the ship rolled and her spool of thread fell to the floor. When she reached down to retrieve it, the ship tilted and the spool rolled quickly to the other side of the cabin, landing in a puddle.

"Merde," she said, glad that no one was around to hear her use such language.

Gabrielle finally managed to grab the spool when it rolled back to her side of the bed, but the thread was soaked. She poked the needle into the front of the shirt and tucked the thread under her pillow for safekeeping. She blew out her lantern and lay back on the bed, watching the lightning crack the sky outside the stern windows.

She missed Jean, worried for his safety above deck in the dangerous weather. She thought of Delphine, pining for her father in New Orleans, of Joseph, wondering where he might be. She feared for her mother, alone with her memories at the Attakapas Poste. And her sisters in Opelousas—would Rose be close to giving birth?

Here she was in the darkest of nights traveling through the Gulf on her way to New Orleans and a host of problems. What lay ahead? Gabrielle wondered. What would become of them all?

She clutched Jean's shirt to her chest, breathing in his scent for comfort. "Dear God," she whispered to the thunder bellowing over her. "Take care of those I love. Watch over us."

It was silence that woke Gabrielle from her sleep. Silence and the lack of movement. Gabrielle felt as if she had been placed inside a cradle and rocked to sleep only to wake when the cradle had stilled.

There were voices above deck, men shouting to one another, and she listened intently to their tone. Had the other ship caught up with them? Her heart stilled, waiting for a sound.

Then the door burst open and Jean strode in, a smile upon his face.

"Wake up, sleepy head," he said, leaning over the bed and kissing her soundly. "We have work to do."

She reached for his shirt to pull him into her embrace but his clothes were soaked. He moved away and pulled the shirt off, revealing the mahogany cross she had given him months before. "I have to make some repairs. Phil is going to take you ashore. I thought you could help with the supplies."

"Of course." Gabrielle handed him the shirt she had mended and the pair of breeches she had placed at the end of the bed to keep dry. "But am I going to be alone with him?"

Jean pulled the shirt over his head and gratefully

caressed the mended sleeve. He then replaced his breeches and tucked his dry shirt into his waist. "He's a good man," he said. "You have nothing to fear from Philibert Bertrand."

There were so many things she wanted to ask him. Was the ship still following? Was he tired from the rough night? Should she find him something to eat? But someone yelled for him above deck and Jean kissed her, then disappeared.

Gabrielle grabbed her clothes from the end of the bed and dressed. This time, she included shoes and Paul LeBlanc's oversized hat to keep the sun from further tanning her face. When she stopped briefly and assessed her hair in the mirror, the woman looking back didn't seem so strange. In fact, Gabrielle was beginning to like this new person.

"Madame Bouclaire," a voice came from the doorway.

Gabrielle opened the door and found Phil waiting to escort her. When he smiled, she almost believed he had come to the same conclusion over her appearance as she had.

"Gabrielle," she told him. "My name is Gabrielle."

Phil bowed gallantly. "Pleasure to meet you, Gabrielle. I am Philibert Bertrand of Poitou, at your service. But please, call me Phil."

He was such a tall, virile man, much like Jean but leaner. Blue eyes sparkled beneath long eyelashes and his feather-fine bronze hair tapered to his nape, where it was tied with a coarse piece of leather.

"Come," Phil said. "You are about to witness what happens to men when there are no women about."

Gabrielle followed him up to the deck, realizing

they were anchored in a secluded cove surrounded on three sides by cypress and tupelo forests. Between the ship and the Gulf beyond lay an island, overgrown and unpopulated. Gabrielle climbed over the side of the ship into the skiff, but her eyes were locked on their destination.

"Don't let first impressions fool you," Phil said. When she gazed at the man who had once threatened to kill her but who was now smiling amiably as he rowed toward land, Gabrielle knew how true his statement was.

"What happened to the ship that was following us?" Gabrielle asked.

Phil shrugged as if the threat had been a mosquito flying about his face. "We lost them."

He leaned forward abruptly and the hairs on the back of her neck straightened as his face came close to hers. Gabrielle realized she still feared the man. "No one catches *La Belle Amie*," he said so strongly, all Gabrielle could do was swallow and nod.

"You're not scared of me, are you?" Phil asked, his features softening.

Gabrielle attempted a smile, but it was difficult. She could still feel the blade at her throat. "No," she said.

Phil grinned. "Liar."

She still felt fear, but his informal behavior warmed her somehow. She preferred men who spoke honestly to women, instead of all that insipid small talk she was used to at the Vincent parties. "Perhaps I would feel more at ease had I not had my life threatened climbing aboard your ship."

Phil's smile disappeared, but not his congenial

tone. "No one climbs aboard our ship unwanted, Gabrielle. No one."

Relief flooded Gabrielle's heart, knowing that Jean would have Phil by his side on his trip to New Orleans, even if she wasn't allowed to go. "I'm glad Jean has you as a partner," she said. "Even if you do have a tarnished past."

Placing a dramatic hand over his heart, Phil grimaced as if injured. "Tarnished? I suppose my partner told you about my discharge from the navy."

"He said you killed a man, but he didn't say why."

"It was actually the nosy captain's wife," Phil said seriously. "She asked too many questions."

The fear returned when Phil's eyes turned cold. Then the corner of his lips curled up in a smile. "It's a joke, no?"

Gabrielle released the breath she was holding, but she didn't feel jovial. "My sides are splitting from laughter," she said soberly.

His eyes narrowed as he studied her, the smile still playing on his lips. "You are so like her," Phil said.

"Like who?"

"Like Phiney," he said softly.

Gabrielle suddenly felt better. "You care for her."

"Of course I do," Phil said, his smile gone. "I watched her grow from a babe."

"We have to get her out of New Orleans," Gabrielle insisted. "Delphine sounded so miserable in her letters. And something's not right. I can feel it."

Phil said nothing, continued rowing and staring at her thoughtfully. When they reached the shore of the island, a land so overgrown with palmetto palms and vines, a new fear emerged. "Where are you taking me?" Gabrielle asked.

The skiff bumped against the sand and Phil hopped overboard and dragged the boat up the small beach. He offered his hand to her but she sat frozen to the spot.

"I'm not going to hurt you, Gabrielle," Phil said softly. "Jean saved my life once. I would kill any man who hurts my friend or his family."

Gabrielle finally met his eyes and found sincerity. But there was a darkness to Phil, something lurking beneath the surface that caused her blood to run cold. How many men had Phil killed since his time in the navy?

She gave him her hand and disembarked from the skiff. Phil then pulled the boat into the bushes and covered it with palmetto fronds. "Come on," he said and headed down the beach.

They had traveled a short distance before he moved into the brush, holding back the foliage for Gabrielle to walk through. When she entered the forest and her eyes adjusted to the dimness, she found a path before her. "Let me go first," Phil said.

They hadn't walked far before a series of shacks came into view. Crates of all shapes and sizes lay about the compound, some covered with tarps. "Contraband," Phil said, winking back at her. "And if you breathe a word of this to anyone, I will tie you to the yardarm and flog you with a cat-o'-nine-tails."

Gabrielle brushed past him toward the first makeshift house. "Liar," she said as she passed.

"So you're not afraid of me anymore, eh?" she heard him say to her rear. "Even with my tarnished past?"

There it was again, that chilling tone he exhibited. No wonder no one boarded *La Belle Amie*. But Gabrielle wasn't going to let him intimidate her. She lifted her chin and turned to face him, finding a smug look that reminded her of her brother-in-law Lorenz, who loved to tease. "I'll bet Jean never told you about me," Gabrielle explained. "About the English soldiers and the throats I slit in their sleep."

Phil crossed his arms and gazed down at her, trying not to smile. "Is that so?"

"If I were you," Gabrielle said with a haughty look, "I'd sleep with one eye open."

Phil tried hard not to grin, but a smile eventually broke free. "I'll keep that in mind."

A feeling of triumph filled Gabrielle, even though she knew it was silly playing teasing tricks with a grown man. Still, she wanted Phil to know she was capable of being part of the crew, even if it was only a war of words.

"The supplies are in Jean's shack, uh, house," Phil said, heading toward the worst-looking habitation in the compound. "I must warn you, he wasn't much for housekeeping."

So this was what became of men in the absence of women, she thought when she crossed the threshold and found a raccoon eating out of Jean's cupboard and three chickens scurrying across the dirt-encrusted floor. The only furnishings were a rustic table, two chairs, and a hammock that had seen better days.

"Jean is usually neater than this," Phil said in his defense. "His mind has been occupied these last few months."

Gabrielle thought again of the fact that she would have to wait aboard ship while the men stole into town looking for her father. She thought of dear Delphine, who did not know she now had a step-mother, a young woman who sympathized with her desire to be at sea. "I have to go with him," she whispered. Turning to meet Phil's eyes, she said louder, "Please, I have to go with him."

She expected an argument, one that repeated what Jean told her on a daily basis, but Phil said nothing, grabbing a cratc off thc floor and hcading back out-side. Gabrielle lifted a similar crate and followed.

They worked in silence, pulling ammunition and food supplies from different areas to the head of the trail. Phil entered one of the houses and returned with some food. "Stay here," he finally said, handing her an apple. "I'll bring these to the skiff."

Gabrielle sat on the steps of Jean's house, listening to the sounds around her. In the distance the Gulf lapped against the island like a soothing lover while parakeets and seabirds colored the sky above her head. By the time she finished her apple, Phil had completed his work. He placed a boot on the porch where she sat and leaned an elbow on his knee.

"I was in love once," he said without looking at her. "She was promised to another so I sought refuge in the navy. The night before her marriage, I had shore leave and the temptation was too much for me to resist."

He paused and looked away. It took everything in Gabrielle's power to swallow the piece of apple lodged in her throat.

"Her fiancé caught us together and challenged me the following morning. I killed my lover's future husband the morning of her wedding."

Finally, the apple slid down her throat but now Gabrielle was having trouble breathing. She fought back an urge to choke.

"I caught a ship heading for the Caribbean and buried my sorrow in rum," he continued. "One night after I picked a fight with half a dozen pirates, Jean rescued me from being beaten to death. He gave me a job and a chance to redeem myself. I owe him everything."

Phil turned and looked at her then and Gabrielle felt her blood stop pumping. "Why are you telling me this?" she asked.

"Because I want you to know that the New World is filled with men like me," he said. "It's a dangerous place."

Now, Gabrielle grasped his meaning. "You want me to stop asking to go into New Orleans," she said, disappointed that he, too, didn't understand. "You want me to stay behind on the ship."

Phil didn't reply. He straightened and held out his hand. "No," he said. "I want you to know what you're up against."

Gabrielle studied the hand before her, wondering what he meant and where he would lead her next.

"Come," Phil said. "I'm going to teach you how to shoot."

Gabrielle touched his fingertips, but she remained confused. "Shoot?"

With an easy tug, Phil pulled her to her feet. "You can't come with us unless you know how to defend yourself."

Chapter Fourteen

Jean landed the skiff on the island's beach and pulled it up to the brush. The ship's other skiff lay hidden among the palmetto thicket, which relieved his mind somewhat, but a nagging fear still played havoc with his logic.

It had been hours since Phil and Gabrielle disembarked to retrieve a few crates of supplies, and night was fast approaching. Only meeting with danger could have prevented their return, although Jean knew Phil would have protected Gabrielle from harm. No one knew of their hideout, yet why else would they take so long? His mind ached from the worry.

"I'm sure there's a reasonable explanation," Mathurin said when he reached Jean's side and recognized the boat.

Jean nodded, afraid to give words to his fears. They headed toward the trail, watching their backs before moving through the forest to the compound. When a gunshot was heard coming from the center of the island, the two men raced through the brush until they reached the clearing.

Jean arrived first, his heart thundering in his chest. As he turned the corner of the first shack, he found Phil standing beside a beaming Gabrielle, a smoking pistol in her hand.

"Just in time," Phil said. "You won't believe how well this woman takes to firearms."

Jean didn't know whether to strangle his partner or hug his wife in gratitude. For the first time in hours he felt relief.

"What's the matter, Jean?" Gabrielle asked. "You look out of breath."

When Mathurin arrived, also panting from the run, the smiles on Phil's and Gabrielle's faces disappeared. "We didn't worry you, did we?" Phil asked.

Jean took a deep breath to fight back his irritation. Now that he knew Gabrielle to be alive and safe, he wanted to throttle Phil. "Of course we worried," he barked. "Have you two not noticed it's almost dusk?"

"Nonsense," Phil answered, slapping Jean on the back. "We have an hour yet before sunset, and I have yet to teach your wife how to handle a sword."

Guns and swords? Jean thought. What the hell was going on here? "What are you doing with a loaded pistol?" he asked Gabrielle.

Gabrielle opened her mouth to speak, but didn't get a chance. "She's an excellent marksman," Phil answered, turning to her with a wink. "Or should I say markswoman?"

Jean moved forward to grab the pistol from Gabrielle's hand, but she quickly stepped back. "I've hit every target," she added. "I know how to properly load it, too."

"What do you need with a pistol?" Jean asked her.

"In case we meet with trouble," she said.

It took a moment for Jean to register her meaning, and when it did, he hung his head in frustration. The woman refused to give up. "You're not going with me," he said, trying hard not to grit his teeth. When he looked up, Gabrielle's arms were crossed about her chest, the hot pistol still clutched in her hand. "You're not going to New Orleans," he repeated.

Tears welled in Gabrielle's eyes, but she blinked them away. Jean watched as she bit the inside of her cheek to control her emotions. "I'm sorry, Gabi," he said, softer this time. "But it's too dangerous."

Gabrielle began to retort, but Phil cleared his throat and sent her a commanding look. He then walked toward Jean, placed his arms about his shoulders, and led him out of Gabrielle's earshot.

"The answer's no," Jean said, wondering when Gabrielle had seduced his partner to her side.

"Listen to me," Phil said. "All I'm asking is that you think about this."

"Think about what?" he returned. "You want me to bring my wife into a city where I could be arrested at any turn? What happens then, Phil?"

"We'll be with you, Jean," Mathurin inserted. "No harm will come to her, I assure you."

"You might be arrested too," Jean said.

"Who would want to arrest an innocent *'Cadjin*?" Mathurin asked. "No one will bother with me."

Jean felt cornered, and he couldn't understand why his best friends didn't see his point. Gabrielle was brave and smart, but she was still a woman. Did they not fear for her safety as he did? Or perhaps it was the depth of his love that caused him to be more protective of her. He had felt the same way about Delphine. When he glanced back at his wife, her arms still stubbornly folded across her chest, he wanted to wrap his own arms about her, keep her isolated from the cruel world surrounding them.

"I want her safe," he repeated. "Why can't you understand that?"

"Because she's not a bird that you can cage," Mathurin said. "She's a woman who wants to find her father, who needs to find him. She shouldn't be holed up inside a ship while you traipse around New Orleans looking for a man you've never seen before."

"She's also the mother now of your daughter," Phil added. "And it's time you brought Delphine home."

The nightmare returned with all its fury. He had planned on visiting Delphine, making sure she was taken care of, that she was receiving the money he sent. Retrieving her was an option. She was thirteen now, capable of choosing between parents. But would she choose wisely?

"If you enter the city as husband and wife at night, you will be less conspicuous," Phil explained. "Gabrielle can wear her cape and the gown from the ship. People will think you are a couple taking in the theater."

"We'll follow you everywhere," Phil continued. "When you slip into Phiney's courtyard, we'll accompany Gabrielle to the Convent to find her father."

"She'll be with us at every turn," Mathurin insisted.

Jean started to relent, but he wasn't yet convinced. "And what happens if the authorities take her too?"

"Jean?" Gabrielle called out.

The three men turned and found Gabrielle packing a ball into the pistol's chamber. She then cocked the pistol and held it skyward. "I can defend myself," she said confidently.

Slowly she turned, aimed the flintlock pistol toward a candle on the other side of the compound, and fired. As the men stared in awe, the tip of the candle blew off.

"Well, look at that!" Mathurin exclaimed.

When Gabrielle swung around, her eyes filled with self-confidence and her short hair tossing about her shoulders, Jean couldn't help but admire her skill and fortitude. She had always been this way with him, but rather quiet and solemn around others, as if she played the part of the proper woman for their benefit. Since joining the crew, Gabrielle had blossomed, become the woman he knew and loved for all the world to see.

How could he say no? Her eyes beamed with pride. Finally, after years of guilt over her family's separation, Gabrielle hoped to rectify the problem she imagined she'd created in Nova Scotia. And damned if she wasn't an expert with the pistol. Mathurin was right. Gabrielle wasn't a woman to be caged for the sake of her safety. For that matter, neither was Delphine.

Jean sighed in defeat. "You never leave my side," he insisted. "You follow my mandates. No arguments."

Gabrielle fought back a smile, nodding as he began a long list of instructions while he walked in her direction. When he reached her side, her eyes glistened with tears of gratitude.

"I won't let you down," she whispered, then threw her arms about his neck and hugged him.

Jean felt uncomfortable showing affection in front of his men, but he placed his hands at her waist and allowed a small squeeze in return. "Come," he said. "We need to get back."

"What about her fencing lesson?" Phil asked.

"Fencing lesson?" Jean asked. "Are we planning on fighting our way into the city?"

Phil threw up his hands. "She's the one who asked."

When Jean's eyes looked her way, Gabrielle felt the impact of that stare all the way to her soul. Poor Jean, she thought, so much conflict raging inside an overly protective man. He probably would have been better off marrying a complacent, docile wife. And if Delphine was the woman everyone said she was, Jean had double trouble.

"I was just curious," she said, hoping to relieve some of his anxiety. "We should go."

They all moved to leave but Jean. He rubbed his hand over his mustache, moving one foot back and forth in the sand.

"Are you coming?" Phil asked.

To everyone's surprise, Jean removed his sword from his sheaf and pointed it toward Phil. "I suppose you were the one who was going to teach her," he said.

Phil cocked his head and grinned. "And why not?"

The sassy dimple appeared as the tip of his sword

teased Phil's collar. "Because you can't fence your way out of a nunnery."

Phil stepped back and produced his sword and the two men began to circle each other. "Watch closely, my dear," Jean said. "I'm going to show you how to conquer an enemy."

"You're dreaming, old man," Phil returned and their swords met.

The two lunged at each other, the clash of steel glittering in the late afternoon sun. They laughed and insulted each other as they advanced and defended, happy, it seemed to Gabrielle, to be facing one another in a fight.

"Are they mad?" she asked Mathurin, but Mathurin only laughed.

"They're boys," he answered. "And boys will be boys."

Phil inched forward in a deft movement and sliced Jean's sleeve.

"I just mended that," Gabrielle yelled.

Jean didn't seem to mind. He advanced on Phil, waving his blade wildly until Phil hit the side of the house. Then with a quick twist of the sword, Jean ripped the sash around his waist and it floated to the ground.

"That was silk," Phil said. "You'll have to pay for that, old man."

"Old man?" Jean asked with a smile. "Don't confuse age with skill."

Phil came forward, eager to prove otherwise, but his anxiousness pushed him off-balance. With two fluid strokes, Jean sent his sword flying, then pressed his blade against Phil's throat.

Gabrielle couldn't help herself; she had never seen anything so extraordinary. She applauded his husband's skill with the foils, then ran behind him to look over his shoulder at Phil. "Now you know what it's like to have a blade at your throat," she said.

Jean released him and Phil caressed the tender spot beneath his chin. "That's the thanks I get for teaching you to shoot?"

Gabrielle raised herself on her toes and kissed Phil on the cheek. "No, this is the thanks."

"Women," Phil said in disgust, although Gabrielle noted a hint of a blush on his cheeks.

"Never be too eager," Jean instructed her as they made their way down the trail toward the bay. "Use your sword to defend and let your opponent advance, let him expend his energy. Only when you see an opportunity do you advance."

When they entered the open beach, Jean handed her his blade. He wrapped his arms around her to show her how to hold the sword. "Stand tall, feet planted firmly," he said. "Keep your blade high in front of you and never take your eye off your opponent."

Gabrielle did as she was told, but the emotions pouring forth lodged in her throat. He was teaching her to fence! He was letting her be part of their operation! Did he have any idea what that meant to her? Finally, she found her tongue. "Thank you," she said.

The familiar worried look reappeared, but Jean dismissed it, returning his sword to his sheaf and heading down the beach. *"Allez,"* he said. "It's time we went to New Orleans."

* * *

Days passed in stormy weather, and Gabrielle longed for the comfort of dry clothes and a cool place to sleep, preferably one with windows and a breeze. But even in the midst of nature's fury, she reveled in the fact that she had become a working asset to the crew. She had helped fix the sails, taken turns at the wheel and become quite good at navigation, and was regularly repairing the men's clothes. They never said as much, but she thought she recognized a trace of approval from the crew.

The ship moved up the Barataria Pass as far as it was able, then two skiffs were unloaded for the trip up the bayou to the Mississippi River. Phil, Mathurin, Jean, and Gabrielle rode in one boat, while two other crew members took the other skiff. A handful of men remained on deck.

They rowed for hours in the moonlight until the bayou enlarged and met the massive river. The men paused at the sight of the mighty water, waiting to catch their breath before entering the harsh currents heading downstream.

"How will we cross this?" Gabrielle asked.

"Quickly," Jean answered. "The current will carry us a few leagues downstream, but that is exactly where we want to be."

A silence fell about the crowd, then Mathurin made the call to action. The boats moved from shore, immediately picked up by the rushing water, and they rowed with all their strength. Gabrielle thought they would never reach the other side without being swept out to the Gulf, but as Jean predicted, they made landfall just north of the city. The men jumped from the skiffs and pulled them up the riverbank.

On the other side of the levee was a secluded shack hidden among a cluster of oak trees. While the crewmen took care of the skiffs, Phil and Mathurin went inside the home.

"Pierre Bourgeois's house," Jean said to Gabrielle. "He will keep our boats hidden for us while we are gone."

"A comrade in contraband?" she asked. "You seem to have friends everywhere."

Jean secured his sword at his side. "I have enemies too."

Gabrielle pulled back the cape that covered her head and body and revealed a loaded pistol and knife in her waistband. "I'm prepared, as you are."

Jean cupped her face in his hands, his dark eyes fraught with worry. "No, *mon amour*, you are not prepared for what dangers lie ahead. That is why you must never leave our sides. Never."

When Phil and Mathurin exited the house, the group headed toward New Orleans along the winding river road where houses sat near the river, their crops extending behind them in long, narrow lines. As they approached the city, the houses increased and the crops disappeared. Suddenly, they were walking down Decatur Street amid the bustle of a portside town.

Jean took Gabrielle's arm, and tipped his hat politely to the people passing them. Everyone smiled in return, except for a couple of shady characters lounging in the shadows, and Gabrielle felt confident with Phil and Mathurin to their rear.

New Orleans was just as Gabrielle had remembered

it, a quilt of many races and nationalities sewn together by a collection of European colonies. Started by the French and French Canadians with help from German immigrants, slaves, and Indians, the Louisiana colony was now ruled by the Spanish government. Immediately to the east were the English in what used to be Spanish Florida, and to the north and northeast their collection of English colonies. Now that the Acadians had arrived, the colony's quilt had grown larger and more diverse. What would become of this gumbo of people, Gabrielle wondered, now that a new governor had arrived, promising to make the territory prosperous?

When they had reached the iron gates of the Ursuline Convent, Jean squeezed Gabrielle's elbow. "I have to find Delphine," he said softly. "Phil and Mathurin will be with you."

"Alone?" Gabrielle asked. "You're going alone?"

A nun approached the gate, so Jean leaned in close. "I must speak with Louise about my daughter and it's best that I do it alone."

"Don't worry," Phil said to her. "The house is one street over and Jean always follows the alley into the back entrance to her courtyard. He won't meet with harm. We will follow him there once we find your father."

"But why can't one of you—"

The nun reached the gate and asked why they had come. Gabrielle explained her situation and asked to visit the infirmary. When the nun opened the gate, Gabrielle turned to speak with Jean again, but in that short amount of time, he was gone.

"Come, *'ti-monde,*" Mathurin said, taking her elbow

and guiding her through the gate. "Let us go find your father."

Her father. Finally, they were standing at the conclusion of her family's endless trials and separation. Yet doubts nagged at the back of her mind, told her something was amiss. As she followed the nun through the Convent courtyard, Gabrielle feared her father wasn't there. And she somehow knew Jean was walking into danger.

Jean jumped over the courtyard wall, avoiding the creaking gate that would announce his arrival. Carefully he slipped into the darkened quadrant, watching the shadows for signs of movement.

The house was dark and silent except for a lone candle in the slave kitchen, probably Carmeline alone at her work. It was too early for Delphine to be in bed and unlikely that Louise, in her nightly desire to indulge in entertainment, would have taken his daughter with her. So where were they?

Removing his sword, Jean entered the courtyard and headed for the house. He had only taken a few steps when he spotted Louise sitting on the bench beneath the house's gallery, her form unusually quiet and still. He couldn't make out her face in the shadows, but he recognized her favorite violet silk gown, the one a suitor had brought her from Paris. He placed his sword back into his scabbard and sighed, grateful that she was at home and that everything remained the same as when he had left. Now, all he had to do was convince her to let Delphine go.

"Louise," he said when he was steps away.

The figure bolted upright and turned. Before Jean's mind could register that Delphine stood before him, she rushed into his arms and wound her own about his neck tightly. "Thank God you're here," she said.

Her tone unnerved him, sent a shiver of fear through his heart. Jean tried to pull her away so he could ask what had happened, why she was wearing her mother's clothes, but Delphine wouldn't let go. Finally, Jean surrendered, holding his daughter close and reveling in the fact that she was safe. He breathed in his daughter's sweet scent, the one that had never changed since she was a babe. He ran a hand through her hair and pressed her delicate head against his cheek.

"My baby," he whispered.

Delphine finally pulled away, wiping the tears from her face. "Maman is dead," she said.

Jean placed a finger under her chin and raised her eyes to his. "When? How?"

Delphine shook her head, reacting like a person in shock. "A month ago, two months, I can't remember now. It was all so sudden. After the duel, she took to her bed and never rose again."

Jean pulled Delphine back into his arms and caressed her hair. She had grown taller since he had left, her head reaching his shoulder like Gabrielle's did. "I'm sorry, pet," he said. "Have you sent word to the Count?"

Delphine nodded against his chest. "I'm not going to France," she said sternly.

"Of course you're not," Jean answered. "You're leaving with me tonight. Tell Carmeline to have your things ready immediately."

She reached inside his coat pocket, pulled out his handkerchief, and blew her nose. "I'm already packed."

Jean smiled, thinking that only Phiney would pack her bags on the chance that he would arrive. Or was there something else at work here? He couldn't explain it, but a fear took hold of his heart. He took her elbows and pulled her far enough away to gaze into her eyes. "What has happened?" he asked.

Delphine swallowed hard. "That horrid man," she whispered, as if afraid to speak his name. "The father of Marcel Prevost. He's been threatening me."

The face of Edouard Prevost came back all too clear. He could still visualize the man goading his terrified son into continuing the duel. "Threatening you?" Jean asked, fury pouring through his veins. "How?"

"He said if the count didn't send word by tonight, he would come for me, take over the house in the name of the governor. Carmeline is bringing the wagon around back. We were about to flee the city."

"This is crazy," Jean said. "He doesn't have the right to do that. Your land is in probate by law."

Suddenly, Delphine's eyes turned fearful and she tugged on his sleeve. "We have to go, Papa," she said. "He can't find you here. He'll have you arrested."

"He will find the end of my blade should he arrive," Jean said.

His words failed to dispel her anxiety. Delphine gripped his hand and tried to lead him toward the courtyard gate. "Please, Papa. We must hurry."

Jean resisted, hoping the bastard would arrive and he could settle the case that was ripping his life in two. "Delphine, don't worry," he told her. "No one is taking you from me."

"*Au contraire*," he heard Edouard Prevost speak from behind him.

Jean turned quickly, drawing his sword, but within seconds the courtyard was filled with men. "That is exactly what I plan to do," Edouard continued. "Just the way you stole my son from me."

A half dozen soldiers drew their blades and approached. Jean pushed Delphine safely behind him, away from the men and toward the outlying kitchen. "Your son challenged me and you damn well know it," Jean said.

"Arrest him," Edouard commanded. "He is Jean Bouclaire, wanted for murder."

"Over my dead body," Jean said.

Edouard laughed. "We can arrange that, Monsieur Bouclaire. But have no fear. Your daughter will be well taken care of by me."

Hatred so intense filled his body that Jean lunged at his attackers, blind to everything but Edouard's smug smile. He managed to injure two of Edouard's men but he had broken his cardinal rules of fighting. Expending his energy and not watching his back, Jean found himself surrounded.

"Are you planning on having your men stab me in the back the way you taught your son?" he yelled at Edouard.

Guilt passed over Edouard's features, but he quickly regained his composure. "Take him," he commanded. "He's a dangerous man. Take him any way you can."

Jean heard Delphine scream just before he felt the

blow at the back of his head. Stumbling to his knees, he turned toward his daughter.

"Gabrielle," he whispered, then his world turned to darkness.

Chapter Fifteen

Gabrielle heard the nun's explanation, but her mind raced to find answers. An anonymous man the nuns had named René LeBlanc had turned violent one day and attacked two men who tried to calm him. He had fled the Convent and was never heard from again.

"Why didn't you believe him when he said he was my father?" Gabrielle asked Sister Marguerite.

"It was that scandalous child who visited here every day," she answered. "Horrible child born out of sin. She incited him into a rage. There is no way to know he is your father."

Gabrielle's cheeks burned from the words, but she didn't have time to retort. Phil, who had leaned against a wall since they had arrived, listening quietly to the nun's explanation, suddenly straightened and towered over her.

"That horrible child is this woman's stepdaughter," he practically shouted. "How dare you speak of Phiney that way?"

Gabrielle rose and took Phil's arm to placate him, but her feelings echoed his. "If Delphine said he was my father, then he was my father," she said, biting back her own anger. "Where did this man you called LeBlanc go?"

The nun paled, then she regained her haughty composure. She stood and appeared ready to leave. "I don't know. We did all what we could for him and he chose to leave this place. If he is your father, no doubt he is well on his way back to the Attakapas Poste."

"No." Gabrielle's head pounded. She was supposed to bring him home; Marianne's vision had indicated as much. He had to be in New Orleans.

"I'm sorry," Sister Marguerite said, and Gabrielle knew the woman spoke truth. The nun touched her arm in a silent apology, then left the room.

"She's sorry," Phil mocked her, pacing the small library. "I'd like to make her sorry."

"Phil," Mathurin scolded him. "Watch your words."

In their disappointment they had failed to notice another nun sitting in the corner, a petite woman whose brown eyes enlarged to the size of pecans at Phil's remarks.

"Do you have any idea where my father is?" Gabrielle asked her.

The petite nun shook her head. "I do know that Delphine has asked about him daily," she said. "If Delphine did not know, he will not be easy to find. She must have checked all the infirmaries."

Gabrielle's panic intensified. Where had Papa gone?

"Please don't be hurt by Sister Marguerite's words," the young woman added. "Delphine is a strong-willed child and Sister Marguerite is an older woman who does not tolerate impudence easily.''

The pride Gabrielle felt for her new daughter doubled, but the fear over her safety and Jean's returned. She couldn't shake her anxiety about Jean visiting the Delaronde house alone. When she turned to share her trepidations with Phil and Mathurin, she found them deep in conversation.

''We're going to the riverfront,'' Phil told her. ''We have friends there who may know of your father's whereabouts.''

Gabrielle nodded. ''What shall I do?''

''Stay here,'' Mathurin said, ''until we or Jean returns.''

The two men placed their hats on their heads and exited the building, leaving Gabrielle alone with her painful thoughts. The petite woman offered Gabrielle something to eat, but she found the tea and biscuits unappetizing despite her hunger.

''May I get some air?'' Gabrielle asked her.

''Of course,'' the nun replied and led her down the hall into a small outdoor area enclosed by brick walls.

The garden smelled of gardenias and night-blooming jasmine, their pungent scent in the stale night air adding to the pounding in her head. What on earth would she do now? she thought madly. Where would she start looking?

She walked around the side of the building to escape the overpowering scents, and her heart stilled at the sight. There before her was the bench where Delphine had appeared in her vision. Beside Delphine had sat her father, listening to the words of Gabrielle's letter.

Tears poured forth and she thought she would choke from the emotions building in her chest. "Where are you?" she asked the night air. "Oh, Papa, where are you?"

Like so many of her prayers spoken during the past thirteen years, there was no answer, no sign that signaled the end to their long suffering. She dropped onto the bench, her shoulders falling from the weight of her grief, burying her head in her hands and sobbing.

Suddenly, an acorn fell from a nearby oak, startling her as it hit the brick pavement. It rolled beneath her bench and her gaze followed the tiny object along its journey, watching as it stopped against a small, white object.

Gabrielle leaned underneath the bench and retrieved a handkerchief, one too small to be an adult's. She examined the miniature cloth, dirty from being exposed for a long period of time. She couldn't make out the initials, so she moved toward the garden's lantern and studied it closely under the light. When she rubbed her fingers across the stitching, she knew at once who had held this handkerchief.

"May I get you something, madame?" the petite nun asked. "Perhaps you would like your tea brought out to the garden?"

Like her vision in Jean's *radeau,* Gabrielle saw clearly why she had feared for Jean's life. Holding the handkerchief, seeing the ghostly images flit across her vision, she knew with complete certainty that Delphine was in danger.

"No, thank you," she said, pulling her cloak over her head. "But I would like to know where Mademoiselle Delaronde resides."

"You mustn't go there at this hour," the nun answered. "You should wait for the men to escort you there."

"I cannot wait," Gabrielle said, passing her but pausing at the door. "Either you tell me or I shall find Delphine myself."

"Follow Chartres one block, then take a right up to Rue Royal," the nun explained as they made their way to the courtyard gate. "Her house is on the corner, riverside, with dark green shutters."

"Merci," Gabrielle answered.

Then ignoring everything Jean had instructed her, she left the safety of the Ursuline Convent and headed out alone into the dark, steamy night of New Orleans.

For the first time in months Delphine wasn't afraid. Edouard Prevost had attacked and arrested her father, removed Carmeline from the house, and had her cornered in the library behind a locked door. God only knew what the dreadful man had planned for her, but she refused to cry. Hate was the only emotion she would give in to now and hate was something she had plenty of.

"You're the lowest form of man I've ever met," she said to him. "You killed your own son. You attacked my father, an innocent man, from the rear. Now you want to molest a child."

"You're no child," Edouard said, angry at her words. "Daughters of whores grow up to be whores."

Delphine attempted to slap him again, but he caught her wrist and squeezed hard. "You and your family will pay for what you have done to me," he said angrily.

"The only person who has harmed you is yourself," she answered, then drew up a knee to hit him in the groin.

Edouard's eyes rolled back at the impact and he winced, but he refused to let go of her wrist. When he stumbled to his knees, Delphine was finally able to release herself and run toward the door, but there was no key to open it.

"Stupid bitch," Edouard called out hoarsely. "You'll never escape me."

Delphine studied the room's contents, hoping to find something to use as a weapon. She spotted the letter opener on the secretary and moved toward it, but Edouard grabbed her ankle and she fell. Slowly, his strength returned and he inched his way toward her, still holding tightly to her leg. Delphine struggled to reach the desk, but Edouard's force was greater. Realizing defeat, Delphine turned and began beating the man with her fists.

With a hard jerk, Edouard pulled her backward and faceup on the rug. He then straddled her, pinning her arms above her head. "You can't escape me, my dear," he said smuggly. "I will ruin you before I leave this place."

Delphine spit into his face, but it only made him madder. He slapped her hard across the cheek and something warm filled her mouth. Still, she would not surrender to fear. "Bastard," she said. "You will never ruin me no matter what you do."

Still wearing his evil grin, Edouard took both of her arms with one hand and ripped the front of her gown with the other, grabbing her breasts with animal force. Delphine shut her eyes and turned away, focusing instead on the feel of Gabrielle's wooden cross on her chest. As Edouard pulled her dress up to her knees, Delphine remembered the afternoon Gabrielle had sent her that cross, the day Parrain remembered his name. Edouard would not have her, she commanded herself. No matter what may come, the foul man would not claim her soul. When she felt his hand slide up her exposed leg, Delphine cringed and shut her eyes. She thought of her father and *La Belle Amie*, imagining herself sailing on the peaceful waters of the Gulf with Uncle Phil by her side.

I won't be afraid, Papa, she said to herself. But her thoughts lied.

Delphine heard Edouard unbutton his breeches, but she refused to look at him. "Look at me, bitch," he commanded her. "I want you to watch me ruin you."

Delphine shut her eyes tighter, but she could have sworn she heard the cocking of a pistol. A draft flitted over her legs and Edouard's grip on her hands lessened.

"Let her go," a voice commanded. "Get off my daughter this instant."

Delphine thought she had gone daft until Edouard released her arms and turned toward the voice. There, standing above them both, was a woman whose face was shadowed by a cloak.

"Who the hell are you?" Edouard asked, rising onto his knees. "How dare you walk in here like—"

Delphine grabbed the brass candlestick from the nearby table and smashed it upon the back of Edouard's head. He stumbled to the floor, freeing her from his hold. Delphine rose, clutching her torn dress to her chest, and moved to the strange woman's side. The stranger instantly pushed her safely to her rear.

To their dismay, Edouard wasn't disabled. He groaned from the pain but managed to stand and face both women. "Bitch," he yelled at her. "I'll have you both hanged."

The stranger claiming to be her mother never moved and never took her eyes off Edouard. "I'll send you to hell first," she said menacingly.

Edouard's eyes narrowed and he rubbed his injured head. "Who the hell are you?"

The stranger pulled back her cloak to reveal a head of ink-black hair cut short at the neck. "I am the pirate Gabrielle, the bold Grania," she said, withdrawing a knife from her waistband with her free hand. "Where is Jean?"

Delphine studied the woman who had stolen her father's heart, the woman whose correspondence had been filled with love and comfort, the daughter of sweet Parrain. Her eyes glared at Edouard as cold as the sea of a new moon, sending a chill down Delphine's spine. Would she actually kill this man?

Edouard met her stare, but only for an instant. Then he reached for his wound and looked away. "I don't care who you are. I'm an official of the Spanish government," he barked. "You have no right to interfere here."

Gabrielle stepped closer, the gun still cocked and loaded, and Delphine caught a glimpse of fear in

Edouard's eyes. "Where is Jean?" she repeated louder.

"The soldiers attacked him from behind," Delphine offered. "He's been sent to the Cabildo."

Gabrielle's eyes grew dark with fury, but again they never strayed from Edouard's face. The man grew more uncomfortable by her stare.

"Sit," Gabrielle demanded, pointing to the secretary with the butt of her pistol.

"What?" Edouard asked.

"You heard him," Carmeline said at the door. Delphine turned to find her servant and friend loaded down with a coil of rope.

This time, Edouard appeared afraid. "You'll never get away with this."

Still staring at the man, Gabrielle inched forward and jabbed the blade to his throat. Her pistol remained aimed at his side, one shot capable of killing him. "I kill anyone who interferes with my family, rat," she said. "One quick move and I will either slit your throat or blow a hole through you. Now, unless you want to have your insides ripped open, I suggest you sit down."

Edouard instantly did as he was told, careful not to upset the blade at his jugular. Gabrielle raised the pistol to his head for emphasis. "Write a letter admitting your guilt. Explain what really happened at the duel that morning, clear Jean of all charges."

Edouard appeared ready to refuse, but Gabrielle poked the knife deeper into his skin and he reached for the quill and parchment.

"Delphine," Gabrielle called out to her. "Change your clothes and be ready to leave."

For an instant, Gabrielle looked back and their eyes met. In that moment that passed between the two women, Delphine felt hope. She still had a family, including an Acadian pirate who chose to cut her hair, and a chance to rescue her father and flee the city. All was not lost.

She ran into the foyer, heading for the second floor, when she bounded into the chest of a tall man. She thought to scream, to warn Gabrielle that the soldiers had returned, when two large arms grabbed her and held her close.

"Phiney, are you all right?"

"Uncle Phil," she cried when she realized who it was. "Gabrielle is in the library with a gun to Edouard Prevost. She's making him write a letter to clear Papa."

"Where is Jean?" Phil asked, his eyes scanning the tears in her clothes.

"The Cabildo," she answered, watching as fury filled his face the more he looked at her gown.

Phil removed his coat and placed it around her shoulders, then he moved past her toward the library. "Get dressed, Phiney," he said. "I don't want you watching this."

He entered the library, but Delphine followed behind. Edouard had finished his letter and was handing it to Gabrielle when they arrived and Carmeline had begun to wrap the rope around his chest. "You'll never get away with this," he said to Gabrielle. "You'll never leave the city."

"You'll never see the light of the next sunrise," Phil yelled and threw a punch to the man's right cheek.

Blood flew from Edouard's face and his head rolled forward as he fell unconscious. Phil grabbed Gabrielle's knife and raised it toward his chest, but she caught his arm. "No," Gabrielle said. "He's not worth it, Phil. We have what we need. Save your energy for later."

"The bastard hurt my Phiney," he bit out.

His words unlocked the emotions Delphine had forced inside herself and tears poured forth. She grabbed the door handle to steady herself, fearful that she might collapse on the spot, but she had to calm him. She couldn't let Phil ruin his life on her behalf. "Please, Uncle Phil," she said, wiping the tears from her face. "Don't kill him."

When he turned to look at her, his eyes were filled with a mixture of fraternal protectiveness and a deep-seated love. She had always known Phil cared, watching over her as she grew from a child, but until now she had never realized the depth of that devotion.

Phil dropped his arm and handed Gabrielle the knife. He took the rope from Carmeline and wound it tightly around Edouard, pulling each circle with a greater force, then gagged him with his handkerchief. While he was busy at his work, Gabrielle walked to Delphine and pulled her into her arms.

So thankful to rest her head and worries on another shoulder, Delphine sobbed into Gabrielle's cloak, while Gabrielle soothed her by caressing her hair. "What about Papa?" Delphine asked between sobs.

"We'll have him free, don't you worry," Phil said, coming to their side. "Do you have a horse we can use?"

"She has a wagon ready for travel," Mathurin

answered, heading up the foyer. "What on earth is going on here?"

Delphine sucked in a breath and composed herself. Tears would have to wait. "It's a long story, Mathurin," she said. "I'll tell you after we get my father out of jail."

"Jail?" Mathurin asked, looking from one face to another.

"Allons, allez," Phil called out and the group made their way through the courtyard to the wagon hidden in the alley. Phil explained his plan and they all listened carefully to his instructions. If all went well, they would rescue Jean and race out of town. But everything had to go as planned.

They waited while Delphine changed her gown, then they all boarded the wagon, Gabrielle holding tightly to Delphine's hand. "I'm fine," Delphine assured her, even though she felt anything but.

Gabrielle sighed, her shoulders drooping from the weight of the events of the past half hour. When she shut her eyes and winced, Delphine knew it had all been a well-acted performance.

"Don't give up now, Gabi," Phil said to her, climbing into the wagon seat. "We have only won one battle."

Gabrielle opened her eyes, inhaled deeply, and nodded, but Delphine could tell Gabrielle was just as scared inside as she was. After all that had transpired with Edouard, now they were faced with the possible failure of freeing Jean from jail.

"You were magnificent," Delphine told her, squeezing her hands. "I'm glad you're here."

Gabrielle smiled, and the woman who looked at

her now was the kind woman Delphine had come to know and love in her letters. "I had good teachers," Gabrielle said, squeezing back. "And a brave daughter to help me."

Mathurin pulled his sword from its sheaf and boarded the back of the wagon where Carmeline lay hidden. Phil whipped the horses into action and the wagon made its way down the alley, heading toward the Cabildo. With one last look, Delphine watched the Delaronde house, and her former life, disappear.

The world had turned hazy but Jean knew he was at the Cabildo. He tried to resist entering the cell, reaching for the soldier's sword, but the pounding in his head made him dizzy and the man beat his hand away. If only he could shake the seasick sensation gripping him. If only he could get back to Phiney.

The soldier threw him into the cell and he stumbled to the floor. Jean attempted to rise, but the floor rose up to meet him.

"Slow down," he heard someone say, but he ignored the voice.

"I have to get to my daughter," he said anxiously, trying to stand. Again, the world tilted and he slid back to the floor.

"All in due time, my friend," the voice said. "You need to rest for a moment and clear your head."

"I don't have a moment," Jean answered, thinking of how his precious angel had been left with that bastard Prevost. "My daughter is in trouble."

Slowly, the man before him came into focus, a middle-aged man with salt and pepper hair and eyes the color of the Mississippi. He reminded Jean of someone, but he couldn't place the connection.

"You're in a locked cell, my friend," the man continued. "You won't help your daughter until you can regain your sense of balance."

Jean surrendered, if only briefly, and pulled his knees in front of him, leaning his head against the back wall. The spot where Edouard's man had landed a blow throbbed, but his world was beginning to clear.

"Who are you?" the man asked with an unnerving tone.

Jean cocked an eye and studied the man seated on the cot. His look was anything but friendly. "I have to get out of here," Jean repeated, standing and forcing down the bile that had risen in his throat.

Slowly, he made his way to the front of the cell and peered down the hallway. One armed soldier sat at a desk at the end of the hall speaking to an unseen man, possibly another soldier guarding the door. Jean's sword lay across his desk next to a set of keys.

"And how do you propose to get out of this cell to retrieve those keys?" the man asked him.

Jean turned to face him and the movement made the world spin again. "I've got to get to my family," Jean said between gritted teeth. He knew it was next to impossible, but he'd be damned if he would sit and do nothing.

A darkness filled the man's countenance and he ran his fingers through his hair nervously. "I have tried repeatedly," he said. "You're not the only one who has family in need."

Jean began pacing the tiny cell, anything to relieve

the anxiety ripping at his heart. "There has to be a way out of here."

Suddenly, he remembered his weapons. Jean pulled off his coat and searched all the places he had hidden his knives, but the soldiers had found them all. When his hand found a warm, damp spot on his shirt, Jean realized he had been cut in the chest. He opened his shirt further to assess the wound, grateful the cut wasn't deep, but now he had problems of a different nature. His cell mate took the opportunity to grab the front of his shirt and throw him back against the wall.

"What the hell?" Jean asked, waiting for the fog to clear before he landed a fist in the older man's face.

"Where did you get that cross?" the man shouted at him.

"Get your hands off me," Jean said, pushing him away.

It was then he spotted a wooden cross, an identical replica of the one he wore, hanging from the man's neck. When Jean's eyes rose to the man's face, he suddenly knew why he had looked familiar.

Chapter Sixteen

"Mon dieu," Jean said. "You're Joseph Gallant."

The man released him when he heard his name spoken and pulled away. "Who the hell are you?" he asked. "And why are you wearing Gabrielle's cross?"

Jean straightened his shirt and took a deep breath. He wasn't prepared to meet his father-in-law, especially under such horrid conditions. "Gabrielle is my wife."

Joseph sent him an accusing look. "What are you doing in jail?"

Jean ran his fingers through his hair in an effort to make himself presentable. "I beg your pardon, monsieur, but I was just about to ask you the same question."

Now, it was Joseph's turn to pace. "I tried to make my way to the Attakapas Poste, but I had no money. In an act of desperation, I stowed aboard a westbound ship, but I was caught and imprisoned."

If Jean's head hadn't hurt so much and he wasn't

standing before his wife's long-lost father, he might have laughed. "Must be a family trait," he said.

The mention of his family made Joseph turn and stare. Jean felt the enormous power behind those worrisome eyes. He understood it well. "They're fine," Jean assured him. "Emilie and Rose are married and living in the Opelousas Poste. Rose is expecting a child so they will join your wife in the Attakapas after the baby is born. Marianne is waiting for you on your land grant. All are in the best of health, except for their heavy hearts. They miss you terribly."

Joseph deflated, falling upon the cot and turning away to hide his tears. "Thank God," Jean heard him whisper. "And Gabrielle?"

Gabrielle, Jean thought, feeling his heart constrict. He shouldn't have allowed her to come to New Orleans, shouldn't have exposed her to such dangers. His predicament was everything he had feared. At least she was safe at the Convent. "Gabrielle is well and safe," Jean said. "Even if she is married to me."

Joseph stood and began pacing again, pausing at the bars of the door and gripping the metal so tightly Jean thought it might break from the weight of his heartache. Suddenly, Joseph straightened as if remembering something vital. "Your daughter," he said. "She's Delphine Delaronde."

Just as his head was beginning to clear, the sound of his daughter's name brought back the pounding. He had to get out of there. Now. *"Oui,"* he answered nervously, taking his turn at pacing.

"Then you must be Captain Bouclaire."

Jean said nothing, but he knew Joseph had made

the connection. Delphine must have told him everything in her visits to the Convent.

"Phiney's in danger," Jean said. "I have to get out of here."

Joseph nodded. "I have a plan."

It took several hours before the two men plotted their escape, then Joseph called the guard over from the desk.

"What do you want?" the stout Creole asked.

"Man's hurt," Joseph replied, tipping his head in Jean's direction. "He dozed off and I can't wake him."

"So, don't wake him," the man said and moved to leave.

"He's injured," Joseph added. "He's received a bad cut on his chest. It looks serious."

The guard came closer but remained steps away from the bars. "Doesn't matter. He's more than likely to hang. He's wanted for murder."

"I don't care if he hangs tomorrow at dawn," Joseph continued, leaning nonchalantly against the heavy metal door. "He stinks. And if he bleeds any more, I'm going to drown in here."

This time, the guard inched closer, peering into the cell cautiously. Unable to view Jean's condition adequately, he approached the bars and gazed inside. Jean lay huddled on the far side of the cell, curled beneath the cot and facing the wall. The guard yelled at him, but received no response. When Jean failed to move when the guard poked him with the tip of his rifle, the man leaned forward against the cell door, his head halfway through the bars.

Joseph moved instantly, locking his arms about the guard's head and holding him immobilized between the bars. The man attempted a shout, but Joseph stuffed Jean's handkerchief into his open mouth. The guard raised his hands in defense, but Jean was at Joseph's side, grabbing the man's hands and tying them against the door with strips of cloth ripped from his soiled shirt.

"Gabrielle isn't going to be happy with me," he said. "She just mended this shirt."

"I'm surprised she's not here helping us," Joseph added. "The last time I saw her . . ."

Jean studied the man who had watched his beloved come into the world, watched her grow from a babe. The same man who had watched Gabrielle being stolen away. Until today, Jean could not imagine such a horror. Now, his Phiney was facing a similar predicament at the hands of Edouard Prevost. There was no moment to lose, but Jean lightly touched his father-in-law's arm in sympathy. Then they both straightened, took the guard's keys and rifle, and headed down the hall, leaving the man tied to the cell's iron bars.

"We have to be quick," Jean said. "The other guard is bound to get suspicious. Our fat friend is making quite a noise despite our gag."

They paused at the end of the hall and Jean slowly peered around the corner. To his surprise, there was no one guarding the door.

"That's odd," he said.

"What is it?" Joseph whispered.

As if the sight of the Cabildo jail left unattended wasn't puzzling enough, seeing Gabrielle rush in the door, a pistol peering out of her waistband and a knife in her hand, made Jean pause in wonder, his chin dropping to his chest. Gabrielle met his eyes and froze, no doubt equally shocked that he was free and armed and standing in the jail's hallway. Finally, they both recovered.

"Dear God, what are you doing here?" Jean asked, feeling his temple burn with fury and concern.

"What is it?" Joseph asked from behind. "Who's there?"

"There's no time to lose," Gabrielle said. "Delphine is causing a distraction. The wagon's around back, waiting for us."

Jean could feel Joseph tense at his back, the reaction to hearing his daughter's voice after thirteen agonizing years. But all Jean could think of was his wife trying to break him out of jail and his daughter outside creating a "distraction."

"Jean, don't think," Gabrielle commanded, tugging at his sleeve. "We have to get out of here now."

He obeyed, feeling better when Phil arrived.

"Well done, old man," Phil said with a grin. "You still know how to fight."

Jean took his sword from the guard's desk, throwing another one to Joseph and following Gabrielle and Phil to the door. "Delphine?"

"Is with Mathurin," Gabrielle answered, scanning the street at the door.

"Time is of the essence," Phil said, checking the other direction. "We need to act now."

Jean turned back to Joseph, who was staring teary-eyed at the woman in front of them. This time, it was Jean who pulled on his sleeve. "Reunions later," Jean said.

Hearing this comment, Gabrielle looked back for an instant, but her mind was concerned with the action on the street. "Who's that?" she asked Jean when he had reached her side.

"A friend," he answered. "He's coming with us."

Seeing that the coast was clear, the foursome followed the Cabildo wall to the back alley, where Carmeline sat perched on the wagon seat. Within seconds, Mathurin and Delphine appeared around a corner.

"Time to go," Mathurin said, his voice commanding haste. But he paused when he spotted Joseph, recognition crossing his features.

"Not now," Jean whispered to him, then took Gabrielle by the elbow and led her toward the wagon seat. There was no time. "We'll take it from here, Carmeline," he ordered. "The rest of you in the back and remain hidden."

The two climbed into the seat and whipped the horses into motion. The wagon bolted through the alley, rushing through the dark city streets in the direction of the river.

Several minutes had passed before Gabrielle could feel her heart pumping again. She was sure it had stopped beating during the rescue, sure that only an invisible force had kept her going through the confrontation with Edouard, then the armed escape from jail. Now that the night became darker on the outskirts of town and the houses became fewer and farther between, Gabrielle's heart slowed to a new problem.

She had left town without her father.

She felt something touch her and glanced down to find Jean's enormous hand covering hers, his thumb caressing the inside of her palm. "Are you still with me?" he asked.

Gabrielle's body had turned numb from the shock of all that had transpired. Still, she nodded.

Jean must have suspected something was wrong for he wrapped an arm about her shoulders and pulled her into his chest. "Everything's going to be fine," he whispered, but Gabrielle knew it to be a lie. They had managed to rescue Delphine and pull Jean out of jail, but she had failed in her personal mission. Failed to reunite her family. Failed to heal the wounds she had inflicted long ago in Nova Scotia.

The road was becoming harder to follow, though she knew they had only another league or so to travel. Gabrielle closed her eyes to ward off the intense pain in her chest, but her body shook from the emotions buried deep inside her. She tried to restrain her tears, to dispel the sobs threatening to bubble to the surface, but the outburst was inevitable. After the first sob broke free, she was lost.

Jean pulled her tighter against him, kissing the top of her head and whispering comfort, but all Gabrielle could comprehend was her failure. Was she never to find her father? Would her family never be reunited? The sobs became aching cries as they broke free, her heart breaking from the heaviness lying there. She felt the wagon slow and stop, but the pain was too much to master. She buried her face in Jean's shirt and sobbed uncontrollably.

"Gabrielle," Jean said, trying to right her, but she wouldn't budge. He attempted to lift her chin, but she couldn't bear looking at anyone, couldn't bear facing the world.

"Gabrielle," Jean repeated. "Look at me."

Gabrielle shook her head, still buried in his chest, but she felt a masculine hand touch her arm. "Gabrielle," another voice said, or was she imagining things? She continued to sob, but something in that voice struck a memory, something in its tone resonated in her soul.

"Gabrielle," the voice to her left repeated, and for a moment she imagined it to be her father. But it couldn't be, she thought madly. They had failed to find him. Joseph had not been in New Orleans and no one knew of his whereabouts.

"Gabrielle," the voice said louder. "Look at me, child."

There it was again, that familiar tone, that voice from her childhood. She calmed her sobs and lifted her head. Jean smiled down at her with a glimmer of hope. Was it possible? she asked him with her eyes. He answered her unspoken question with an affirmative grin, but Gabrielle was too afraid to turn around, too fearful of being crushed once more.

She felt the touch on her arm slide down and take her hand. "Gabrielle," the voice whispered again, and she knew she wasn't dreaming.

Gabrielle turned to find a man standing before her on the ground, his tall frame almost meeting her face to face. He had the height of her sister Emilie and the gentleness of Rose, but Joseph Gallant owned every trait that Gabrielle possessed. All the days she had worried of forgetting her father disappeared. She knew this man as if they had spoken yesterday.

"Come here, my Tide Chaser," he whispered, tears pouring down his face.

Gabrielle jumped from the wagon seat and threw herself into her father's arms, strong arms that enveloped her and comforted her. He pulled away briefly to gaze into her face, studying her as if she might be a dream, then kissed her forehead and hugged her again.

"Oh *petite chou,*" he whispered. "I have found you at last."

He embraced her for what seemed like an eternity, then held her at arm's length to examine the woman she had become, cropped hair included. "I can't believe it," he said, smiling through the tears. "My child is a pirate."

"I'm not a pirate," she said, glancing at Jean, who was busy holding his own daughter, checking to make sure she was safe. "I'm a smuggler's wife."

"I don't care if you're the Queen of England," Joseph said, taking her into his arms once more. "You are a sight to behold."

They held each other tightly, Gabrielle now crying tears of joy into her father's shoulder. "I thought I would never find you," she whispered.

To her surprise, Joseph laughed. "Nothing could keep me away from my little girls," he said emotionally. "You don't think a few Englishmen would separate us forever, do you?"

Thoughts of the exile flooded her senses and she

recalled how they came to be separated. Before she had time to let the guilt filter through her joy, Phil was at their sides, his sword drawn protectively.

"I hate to break up the reunion," he said, "but we need to get out of here."

No sooner had his words been spoken than the sound of several men on horseback was heard coming down the river road. All of the men instinctively pulled their swords, including Joseph. They stood facing their attackers in one line.

"Stay back with the women," Jean told Joseph. "Let us handle this."

Joseph didn't budge. "Don't confuse age with skill, my boy. I have fought worse enemies than this."

Gabrielle pulled her pistol from her waistband and glanced at Delphine. "Stay behind me," she commanded, but Delphine only joined the line and extended her hand.

"Hand me your knife," Delphine said confidently.

Gabrielle glanced at Jean, who appeared ready to be inflicted with palsy, but he didn't have a chance to object. "Gabrielle, Delphine, hide behind the wagon," Joseph commanded.

There were four men approaching, four men to match theirs. Two armed women would come in handy.

Gabrielle handed Delphine the knife, then turned back toward her husband and her father. "No one is going to separate my family again," she said firmly. Glancing back at her new daughter, she added, "Delphine and I will see to that."

As the men came closer, Gabrielle realized they were officials of some kind, but wore uniforms different from the Cabildo guards. One man was elegantly dressed, unusually so for a person coming to arrest fugitives in the middle of the night.

"Captain Jean Bouclaire," the man to his side announced. "Show yourself."

Gabrielle stopped breathing, wondering what would transpire next. Jean stepped forward, still holding his sword before him. "I am Jean Bouclaire," he answered.

"Are you the man wanted for the murder of Marcel Prevost?" the man asked.

"I am," Jean said.

Delphine gasped at her side and Gabrielle forced herself to breathe. This wasn't happening. Not after all they had been through and how far they had come.

Then she remembered the letter.

"If you please, monsieur," Gabrielle spoke up. "I have a letter that will clear Captain Bouclaire's name."

Every man standing in the line turned astonished eyes upon her. All except Phil, who was grinning knowingly.

"Bring me this letter," the well-dressed man said in French with a Spanish accent.

Gabrielle tucked the pistol into her waistband and approached the gentleman. When she reached his side, she noticed the delicate lace at his throat and the fine silk waistcoat and coat adorned with an insignia. She handed him the letter and a gem-encrusted hand accepted the parchment.

He read the letter silently after the man to his left produced a candle from his saddle and provided the light. Then the aristocrat turned his heavyset eyes to hers.

"This clears Captain Bouclaire's name," the man said. "But it is written by a man I do not trust. Therefore, it is worthless."

Gabrielle's hopes faded. They would have to resort to fighting to break free of the authorities after all. She wondered what to do next, how to flee back to the safety of the group, when the man spoke again. "That is why I am here, madame."

Now, Gabrielle was completely confused. "I don't understand, monsieur," she said.

"You are speaking to Count Don Alexandre O'Reilly," the man to her right announced. "Governor of the colony of Louisiana."

Gabrielle fought to keep her jaw from dropping open. She didn't know whether to bow or curtsy. She chose the latter, her eyes falling to the man's well-tailored legs in subservience. "Your Highness," she said, praying her ignorance wasn't showing.

"Madame," O'Reilly said softly, a trace of a smile on his lips.

"She is my wife," Jean said, approaching the governor and returning his sword to his sheaf. "Madame Gabrielle Bouclaire."

"Daughter of Joseph Gallant," her father added, following on Jean's heels.

The men bowed their heads respectively to the governor and he, in turn, returned the salute.

"I will not detain you long," the governor said. "I only wish to inform you that all charges have been dismissed."

Jean's face exhibited surprise, but he remained guarded.

"We received a letter from Antoine Vincent, a man of which I hold great esteem," O'Reilly continued. "He explained Prevost's lies and I had my men look into his affairs. We also inquired as to your reputation in town, monsieur, and the public sentiment was in your favor."

The governor leaned forward in his saddle. "I also hear you have access to wonderful spirits coming from the Caribbean."

At this Jean smiled broadly. "Your Excellency, I would be honored to deliver some of my finest spirits for your perusal and allow you to determine their quality for yourself."

O'Reilly straightened, quite pleased with the transaction. "You are free to go, Captain," he said. "Edouard Prevost will not harm you or your family anymore."

"And may we still conduct business in Louisiana?" Phil piped in from behind.

The governor turned his horse to leave, but he left them all with a parting thought. "I'll make that decision after my rum arrives."

The governor's party left the clearing, heading down the river road toward New Orleans, and everyone breathed a sigh of relief. Gabrielle could still feel the embarrassment burning in her cheeks.

"Did I say the right thing?" she asked. "Did I call him the right name?"

"It doesn't matter, *'ti-monde,*" her father said, kissing the top of her head. "The worst is over. Now, it's time to go home."

* * *

Once aboard ship, Gabrielle, Joseph, and Delphine took turns freshening up and donning clothes from Jean's stash. After Jean brought the schooner to full sail and met the Gulf waters, he joined them in the main cabin with an enormous platter of food and wine.

"And then what happened?" Joseph asked Gabrielle. "How did Lorenz finally convince Emilie to marry him?"

Gabrielle finished her story of her oldest sister and Lorenz Landry, the Acadian man she had known since childhood. They were thrown together upon reaching Louisiana, Lorenz asking Emilie several times for her hand in marriage only to be turned down again and again. But all turned out happily in the end.

"You know how stubborn and impulsive Lorenz is," Gabrielle said of her brother-in-law. "Emilie was worried he would do something foolish and get himself exiled from Louisiana. She was so fearful of being separated like Maman is from you."

Joseph's eyes turned dark and he stared down into his hands folded solemnly in his lap. "I'm sorry, Papa," Gabrielle said. "I didn't mean to make you sad."

Joseph looked up, his eyes glistening despite the pain lingering behind them. "I'm not sad, *petite chou,*" he said, taking her hands in his. "I am grateful this horror is coming to a close."

"You must be so excited to see your wife again," Delphine added, her face beaming.

"More than you know, Phiney," he said. "You

would think a person could wait a few more days after waiting thirteen years, but I feel like I shall jump out of my skin."

"We shall be there in good time," Jean offered. "We are full sails ahead."

Joseph squeezed Gabrielle's hand. "Tell me more of the family. Keep my mind occupied while we wait."

"There's so much to tell," Gabrielle said.

"Rose," Joseph offered. "She is with child?"

Suddenly, Gabrielle felt as giddy as her father, anxious to be near her dear sisters and mother. She missed them terribly. "Rose should have the child soon, maybe as early as next month. Perhaps we could travel up to the Opelousas Poste to see them."

"Absolutely," Joseph agreed. "And this Coleman Thorpe, is he a good husband?"

"A fine man," Jean said. "I've known him a long time and hope to do business with him one day."

Joseph's eyes sparkled with pride, but there was a hint of something else behind his thoughts. "What kind of a name is Coleman?"

Suddenly, Gabrielle remembered her brother-in-law's nationality, the reason it had taken Rose all of last summer to convince the family he was worthy of her hand. Coleman *was* a fine man, but he also was English. How would her father, who had been captured, imprisoned, and exiled by the same people, feel about being related to one?

"He owns a farm in the Opelousas Poste, and has inherited quite a bit of money since his father's death," Jean added, sending Gabrielle a concerned look. She realized Jean had come to the same conclusion as she.

"He built the house that Maman and I live in on your land grant, a beautiful place," Gabrielle said. "When I left, he was having other homes built for himself and Rose and for Emilie and Lorenz."

"Money is nice but it doesn't necessarily make a good bedfellow," Joseph answered. "What is his background?"

Jean and Gabrielle exchanged glances, wondering how to break the news. Delphine sensed something passing between them and eyed them curiously. As if feeling the need to offer assistance, she added, "I've met his solicitor in New Orleans after you discovered your identity, Parrain. He was very kind and said he would get word to the family, in addition to looking out for you."

"He did get word," Jean said. "Which is why we're here tonight. If it wasn't for that letter, we never would have known you were in New Orleans."

Joseph nodded silently, then crossed his hands across his chest. "He sounds like an admirable man, but what's his nationality? Thorpe doesn't sound French to me."

"It's not French," Gabrielle said softly.

"Oh?"

Gabrielle peered over at Jean, who raised his eyebrows. The truth had to be told, but she dreaded telling it.

"I suppose the next thing you're going to say is he's English."

Gabrielle held her breath, fearful to affirm the inevitable. But when she met her father's eyes, the sparkle had intensified.

"Gabi," he said, breaking into a smile, "Coleman's

family took care of me in Georgia when I was traveling through the colony on my way to Louisiana. I owe them my life."

Gabrielle had forgotten that Coleman had written to his cousins in the English colony, asking them to watch out for her father. Because of that letter, Coleman's family had not only invited Joseph in, but nursed him through a fever and armed him with food, weapons, and ammunition for the trip through the Southern backwoods. Coleman's assistance was the reason he and Rose had married. It was the key that had unlocked Marianne's heart to him.

"Then you're not upset?" Jean asked. "Because he's English?"

Joseph sighed and leaned back against the bedpost. "Not all men can be blamed for the actions of their crown," he said. "I judge a man by his heart and soul, not by the uniform he wears or the language he speaks."

"Or the fact that he gets thrown into jail on occasion?" Jean offered with a grin.

Joseph shook his finger at his son-in-law. "Don't ever let that happen again."

Delphine took Jean's hand and nuzzled against his side. "It won't, Parrain. Now that he has me onboard to look after him."

Biting the inside of her cheek, Gabrielle stifled a laugh. But to her surprise, Jean wrapped an arm about his daughter, kissed the top of her head, and appeared resigned to the feminine additions to his life. He glanced at Gabrielle and sighed defeatedly.

"Is it so bad having us at your side looking out for you?" Gabrielle asked.

"It's what I've always wanted," Jean argued. "But is it so wrong of me to want to keep my family safe?"

"That's impossible," Joseph said. "Nothing can ever guarantee that."

A pronounced melancholy fell about the room and Gabrielle suddenly remembered the look on her father's face thirteen years before, when he had waved to them from the bluff while they sat huddled on the cold beach. His look had exhibited such a wide range of emotions. Gratitude that his family was safe. Fear over their future. Outrage at the loss of their farm and land.

Never in her young life had Gabrielle witnessed her father's helplessness. He had always been the epitome of strength and safety. It had frightened her to the core.

"Perhaps you're right," Jean said softly. "Perhaps we are all fooling ourselves that we have control over our destinies and the fate of those we love."

Jean's words echoed in Gabrielle's mind and cut a path all the way to her soul. She had interfered with her family's destiny. Because of her foolish actions on the beach that day, she had ripped them apart. Joseph's hand still held hers, but Gabrielle couldn't bear to look at him.

"I want to see the stars," Delphine announced. "I know it's late, but may I take a turn on deck before we go to sleep?"

"Of course you may," Jean answered. To Gabrielle, he added, "We'll be right back."

A knot lodged itself in Gabrielle's throat so all she could do was nod. When Jean and Delphine closed the door behind them, she felt her father squeeze her hand. "Gabi, is something wrong?"

Gabrielle still couldn't manage to look him in the eye. Guilt raked her being.

"Is it Jean?" he asked, although there was more surprise to his tone than alarm.

"No," she whispered and the words forced the knot loose with tears following behind. They poured down her cheeks.

"Is it Marianne?" This time, the alarm in his voice was acute.

"No," she answered. "Maman is fine."

"Then what is it, my child?"

Gabrielle swallowed hard, but the tears continued unabated. "I have done something terrible," she managed to whisper.

She felt a hand brush the loose strands of hair off her face. "What have you done?"

Ruined your life, she thought.

"Gabrielle," he said in the paternal voice she knew as a child. "What is it?"

"I am the reason we were separated."

Chapter Seventeen

A silence followed and Gabrielle shut her eyes to the pain of her confession, but Joseph placed a finger at her chin and forced her head up. "Look at me," he said gently. Gabrielle opened her eyes, but her father wasn't angry. "You can't be serious."

"You told me not to go down by the water," she said, the tears still flowing. "I went to look at the frigate and Maman had to come looking for me. When she finally reached me, we looked back up the bluff and you were gone. Then they started loading us on the boat."

"Gabrielle," Joseph said calmly. "You're not the reason we separated."

"But if I had only done as you told me to do. . . ."

"We still would have been separated."

Gabrielle pulled her sleeve across her nose, wishing she had Jean's handkerchief. She wanted to believe her father; she ached to believe him. But with all the confusion of the exile, she knew her actions had contributed to their dilemma.

"But I . . ."

Joseph took her hands once more and moved so they faced each other squarely. "I was with your grandfather, my father," he began. "When they trapped us inside the church, he grew very ill, more than likely from the shock. When they marched us down to the beach, right after I spotted you and your mother and sisters, my father took one look at the chaos around us and collapsed."

Joseph paused in an effort to regain his composure, glancing down at their joined hands. No one had known of Grandpapa Gallant's fate; they had received word on only a few members of their extended family.

"What happened?" Gabrielle asked.

"While I was trying to help him, the soldiers pushed us forward, yelling at us to continue down the path," Joseph continued. "I was furious. Angry from being treated like cattle and betrayed in such a barbaric manner, angry at the cowards who hadn't the courage to face us like men, I punched the first Englishman I saw. The next thing I knew I was hit from behind and the whole world went dark. When I woke up, you were gone, having sailed with the tide. And my father was dead."

Joseph's auburn eyes met hers, the same eyes that had twinkled when Marianne sang his favorite song or Gabrielle presented him with a new crystal found by the waterside. They were the same eyes she had known and loved in Nova Scotia years before, but now a fathomless darkness lingered there.

"You see, my dear," he said softly as if each word caused great pain, "*I* am the reason we were separated."

This time, Gabrielle squeezed his hands. "No," she insisted. "You did nothing wrong. The English did this to us."

"I shouldn't have gotten angry."

"How could you not have?"

Gabrielle raised her father's hands to her face while the pain of thirteen agonizing years of separation, years of wondering and wandering, rose to the surface and broke free in a torrent of tears. Then they hugged each other tightly, savoring the connection between father and daughter, the bond created at conception and nurtured through childhood. The link that no army could sever.

The moon disappeared and the soft, erratic breeze caused the sails to flap lightly in the early morning air. Jean was exhausted, but it felt good to be at the helm, good to feel the Gulf air on his face, even if they were now traveling slower than before.

He heard Gabrielle approach before he saw her, felt her hand inside his before he had time to turn. Like Delphine, she leaned against his upper arm, she, too, exhausted from the day's activities.

"You told him, didn't you?" he asked her.

Gabrielle didn't respond, but he could sense both her mental and physical exhaustion. "He told you that you didn't cause the separation, didn't he?"

"Yes."

Her tone wasn't what he had expected. Jean assumed she would be free of her guilt once she heard the truth, but her voice exhibited a dire sadness.

He pulled an arm about her and hugged her close. "What's wrong, *mon amour?*"

"I thought I would feel relieved when I found him," she said. "I do, but I also feel sad."

Jean kissed her forehead, savoring the smell of her hair. "Why do you feel sad?"

"Because he missed watching me grow up. He missed it all. And my parents lived the best years of their lives in exile, away from each other."

She felt so limp in his arms, so small and helpless. Jean caressed her arm. "Why don't you get some sleep," he offered. "You'll feel better in the morning."

Gabrielle shook her head. "So much has happened. I can't stop thinking about it all."

Jean looked around for the crewman on duty. "Maurice," he shouted. "Take the wheel."

Relieved of his position, Jean walked Gabrielle to the bow of the ship, still holding her close. He removed his coat and placed it on deck, then motioned for her to sit down. When he joined her on deck, he wrapped his arms back around her shoulders and pulled her into his chest.

"Who is that?" Gabrielle asked, looking out at the ship's figurehead, a Grecian beauty with long, flowing black hair.

"That's Gabrielle, the bold Grania," Jean said.

In the darkness he could feel her smile, but it was a feeble one. His love's strength was waning. "Delphine told me all about your bravery with Edouard Prevost," he explained. "I think perhaps I should resign as captain. I can't possible compete with such talents."

"Don't be absurd," she whispered. "I did what I had to do."

"You stood your ground and you didn't take your eyes off him." Jean was so proud of his wife, he thought his chest might burst. She had saved his daughter's life. "You're quite a woman, Gabrielle."

She managed to look up, touching his dimple lightly with her fingertip. "Does this mean you approve of me being here?"

He captured her finger with his lips, sucking gently on the soft, tender skin. "Yes, I'm thankful you're here." Thinking back on how she had boarded his ship, he added, "I'm thankful you know how to swim."

Gabrielle smiled, but her eyelids fluttered. She dropped her head back on his chest and nestled her hand in the folds of his shirt. "I love you, Jean," she said softly.

Lying there in the light of a thousand stars, with the gentle rocking of the ship, Jean thought back on what Joseph had said in the cabin. Life was unpredictable and nothing guaranteed a person's safety. He was foolish to place those he loved onshore and out of reach of harm's way. Delphine had been closer to danger than she would have been in his care aboard ship. Gabrielle would have withered away alone in the Attakapas, hungry for the sound of the sea. They needed each other. For what precious time they had on earth, they had to spend it together, despite what dangers they might face.

Jean gazed down on his wife, who in a few days' time would witness the reunion of her long-splintered family. He kissed her nose, then her lips.

"I love you too, Gabrielle," he said.

But she was fast asleep.

The air felt lighter that morning, free of the usual humidity pressing at Marianne's lungs. The birds appeared well before dawn, announcing the arrival of a beautiful day in the Attakapas.

Marianne rose and brewed a cup of coffee, then sat on the back gallery watching a great blue heron perched at the bayou's edge, waiting for breakfast to swim by. She had seen that bird every day, welcome company for a woman who spent half her lifetime waiting. But when he snatched up a fish and flew away, something in the air that morning gave her hope, made her imagine the waiting would soon come to an end.

Draining the coffee in her cup, she willed away the thoughts. Her precarious heart couldn't stand more disappointment. It was best to keep waiting and watching, but not wish for more than life was willing to give. Yet she couldn't resist. She swirled the remnants of the coffee around the cup, then turned it upside down to drain the liquid. When she righted the cup, the leftover grounds had left a distinct line around the rim. A perfectly straight line.

Marianne gasped. It had been years since she had seen a perfect line in her grounds, an indication of great fortune. And this line had the image of a boat on one side above the line, a sign that family was coming to visit.

Her head a conflict of emotions, Marianne entered the house and placed the cup on the table. Her mind pleaded for her not to crave what may never come to pass, but her heart couldn't help but be lifted by the prospect of Joseph's arrival. And then there was Gabrielle. Even though she instinctually knew she had done the right thing by sending her daughter off with Jean, she worried incessantly for her safety.

Marianne gripped the back of a chair and cringed at the weight of her troubles, felt the world pressing heavy upon her shoulders. Would her sorrows never end? Would her family ever be reunited?

She thought, too, of the Attakapas community, so many people worried over her state of mind. Her widowed neighbor, Raymond Sonnier, visited every day, indicating she was close to losing her sanity. He had even gone so far as to suggest marriage to relieve her suffering. Marriage? Marianne laughed at the image. As if she would consider marrying another.

"I won't go," she said aloud to no one. "Forgive me, Joseph, but I can't do this anymore."

Even as the words left her lips, she knew she would still load her basket with food and travel down to the live oak tree, still wait until dusk for Joseph to arrive. But after thirteen years, she wondered if she could endure one more day of hoping, one more day of waiting.

The sound of a buggy was heard on the road outside, thankfully breaking her from her melancholy. Marianne prayed it wasn't Raymond coming to check on her, to hint of his growing attraction and to encourage her not to wait at the tree that day. She wasn't up for conversation from anyone.

"Maman?" someone called out, and Marianne's heart leaped. Tears rushed to her eyes when she recognized the sound of her firstborn's voice. She threw open the door, clutching her heart at the welcome sight of her family.

"Maman," Emilie shouted, jumping from the wagon and rushing into her arms. "Oh, Maman."

The two women tightly hugged one another, crying and laughing at the same time. Marianne peered over Emilie's shoulder to see Lorenz and Coleman helping a very pregnant Rose out of the wagon.

"Rose," she exclaimed, rushing to the wagon. "What are earth were you all thinking?"

"I'm fine, Maman," Rose said, placing her feet on the ground and instantly wrapping her arms around her mother's waist. "I would have walked here if I had to."

Something was amiss, Marianne thought. Why had they risked Rose's health? When she met Lorenz's gaze and caught his guarded smile, she feared the worst. "What is it?" Marianne asked. "Why have you come?"

Rose pulled away from her mother's embrace, but she refused to let go of her hand. "We wanted to see how you are."

"Where's Gabrielle?" Emilie asked from the threshold.

Marianne couldn't place why, but her children seemed anxious. "Why are you here?" she repeated.

"We were worried about you," Coleman offered.

"Worried?" Marianne asked, looking from one to the other for answers.

"Your neighbor wrote us a letter," Lorenz explained. "He said Gabrielle is gone and you're not well. We came as soon as we received the letter."

She should have been furious that Raymond had risked the life of her precious baby for the sake of his loneliness and the rumors of a small town. But truth be told, Marianne was thrilled they had come.

"Come inside," she said. "I'll make a new pot of coffee and explain everything."

"Where's Gabrielle?" Emilie insisted as they entered the house.

"With Jean," Marianne said. She then recounted how the letter had been sent by Coleman's solicitor and intercepted, of Gabrielle stowing away on Jean's ship and their plan to retrieve Joseph from New Orleans.

"You let Gabrielle leave with that pirate?" Emilie nearly shouted.

"He's a good man, Emilie," Rose said, sending her mother an approving smile. "She did the right thing."

"But she's on his ship," Emilie insisted, amazed that the others weren't as concerned as she was. "Gabrielle is unchaperoned on a ship full of pirates."

"He's not a pirate," Coleman added. "He's a smart businessman."

"Besides, being on a ship is exactly what Gabrielle wants," Lorenz said. "You know how much she loves the sea."

Emilie crossed her arms about her chest, refusing to give in.

"Bringing Papa back is what Gabrielle needs," Rose said softly. "Maybe now she will be at peace."

A silence fell among the group, each one knowing the guilt Gabrielle had carried since the exile. Leave it to Rose to speak the words of truth, Marianne thought. Her petite, quiet daughter was always amazing everyone with her strength and wisdom.

"Are you well?" Marianne asked Rose, who seemed tremendously uncomfortable with the mammoth weight around her middle.

"I feel like I have swallowed a giant pumpkin," Rose answered.

Everyone laughed but Coleman, who turned pale at the conversation. Marianne knew he feared the birth, having lost his mother and brother in childbirth years before.

"Excuse me," Rose said, heading for Gabrielle's room. "Nature calls."

When Rose closed the door behind her, Coleman came to Marianne's side. "She's so big," he whispered. "I never would have let her come, but she insisted she would run away in the middle of the night and walk here if I didn't bring her."

"You did the right thing," Marianne said, taking his hand. She knew she had to comfort his fears, but she had plenty of her own. Her daughter was indeed very large for her small frame. "She'll be fine, Coleman. I'll take care of her now. I've helped bring lots of babies into this world."

Her words hit their mark, for Coleman brightened. He nodded, but Marianne knew that when the day came, Coleman would be in as much pain as Rose.

"Marianne," Lorenz said. "Forgive me, but why is the town worried about you? Why are you spending so much time by the bayou's edge? Your neighbor said—"

"My neighbor worries too much," Marianne insisted, fury now filling her brow. "He also wishes to marry me."

Emilie gasped. "You can't!"

"Of course I can't," Marianne said. "I will wait until my dying day for your father if I have to."

"But why at this oak tree?" Lorenz asked. "Why every day at all hours?"

Marianne sighed, wondering how to explain her vision. Her family knew she experienced such etheral images, but she wondered if they would question her sanity too. When she gazed down at the table before her, staring back at her was her coffee cup, a perfect straight line beneath its rim and a boat sailing above. It was then she realized that in her vision they had all been together, as they were now.

"I had a vision in Opelousas," she explained. "I saw your father returning to us, coming up that bayou with Jean and Gabrielle at the helm. We were all by the oak tree. All of us standing together, like we are now. Waiting."

No one said a word, but Marianne heard Rose returning to the main room. "I'm not crazy," she said, although she wondered if that were true.

Tears fell down Emilie's face and she looked away. "Where is this tree, Maman?" she asked.

"On the land grant, between the house and the bayou."

"Should we pack a lunch?" Rose asked.

Now, it was Marianne's turn to cry. She reached for her daughters' hands and they each took one. "I'm not crazy," she said again, believing it this time.

"No one present said you were," Lorenz said, his eyes gleaming with unshed tears.

"The day is advancing," Coleman added. "Let us go find this magical oak tree."

They made their way to the enormous oak, pausing to let Rose catch her breath. Coleman placed a large blanket on the ground and then withdrew fruits, breads, and wine from the basket. As the sun headed toward its zenith, they all told Marianne of their months in the Opelousas Poste, bringing in the crops and waiting for the arrival of the first Gallant grandchild.

When the shadows began to lengthen, Marianne leaned against the trunk of the tree, grateful to have her family near her again, and began to sing "La Claire Fontaine." Trying to dispel the anxiety taking hold of her heart now that dusk was approaching and Joseph had not arrived, she closed her eyes and concentrated on the words her mother had once sung to her.

She initially didn't know what caused her to stop, but a powerful force ran through her, pressing the breath from her lungs. Marianne rose, watching the bayou, wondering why her skin felt chilly when the temperature rivaled summer.

"Maman?" Emilie said, also rising and coming to her side.

Marianne barely made out the sound, but she recognized it immediately. Distant and faint, she wondered if the others heard it too or if she had finally lost her mind.

"What is it?" Rose said, struggling to her feet.

Both daughters took Marianne's hands and gazed at the bayou together. Emilie shivered, as if she felt the force rippling through the air too. Then Rose gasped as the sound became clearer. The sound of an Acadian singing.

Marianne released their hands and moved slowly down the bank. The dream she had nurtured in her breast for thirteen years was finally coming true. She knew it. He was here. Joseph was in Louisiana. They had found each other at last.

She sensed his presence before the *radeau* turned the bend and Joseph came into view, his smiling face beaming from the bow of the boat. As in a vision, Marianne walked in a mental mist toward the water's edge, her eyes never leaving her true love's face. She heard Jean relay commands to bring the boat closer to the bank and Emilie crying behind her, but all Marianne could comprehend was that Joseph had finally arrived. Her husband was right before her.

When Joseph jumped over the side of the boat and began moving through the waist-deep water toward the bank, Marianne's feet moved into action. She walked faster toward the water's edge while he struggled to clear the bayou. They met where the bayou kissed the cypress knees and rushed into an embrace.

An intense joy filled Marianne as Joseph enveloped her in his arms, raising her off her toes and turning her in the air. She clutched his shoulders, ran her fingers through his hair, then squeezed him so tight they both broke out into laughter—or was it crying, she wasn't sure. He took her face in his hands and kissed her soundly, then covered her face in kisses and hugged her once more.

"Oh, my love, I will never let go of you again," he whispered before capturing her lips once again.

Marianne buried her face in the curve of his neck

and savored the feel and smell of him, running her fingers across the length of his chest and onto his face to make sure he wasn't a vision. But he was real, capturing her fingers and kissing her again and again. For the first time since the exile, she was whole. Marianne Gallant was finally home.

Joseph never let her go, but he peered over her shoulder up the bank. "Emilie?" he said, his voice breaking.

Marianne pulled back and led him to the tree where his family waited. Emilie held a hand over her mouth to contain her sobs, and Joseph quickly embraced her, one hand still holding on to his wife. "My beautiful Emilie," he whispered.

"Oh Papa," she cried into his shoulder.

Rose slowly approached, eying him curiously. She had been too young to remember much of her father.

"Rose," Joseph announced. "I would have known you anywhere."

"Papa," she said, filling the space Emilie had left. He kissed the top of her head and she laid her cheek against his chest.

"I'll wager you're as sweet as the day I left you," he said, holding her close.

"That she is," Lorenz offered.

Joseph looked up at Lorenz, whose cheeks were stained with tears. The last time they were together was the day the English had trapped them in the church at Grand Pré. Lorenz, then twelve, had cried from fear and Joseph had told him not to be ashamed, that even grown men were wont to shed tears. Now, reunited, the two men seem to speak the same words with their eyes.

Lorenz reached out his hand and Joseph took it, but within seconds the two men embraced. "I'm honored to have you as a son," Joseph said, releasing him. "Thank you for taking care of my family."

"It has been my greatest honor," Lorenz said.

"Papa," Rose said meekly. "I want you to meet my husband."

Joseph had no problem finding Coleman among the dark Acadians. His blond hair and blue eyes announced to the world his nationality. Yet when their eyes met, an understanding seemed to pass between them.

"Monsieur Gallant," Coleman said, offering him his hand. "It is my pleasure to meet you."

Grasping the Englishman's hand firmly, Joseph smiled. "My name is Joseph. Or do you not understand French?"

"He speaks French, Papa," Rose interjected.

Coleman leaned close. "I now dream in French," he said with a grin.

"Welcome to the family, son," Joseph said. "And thank you for all you have done to have us reunited. I am deeply in your debt."

"No," Coleman said proudly. "Your family has given me great joy. The debt is all mine."

Marianne suddenly remembered Gabrielle. Still holding on to Joseph's hand, she turned and scanned the bayou, but the *radeau* was empty.

"I'm right here, Maman," Gabrielle said, coming out of the grove of cypress to everyone's left.

Gabrielle took Marianne's free hand and kissed her cheek while wrapping an arm about her mother's neck.

"I was so worried," Marianne said. "I have missed you so much."

Emilie and Rose quickly surrounded Gabrielle, commenting on her hair and the clothes she wore. Jean was right behind with a young lady Marianne had not seen before.

"Everyone," Gabrielle announced. "This is Delphine Delaronde, my stepdaughter."

Marianne squeezed her hand and kissed her again. "Congratulations, my dear," she said. "I'm so happy for you but so sorry I missed the ceremony."

"I know, Maman," Gabrielle said. "You were there in spirit."

Emilie instantly folded her arms about her chest and sent Jean a scrutinizing stare. "Jean?"

Jean grinned at the overprotective sister who had been in charge of her family since the separation. Marianne nearly burst into laughter when he folded his own arms and gazed down at her, his dimple a deep indentation. "Emilie?"

"I hope you made an honest woman of my sister," she said, giving him the eye.

"We had a priest, if that's what you mean," Jean said.

Emilie relaxed. "That's exactly what I meant," she said, then offered her new brother-in-law a kiss.

Gabrielle reached for Rose's hand, and Joseph did the same to Emilie. Joined together in one continuous family line, Marianne looked at her grown daughters and the man she had adored since the first day she spotted him walking back from the apple groves. Her heart swelled from the emotions, a joy so overwhelming she had trouble breathing.

"Maman," Gabrielle said, breaking the silence. "I think your youngest daughter has something to tell us."

They all turned toward Rose, including the men, and she swallowed hard.

"What is it, Rose?" Marianne asked.

Rose blushed, then the blood drained from her face instantaneously as she grimaced. But she said nothing.

"She's about to break my hand," Gabrielle offered. "I think she's having this baby."

Chapter Eighteen

Within seconds of Rose admitting she was having pains, her water broke and all chaos erupted. Marianne barked orders for water, a knife, and plenty of sheets, while Coleman scooped Rose up in his arms and carried her objecting into the house. Rose refused to let her father out of her sight so he remained on one side of the bed holding her hand while Coleman took the other. Marianne supervised the birth, and Gabrielle, Emilie, and Delphine acted as her assistants.

Lorenz and Jean left to find Felicité to reunite her with Mathurin, and Gabrielle was thankful for two fewer people among them. The room had become unbearably hot as the late afternoon sun poured through the west window and it was difficult concentrating with so many talking at once.

"Why didn't you tell me?" Coleman asked his wife. "My God, Rose, you should have told us."

"It didn't hurt this much last night," she offered and Marianne went pale.

"Last night?" she practically yelled.

"If I had told you, Coleman wouldn't have allowed me to come."

"You're damn right I wouldn't have." Now, that Coleman was nearing hysteria, he had resorted to speaking English.

"Calm down, everyone," Gabrielle said. "She's having another pain."

Once they had placed Rose on the bed, she made no pretenses when the pains arrived. To everyone's surprise, they occured only minutes apart, some right behind the other. Now, when the pain began, Rose leaned forward and grabbed Gabrielle's forearm and began to push.

"So soon?" Emilie asked her mother.

Marianne felt Rose's belly, which had become rock hard. She took Rose's other hand and pulled her farther toward her. "It's time," she announced.

Gabrielle was told births took a long time, especially firstborns, but leave it to tiny, delicate Rose to break that rule. After four pushes, Gabrielle spotted a head of blond hair emerging.

"It's a boy," Marianne shouted when she had pulled the baby free.

They all cheered and Coleman captured his wife's face and kissed her repeatedly. "Thank God," he said. "Thank God you're all right."

"I told you not to worry," she said, but Rose was far from danger's door. It wasn't long before another spasm hit her and she buckled under the pain.

"It's the afterbirth," Marianne told Coleman, who looked ready to faint. She quickly wrapped the blue-eyed baby in a blanket and handed him to Emilie.

When Rose leaned forward and let out a yell, Gabrielle nearly fainted herself.

Marianne put a hand on Rose's belly and the blood drained from her face. "Do you have twins in your family?" she asked Coleman.

"My uncle was a twin, why?"

Gabrielle couldn't contain her wonderment any longer. She peered beneath the sheet and screamed just as a head of jet-black hair poked its way through the birth canal. "It's another one," she heard Delphine cry, her stepdaughter as excited and amazed as she was.

The tiny baby entered the world and let out its own scream. "This one's a girl," Marianne announced, wrapping the baby and handing her to Gabrielle. "With that voice, she's definitely a Gallant."

"I love you two very much," Rose said to her sisters, who were cooing over the babies, "but hand over my children."

Gabrielle and Rose placed the two babes in her arms and they nestled comfortably against her breast. Coleman stared at his wife and children as if in a daze. *"Mon dieu,"* he said in French, which made everyone laugh.

"One of each," Joseph said, remarking on how each child took after each nationality.

"The boy will be named Richard, after Coleman's deceased father," Rose explained. "I want to name the girl Josepha Marianne, after the heroes in my life."

Marianne bent down to examine her grandchildren, while Joseph held her close, both of their eyes filled with tears of pride. Gabrielle watched in amazement as her parents, so long separated, together witnessed the first moments of the next generation, still holding tightly to one another's hand.

"Born of English and Acadian descent on Louisiana soil," Joseph said. "What do you suppose that makes them?"

"Cajun," Coleman said with a grin.

Everyone laughed but Joseph, who turned to each one for an explanation.

"When we first met, Coleman had trouble pronouncing our nickname that shortens Acadian to 'Cadjin,'" Gabrielle explained. "He thought we were saying 'Cajun.'"

"Cajun?" Joseph said with a laugh. "Is that what we are now, Cajuns?"

"Why not?" Marianne said, gazing at the blue eyes of her grandson and the black eyes of her granddaughter. "It's as good a name as any."

Gabrielle helped Marianne change Rose's bedding, then assisted Delphine into a chair to rock a fussy Josepha to sleep. Rose had finally closed her eyes, but Coleman remained at her side, stroking her hair with one hand while he lovingly held his peaceful son in the other. Lorenz had returned, his eyes ablaze at the sight of new life, and he pulled Emilie into a corner to huddle like lovers, planning their own family, no doubt.

In the center of it all stood Joseph and Marianne, their eyes savoring every aspect of each other, their fingers holding and caressing what until now had existed only in dreams. Gabrielle had forgotten how affectionate her parents had been, how completely devoted they were to each other. Her Aunt Lisette had said they had fallen in love at first sight, that no couple in the village of Grand Pré had ever been so in love.

Gabrielle suddenly ached for Jean. She wondered if he was still at the Dugas house reuniting Mathurin with his daughter. She stole to the back gallery to search for him and found him leaning against an outside post, studying the bayou.

"A boy and a girl," he said softly as she approached. "Can you believe it?"

In the oncoming twilight, it was difficult to make out his eyes, but his voice held a trace of awe at the events that had transpired that day. She slipped her hands around his waist and he pulled her against his chest. He held her tighter than usual, which confirmed her suspicions that the reunion had stirred him deeply.

"I am a lucky man," he whispered. "I have an amazing family."

Gabrielle knew Jean loved her. He showed her he did in multiple ways every day. Yet she still longed to hear him say the words. Despite her logical mind telling her it wasn't necessary, she needed to hear those three simple words, the verbal affection that flowed so freely between her parents.

"Jean," she asked, her heart beating loudly in her chest. "Do you love me?"

He was silent for several seconds and she instantly regretted asking. "It's all right," she said with a sigh. "I know, you're a man of action."

"Gabrielle, I'm not one for words," he insisted. "I don't say them well."

Gabrielle moved back, commanding herself not to

feel disappointed, especially on a blissful day such as this. But his lack of affirmation pained her.

She wasn't a foot's length away when Jean grabbed her hand and tugged her back into his embrace. With his other hand, he cupped her face, nearly melting her heart with his loving gaze.

"I fell in love with you the first day we met," he said heatedly. "I have never loved anyone but you. And I will love you, Gabrielle Gallant Bouclaire, until the day I die."

Gabrielle swallowed hard, trying to tame her wild heart thundering in her chest. "Those words will do," she whispered.

They stared at each other for what seemed like an eternity, while the night birds chased mosquitoes above their heads and the Evening Star rose bright on the horizon. Jean caressed her cheek with his thumb while drinking in the sight of her, and Gabrielle reached up to touch the dimple she so dearly loved.

The world slowed and time seemed to stop. Jean dipped his head to hers and gently met her lips, then deepened the affection while his hand at her waist melted them together.

"I love you, Gabrielle," he said while her parents' laughter drifted from the house and surrounded them in its comforting embrace. "I love you."

AUTHOR'S NOTE

In the town of St. Martinville, on the banks of Bayou Teche in what was once the Attakapas Poste, there is an enormous oak tree known as the "Evangeline Oak," the spot where an Acadian woman named Emmeline Labiche apparently waited for her lover, Louis Arceneaux, separated from her during the exile from Nova Scotia. Many people believe that this couple was the basis for Longfellow's epic poem *Evangeline,* a tragic tale of separated Acadian lovers, although some scholars have declared it a regional myth. Regardless of its validity, the oak tree remains, a testament to the courage and perseverance of a people scattered throughout the world and reunited on a faraway bayou.

The Chitimacha holy tree is another local legend, although there really is such a tree, a large cypress that fronts a bayou and complements a midden not too far from St. Martinville. I have interviewed a resident of the area who swore he visited the tree three times while fishing and three times the tree brought him rain before he had time to reach his boat.

ABOUT THE AUTHOR

Cherie Claire never had problems dreaming up great characters for her Louisiana historical romances. A native of South Louisiana, she was raised saturated in the colorful culture and traditions of the Bayou State. A journalist, Cherie makes her home in southern California with her husband and her two sons.

Cherie loves to hear from readers.
Visit her Web site at
www.geocities.com/BourbonStreet/Bayou/4745

Celebrate Romance With Two of Today's Hottest Authors

Meagan McKinney

__In the Dark	$6.99US/$8.99CAN	0-8217-6341-5
__The Fortune Hunter	$6.50US/$8.00CAN	0-8217-6037-8
__Gentle from the Night	$5.99US/$7.50CAN	0-8217-5803-9
__A Man to Slay Dragons	$5.99US/$6.99CAN	0-8217-5345-2
__My Wicked Enchantress	$5.99US/$7.50CAN	0-8217-5661-3
__No Choice But Surrender	$5.99US/$7.50CAN	0-8217-5859-4

Meryl Sawyer

__Thunder Island	$6.99US/$8.99CAN	0-8217-6378-4
__Half Moon Bay	$6.50US/$8.00CAN	0-8217-6144-7
__The Hideaway	$5.99US/$7.50CAN	0-8217-5780-6
__Tempting Fate	$6.50US/$8.00CAN	0-8217-5858-6
__Unforgettable	$6.50US/$8.00CAN	0-8217-5564-1

Call toll free **1-888-345-BOOK** to order by phone, use this coupon to order by mail, or order online at **www.kensingtonbooks.com**.

Name _____

Address _____

City _____ State _____ Zip _____

Please send me the books I have checked above.

I am enclosing $_____
Plus postage and handling* $_____
Sales tax (in New York and Tennessee only) $_____
Total amount enclosed $_____

*Add $2.50 for the first book and $.50 for each additional book.

Send check or money order (no cash or CODs) to:

Kensington Publishing Corp., Dept. C.O., 850 Third Avenue, New York, NY 10022

Prices and numbers subject to change without notice.

All orders subject to availability.

Visit our website at **www.kensingtonbooks.com**.